# DEADLY TREASURES

## OLIVIA WELLS MYSTERIES
BOOK 2

### JANE MCPARKES

PENCREEK
PUBLISHING

*In loving memory of Mary Cecilia Smith*
*My very own Auntie Molly*

# 1

In spite of the warm evening, Olivia shivered and forced herself to relax back against the leather interior of the taxi. The driver didn't even draw breath as he swerved violently to avoid a very clean SUV hurtling round a blind bend towards them in the middle of the road. She clung on to the handle above the rear door and winced at the competing blasts of horns and torrents of abuse that were exchanged through the open windows.

'Blimmin' emmet arseholes!' the driver yelled, gesticulating wildly and then beaming at Olivia in the rear-view mirror, apparently satisfied that he had taught the tourist a valuable lesson in the art of driving down narrow Cornish lanes.

'Now where were we? Ah yes.' The driver grinned at Olivia again as she seized the opportunity to straighten her fancy jewelled headband that had assumed a jaunty angle over her right eye. 'You're off to this posh do at Peneglos Hall the whole of Falmouth is talking about.' His dark eyes, twinkling in the mirror from a face tanned deep brown by the hottest

Cornish summer in fifteen years, rested on her outfit. 'Fancy dress is it, love?'

'Yes, 1920s flapper and black tie,' Olivia confirmed, tugging the heavily beaded and tasselled sleeveless dress over her knees. 'Not my usual style, it must be said.'

Once he was stationary at a junction, the driver twisted around in his seat, and tipped his denim cap back on his head with a wide smile. 'Well, I think you look proper hansum.'

'Thank you.' She reddened and changed the subject. 'Do you know the Hall then?'

'Too right I do.' He pulled out on to the main road that led to Falmouth and accelerated sharply. 'I lived over that side of Falmouth when I were a nipper and me and my mates used to ride our bikes out there and play in the grounds. The old boy didn't mind us playing in the woods or down in the cove, as long as we kept out of his way.' He gave Olivia a conspiratorial smile. 'It was heaven for us kids.'

She smiled back. 'His name was Charles. Was he still living in the house back then?'

'Nah. It was practically falling apart so he'd moved into the gardener's cottage.' He stopped the car to let an elderly couple cross the road. 'The old boy only cared about that walled kitchen garden, by all accounts. Even employed a weird, beardy gardener bloke to help him look after it. It's a good job his great nephew came back to take over after he died. Can't say we were surprised though. He was always good to Charles.'

The driver fell silent as he weaved the vehicle through the streets of Falmouth, passing the colourful front gardens of the houses and cottages lining the roads that eventually disappeared and gave way to verges thick with cow parsley and poppies.

'Apparently the nephew has done a proper job with the old

place. Word is, he got some fancy American architect in to oversee it, and she's done a grand job turning it into a swanky hotel that's all green and eco-friendly...' His voice trailed off as he caught Olivia's eye in the rear-view mirror. 'Oh my, that's not you, is it, love? You have got a bit of an accent.'

She laughed. 'Guilty as charged, I'm afraid. But I was born and brought up in Penbartha, and only spent seven years in Manhattan.' She watched as the back of the driver's neck turned crimson. 'I'm Olivia, by the way.'

He coughed. 'And I'm Jack. The missus always says I should think before I speak. No offence, love.'

'None taken.' She leant forward. 'But you're right about the Hall being in a sorry state and it looks like the Falmouth grapevine has got it spot-on as usual. The nephew is called Ruan, and he and his partner, Lucinda, had the most fantastic plans for the Hall. My job was to honour the vision and techniques of the original architect and craftsmen while bringing it up to date with the high energy-efficient standards of twenty-first century living. That's what my business specialises in – breathing new life into old buildings in cutting-edge and sustainable ways.' She sat back in her seat. 'It's been a bit of a race against time to get it ready for the summer season. We've had less than eighteen months to get it all done.'

'All the more reason to enjoy tonight then.' He winked at her in the rear-view mirror. 'My daughter's looking for a waitressing job over the summer before she goes to uni. You couldn't put in a good word for her, could you, love?'

'I'll see what I can do. Get her to call the Hall next week and speak to Lucinda.' Olivia gazed out of the car window for the next couple of miles, watching a small flotilla of white-sailed boats chasing diamonds of sunshine across the aquamarine waves, and wondered whether Jago would manage to get his own boat out on the water for the summer. Her stomach squeezed. That all depended on whether he even made it down to Cornwall this time. And based on his recent track record, she wasn't convinced he would.

Eventually, they turned off the open coast road onto a smaller lane, bumped over several potholes, and drew to a halt in front of a large black, glossy sign announcing Peneglos Hall in gold lettering.

'Oh my!' Jack breathed. 'Even the old stone pillars and rusty gates are looking grand! I'm more used to seeing them hanging off their hinges and covered with brambles and nettles.'

His words brought Olivia out of her thoughts and she opened the window as the taxi nosed up the meandering tree-lined driveway bordered by towering rhododendrons and the delicate nodding hydrangeas in every shade of blue, pink and white. Although it was after seven o'clock, the heat from the sun in a cloudless sky was still strong and Olivia welcomed the slight breeze encouraged by the movement of the car. She inhaled the sweet scent of the flowers that mingled with the dusty smell of dry pollen and leaves in the warm air.

Eventually, the trees on either side of the drive thinned out to cow-dotted fields and Olivia leaned forward expectantly, a small bubble of excitement mingling with her nerves, eager to catch her first glimpse of the old Georgian country house in its full glory and see it through the eyes of the guests.

And there it was. Peneglos Hall glided into view, sitting upright and proud, just like its first owner. It was a large square building, built of local granite, now silvered with age, with elegantly tall multi-paned windows on each of the three floors. From its elevated position the windows on two sides of the house overlooked the magnificent gardens and distant farmland and the other two sides enjoyed fabulous views over the gently sloping gardens to the glittering blue expanse of Falmouth Bay and beyond.

The taxi followed the main drive until it reached a gravelled parking area, already filled with cars. Olivia was far more familiar with taking the second narrower driveway to the left, which led around to a large cobbled area in front of the coach house and stable block. Now she relished crunching to a halt in front of the sweeping granite steps that led up to a classic portico entrance.

'Bloody hell.' The taxi driver's mouth fell open. 'You've done all this in less than eighteen months? After all those years of neglect?' He shook his head. 'I'd heard it was posh, but this is like something out of *Downton Abbey*!'

'It's beautiful, isn't it?' Olivia agreed as she stepped out of the taxi, grateful for Jack's help as she negotiated her beads, tassels and the high heels of her T-bar sandals.

'It is.' He handed her the overnight bag he had stowed in the front passenger footwell and looked at her more closely. 'Are you sure you're okay, love? Your face looks more like you're going to a funeral than a fancy party.' He winced. 'I've done it again, haven't I? Me and my big mouth. Of course you're nervous. It's a big night for you professionally, isn't it.' He slipped his business card into her hand and patted her arm. 'There you go, love. Make sure you have a super time. Call me if you need a lift back tomorrow.'

She smiled. 'Thank you.'

A member of staff, dressed in the hotel uniform of black trousers and a black and white striped shirt appeared to take her bag with a cheerful smile and warm promise that he would take it to her room. Olivia waved at Jack and then took a deep breath before she approached the open front doors, wondering whether the sense of nervous anticipation threatening to overwhelm her was, as Jack had said, apprehension on behalf of her clients showcasing their boutique hotel for the first time, or something more fundamental and closer to her own heart.

She stepped through the vestibule into a vast square stone-flagged reception hall. Natural light flooded through a large, carefully restored roof lantern, bouncing reflections off the crystal vases filled with stunning arrangements of local flowers that stood on two long side tables. A grand staircase with gleaming oak bannisters and handrails swept up and around the walls upon which hung family portraits, now restored after decades of neglect and decay, all watching over the evening's events in their ornate gilt frames.

She stood for a moment and looked around, savouring the warmth and excitement of the evening and one of her favourite activities – people watching. Tanned and toned women in their flapper dresses, wafting expensive perfumes exchanged air kisses and pleasantries with men in dinner jackets and bow ties and Olivia smiled. It looked as if the finest of Cornish society and beyond were here tonight. And that was where Lucinda excelled, Olivia realised, just like her own godparents had always done. None of them were respecters of social conventions, and the local dignitaries and landowners happily mingled with the craftsmen, builders and local designers who had worked on Peneglos, and the local farmers, fishermen and suppliers who had helped bring their vision to life.

Music, laughter and general chatter floated through to the hall from a series of interconnecting reception rooms and spilled out onto the terraces and formal lawns at the side of the house. It was a long time since Olivia had attended a glamorous cocktail party. There hadn't been much opportunity since she'd been living back in Cornwall and she hadn't missed them. Tramping around building sites in boots and a hard hat and attending planning and client meetings was much more her forte. The fact that the party was being held to celebrate the opening of her new business's biggest renovation project to date had made it impossible to refuse.

'Hey, Olivia! Come through. We have guests who are dying to meet you,' a familiar voice called from one of the main drawing rooms. Olivia whisked a crystal flute of champagne from the tray of a passing waitress and gulped down the sharp, clear bubbles, feeling them tickling her nose before she took another deep breath and weaved her way through the throngs. She nodded and smiled at the people she recognised until she reached the main drawing room where she stopped for a moment to take everything in.

Here, as in all the other rooms in the Hall, there was a complete absence of the classic swagged elegance of similar Georgian style houses. Instead, Olivia and the designers had allowed the marble fireplaces and magnificent countryside and sea views from the floor-to-ceiling windows provide all the necessary drama and the basis of the colour palette throughout the house. Local artwork on the walls oozed style and a simple mix of antique and contemporary furniture, oversized armchairs and sofas provided comfort for their older guests. Olivia's gaze eventually settled on Ruan and Lucinda who were standing among a circle of guests, looking every inch the Lord and Lady of the manor.

Olivia had liked both of them from their very first meeting. Ruan was the more flamboyant of the pair. In Lucinda he had found a business and life partner who fizzed with fun but was creative and professional at the same time. As a couple they were completely in tune with each other and with Olivia and Rocky's commitment to sustainability and the environment. They had taken on board all the experts' suggestions with great enthusiasm and added their own ideas until their joint vision was simply amazing.

Both in their late thirties, Ruan was handsome, charming and appeared comfortable in his dinner suit and black tie. Lucinda was fun and stylish, with a strong face and wide mouth. She laughingly blamed her love of puddings and all things sweet for her slightly plump figure, but she looked magnificent in her carefully designed flapper dress, fashioned out of vintage fabric that made the most of her attributes. She described herself as big-boned and big-hearted and tonight she radiated happiness as she threw her arms round Olivia.

'Darling! You look fabulous!' Lucinda pulled her to one side. 'I'm so glad you're here! Some of the men are asking the most technical questions and I haven't a clue!'

Olivia looked around the room. 'Where's Rocky?'

Lucinda let out one of her famous belly laughs. 'The last time I saw him he was on the terrace, surrounded by a gaggle of beautiful women. I overheard him talking about biomass boilers and photovoltaic panels and they seemed to be hanging on his every word, but I don't think it's our green credentials they're interested in.'

Olivia followed her gaze out through the doors and on to the stone terrace where her best friend and business partner, usually a man of few words, was deep in conversation with a group of glamorous and captivated women.

'Olivia, I'd like to introduce you to Andrew Warner. We used to work together in London and he's really interested in what we've done here.' Lucinda tugged gently at her friend's arm and whispered in her ear, 'Don't look so worried. It's going really well.'

Olivia nodded and turned to smile at her fellow guest, who was in his early fifties with a small mouth set in the arrogant expression of someone who was supremely confident in his abilities.

'Lucie is always singing your praises, Olivia. I'm so pleased to meet you.' He shook her hand energetically, the sunlight glinting off his fancy watch and almost blinding her.

'So, are you in the hotel business too?'

'I am. And I've recently been approached by a hotel group who want to explore the green agenda. They're thinking of demolishing one of their existing hotels and rebuilding it from scratch. Would you be interested in arranging a meeting?'

Olivia tried not to wince. 'I'm afraid we don't get involved with demolition and rebuild. We specialise in restoration and retrofit.' She forced a polite smile. 'It's all part of our commitment to sustainability.'

Andrew inclined his head. 'Ah, the two most important words in the language of today's tourism industry. Luxury and sustainability.'

Olivia nodded. 'Well, it is here in Cornwall. I can't speak for the rest of the country. And I can only take credit for the bare bones of the building. The rest is down to our incredible teams of craftsmen and designers.'

Andrew was still gazing round the room. 'It must have cost a fortune.'

Olivia brushed that comment away with another smile, and was relieved to see a familiar figure drift into the drawing room.

'This is the woman you want to talk to about sustainable interior design. Meet Kyra McLeod. We used to work together in Manhattan and now she's opening a studio in London. Kyra, this is Andrew Warner, who might be interested in your interior design services.'

As soon as he'd been whisked away for a tour of their

work, Olivia was approached by an endless succession of other guests, all wanting to talk to her about their own projects but, as soon as she was able, she slipped out of the tall double doors, her eyes searching for just one person.

The terraces and formal lawns looked magical on this warm midsummer evening and Olivia leant against the stone balustrade and looked down across the sun-washed gardens. They were filled with a mixture of indigenous and tropical plants and flowers that had been the pride and joy of Ruan's ancestors. Some of the guests were wandering along the gravel paths that meandered through the beds, their legs and clothes brushing against the sweet-smelling lavender, verbena, alliums and rosemary, all releasing their fragrance into the warm air and lending the evening an exotic feel. She wondered briefly how many of these chosen guests were even interested in the sustainability element of what Lucinda was trying to achieve and how many were just there for the luxury. *Stop being such a cynic, Wells,* she told herself sharply. She shifted her gaze to the wildflower meadows that led from beyond the gardens down through the valley to a private cove, invisible from the Hall, and then out to the ocean that stretched in front of her for miles. A pair of skylarks suddenly swooped in and out of the meadows and she took a deep breath of sea air laced with garden scents, hoping it would settle the butterflies still swooping in her stomach.

'It's amazing what Mum and Dylan have managed between them in the gardens, isn't it?'

Jolted from her thoughts, Olivia turned with a smile to Kitten who was standing next to her in a vintage cream and ivory dress, embellished with silver beads. The high neckline and sleeveless bodice showed off her petite figure to perfection, her pale, flawless skin and blonde hair, fashioned in a Gatsby-style pixie cut, making her look every inch a 1920s flapper girl.

'It is and they make a great working partnership. Needless to say, Dylan is keeping a very low profile tonight, but I'm sorry Cassie's not here.'

Kitten shrugged. 'I tried to persuade her, but she'd made her mind up. Said she was happier at home looking after the dogs for you and Jago.' Olivia's face didn't flicker. 'I told her Rocky and I would look after her, but you know what she's like these days.'

Olivia did, and understood why. 'How's Rocky coping with all his adoring fans?'

Kitten rolled her eyes. 'He's loving every minute of it! Talking about the subjects closest to his heart. Who knew sheep's wool insulation and lime plaster were so sexy?' She moved closer to Olivia. 'One of the many things I love about that man is his complete inability to read women. He actually believes they're as interested in retrofit and refurbishment as he is. And not because he is drop-dead gorgeous in that tux.'

Olivia laughed. All these months on, she was still surprised and delighted that Rocky and Kitten were such an unlikely but happy couple. He was her oldest friend and she'd never seen him so content.

Kitten glanced at her watch. 'I suppose I'd better rescue him. Gabe and Lexie are eager for people to start eating soon and I'm starving.' She looked sharply at her friend. 'If you chew your lip much more, you'll draw blood. Jago will be here, Olive. When has he ever let you down?'

A movement out of the corner of her eye caught Olivia's attention and she felt a familiar lurch in her chest. Even at a distance Jago was unmistakable, with his tall, broad-shouldered body, handsome features and a head of thick, prematurely silver hair. He was moving towards her through the throngs, his strides long and purposeful, looking comfortable in an immaculate black tuxedo, black bow tie and highly polished shoes. Blue eyes, piercing even in his unusually pale, strained face, locked on to hers and he gave one of his rare lop-sided smiles. Another familiar sensation fizzled through her and she smiled back.

Ruan and Lucinda halted him as he passed by and introduced him to two figures in chef's whites who were directing people through to the dining room to eat. A frown creased his brow and every now and then he pinched the bridge of his nose in an impatient gesture, his eyes looking out on to the terrace rather than at the people who were talking to him.

Olivia stiffened as cold fingers closed round her heart. This wasn't the Jago she knew. This was Jago the barrister; the cool, authoritative courtroom lawyer cross-examining an unsavoury witness. He stood grim-faced and rocking on the balls of his feet, his gaze distracted as Ruan beckoned a waitress over with a tray of champagne.

'I told you he'd be here!' Kitten patted her friend on the shoulder. 'He probably had trouble charging his car on the motorway. You know what the service station EV points are like. You can relax now.'

Olivia was just about to say something in reply when the peaceful air was suddenly filled with a cry and a shattering crash as the waitress, champagne, glasses and silver tray all hit the floor at the same time.

# 2

Jago snatched two champagne flutes from a passing waiter and handed one to Olivia, before swallowing his in one gulp and looking around for another.

'What was all that about?' Olivia handed him her own flute, which went the same way.

Lucinda jumped in. 'Absolutely nothing! We were just introducing Jago to Gabe and Lexie, when I think the heat must have got to the waitress and she had a funny turn and hit the floor. Lexie's taken her to the kitchens for a glass of water and a sit down. She'll be right as rain in a moment.'

Jago wasn't so sure. The look that had crossed the waitress's face wasn't one of heat exhaustion. He looked around. 'Do you think we should check on her?'

'Not at all!' Lucinda kissed his cheek warmly and guided them through to the dining room. 'Thanks for being so caring, Jago, but you must be ravenous after that long drive and Gabe's anxious that everyone sees the food at its best. Come on through and be prepared to be impressed!'

'Wow!' Olivia exclaimed. 'I knew Gabe and Lexie were planning a feast, but I didn't expect it to look like a de Heem painting!'

Jago blinked. Art wasn't really his thing, despite Olivia's good-natured efforts to educate him. 'A what?'

She nudged him. 'Jan Davidsz. de Heem. The Dutch still-life baroque artist? Amazing oil paintings of overflowing banquet tables? We've seen his work at the National Gallery. And I went to an amazing exhibition at MOMA when I was living in Manhattan.' She must have seen his eyes glaze over because she laughed and handed him a white china plate. 'Just eat, Jago.'

Jago did as he was told. It was a long time since he'd eaten and his stomach was rumbling from the mouth-watering mix of smells that were coming from the nearest trestle table, which seemed to be loaded with meats, cheeses and crudités artfully arranged in piles that overlapped and intertwined. Every gap was filled with greenery, sprigs of herbs, nuts and what looked to Jago like garden flowers. Serving boards of different heights, trays and three-tier stands were dotted between the tables, filled with artisan breads, crackers, bread sticks, dips and condiments. As he loaded his plate, carefully leaving the garden flowers behind, he glanced across at Olivia who was admiring the adjacent table where the chefs had created an equally stunning dessert table, full of pastries, cupcakes, florentines and lots of things he didn't recognise but looked delicious. He would get to them later.

'Are you enjoying our food?' A heavily accented deep voice interrupted him. 'All farmed and produced within a ten-mile radius of the Hall!' A carefully groomed, muscular figure in a white chef's tunic and smart black trousers appeared at their side. 'Do I take it you approve of my tablescaping?'

Jago's mouth was already full, so Olivia answered for him, her voice warm with praise.

'It's fabulous, Gabe. Like painting with food!'

A wide smile spread over the chef's handsome Italian features. 'What a lovely way of putting it! I will remember that forever.' He caught hold of Olivia's hand and brought it up to his lips theatrically for a moment. 'Painting with food.' He turned to Jago. 'Your Olivia is not just a beautiful face, no?'

Jago tensed and swallowed his food. 'I'm afraid our introductions were somewhat interrupted.' He took in the surprised look on Olivia's face and knew he was being curt, but for once, he didn't care. 'I'm Jago Trevithick.' He thrust a hand at the other man.

Gabe didn't miss a beat and he shook the proffered hand vigorously. 'And I'm Gabe Marotta. Pleased to meet you at long last. I've heard so much about you from Olivia. I'm surprised we haven't met before but Olivia says you've been too busy working in London.'

Jago glowered at the implied criticism, which he had to admit to himself, hit a nerve. 'Olivia understands that's the way it is sometimes in my line of work.' He held Gabe's gaze, which didn't flicker.

'Molto bene! I did wonder for a moment if that waitress had recognised you from court or something and that was why she dropped the tray...' Gabe left the words hanging in the air.

Jago's stomach clenched and he stared at Gabe coolly. 'I really don't think so. I doubt someone like her would get caught up in the sort of cases I deal with.'

Lucinda breezed past and caught hold of Gabe's arm. 'You're not still talking about that silly waitress are you, Gabe?

Because it turns out she hadn't eaten all day and went all faint in the heat. She's fine now and I'm sending her home.' Her face lit up with one of her brightest smiles. 'So, please carry on mingling, you two, while I introduce Gabe to someone, if you don't mind.'

They hurried off together and Jago returned to his plate of food, his usual confidence and self-assurance shaken, trying to ignore the look of concern on Olivia's face. They weren't left alone for long. Various guests were eager to talk to Olivia and she abandoned her own food to answer another dozen questions from people interested in her work. Eventually Jago caught her by the elbow, whisked another two champagne flutes from the tray of a passing waiter, handed one to Olivia, and gulped his back in one.

'Jago, are you sure you're alright? You're behaving really strangely. Has something happened?'

He looked down at her lovely face, which was now creased with worry. He could tell from her healthy glow, the fine dusting of freckles and the threads of gold running through her hair, that she'd been out in the Cornish sunshine, running, walking and gardening at every opportunity. Her incredible dark eyes, flecked with amber, added to her striking appearance, and tonight, dressed in a vintage dress of copper and golds, and with her mass of dark curls held in place by some sort of headband, he decided she looked like an exotic princess. He'd been so looking forward to seeing her again, but now he felt their reunion had been spoiled by the waitress incident. And Gabe's glib remarks.

Jago helped himself to another glass of champagne and leant down to kiss her, breathing in her familiar perfume. 'Everything's fine, I promise. Let's just enjoy ourselves.'

Her expression didn't clear and he realised he was going to have to come up with some other tactic to allay her worries.

He slipped an arm around her waist and drew her into his side, burrowing his nose in her hair and kissing her just behind her left ear. Running his hand down the low back of her dress had the desired effect and she shivered and moved closer.

'When d'you reckon we can go and check out the bedroom?'

He could feel her laugh travel through her body. 'It's far too early! Behave yourself. I think we've got speeches to come.'

Jago groaned. He'd heard enough speeches over the last six weeks. Tonight, he just wanted to enjoy being back with Olivia.

'Break it up, you two!' Rocky moved between them, slapped Jago on the back and kissed Olivia's cheek. 'Bit of a dramatic entrance wasn't it, even for you, Jago?'

Jago saw the look that passed between the two friends and decided to try and shrug it off. 'What can I say?' He pointed to Rocky's empty champagne flute. 'Fancy another?'

Rocky pulled a face. 'No thanks, mate. Can't say it's really me. I've heard there's some local beer outside, so I'm going for that before the speeches start. Want one?'

Before Jago could nod his head, there was a tinkling of a spoon against glass and the waiting staff ushered the guests into the entrance hall where Ruan and Lucinda stood beneath the huge portrait on the wall.

Lucinda coughed and everyone fell silent.

'We prepared this speech together and Ruan was going to deliver it, but he's feeling too emotional to do it justice.' She glanced up at him and they exchanged a nervous smile. 'I just hope you will all bear with me.'

A murmur of support rippled around the guests and Lucinda flushed and spoke movingly about his grandfather's life, travels and his love of the Hall and gardens. She described Ruan's initial shock at his legacy and his decision to buckle down and build on his family's heritage. Then she turned and pointed to the portrait behind her.

'For those of you who don't already know, this is Joseph Braithwaite, Ruan's five-times maternal grandfather. He started his career as a crew member on a privateer ship in the 1770s. They were basically pirates, licensed by the government to attack foreign vessels in wartime and keep them away from English shores. In return, they kept or sold whatever they seized. He then went on to join the merchant navy where he honed his skills in evading capture during the various wars with France and Spain. When Falmouth was chosen as the new base for the packet service in 1780, and new routes were established to carry important mail, documents, goods and some passengers to the far-flung corners of the world, Joseph and his ship were an obvious choice.

'And unsurprisingly, given his past, Joseph was quick to exploit any and every opportunity to engage in unofficial trading activities which supplemented his official wages very nicely. Suffice it to say he and his family enjoyed many of the more exotic treats in life, that weren't normally available in Falmouth back then.'

Jago zoned out and directed his gaze at the recently restored portrait of Joseph. A stern face with a defiant gaze and a fighting chin stared back at him. He wore a full navy dress coat edged with gold lace and lots of brass buttons over white breeches, white waistcoat, white cravat and a black velvet kerchief. He looked arrogant and contumacious, Jago decided. Above the law. And he'd had enough of people like that.

Lucinda came to the end of another entertaining story

about Joseph's escapades and smiled at the guests. The entire audience was listening intently, smiling and laughing with her. 'Unfortunately, Joseph was forced to curtail his activities in the 1820s when the Admiralty took over the running of the packet service, and he could see the writing on the wall so far as his somewhat unconventional money-making ways were concerned. And so, he retired here from over the water at Flushing and built this beautiful house as a testament to his successful career.'

Out of the corner of his eye Jago saw Kitten nudge Olivia. He guessed that Kitten wanted Lucinda to move on from the history of the Hall to talk about its future. Olivia shushed her. That was the difference between the two women, he thought fondly. Olivia was content with saving old buildings. Kitten was far more ambitious. She wanted to save the planet.

'And so, with the help of a wonderful team led by Olivia Wells and Rocky Berryman, we have undertaken an eighteen-month programme, which has seen its transformation from a neglected old house to an elegant boutique eco-hotel. I'm sure you will all agree that we have retained the dignity and grandeur of its past. The Hall has been standing for nearly two hundred years, through good times and bad. It's seen births and deaths, wars and shipwrecks, sadness and triumphs and it's still here to tell the tale.' The guests clapped as they all stood enraptured by Lucinda's ability to spin a good tale.

'Peneglos Hall has a wonderful story to tell. But now we are about to write a new chapter. We are serious about luxury and we are serious about sustainability. We're committed to being the greenest hotel in Cornwall, to having a low impact on the environment and providing a positive experience for our visitors, local businesses and the whole of the local area. In short,' Lucinda caught hold of Ruan's hand as he stood proudly beside her, 'we are all here tonight to do three things for Peneglos Hall. To honour its past, celebrate its present and preserve its future!'

The hall broke out into applause. Jago stole a quick look at the faces of Kitten, Rocky and Olivia, expecting the former to be more than a little put out by the way Lucinda had glossed over all the sustainability measures that had been such an important part of the renovation programme. But they were all smiling, surrounded by guests congratulating them and he breathed a sigh of relief.

---

It had turned into a gloriously golden evening and Jago finally felt himself relax as he stood slightly to one side while Olivia chatted and mingled with other guests. A few of the well-groomed and beautiful women, who seemed to be Lucinda's friends from London, tried to talk to him, but he just wasn't in the mood for small talk. He was only interested in talking to one woman. And she was firmly in professional mode: chatting with potential clients, explaining what they had done at the Hall, suggesting ways they could improve energy efficiency in their own homes and workplaces. Jago imagined this was how she must have been at the glamorous events she'd attended in Manhattan and it was so different from the Olivia he knew, whose idea of dressing up was changing out of her running gear into black skinny jeans and vintage Liberty shirts.

Eventually, Ruan and Lucinda made sure that all business talk subsided and the party continued into the night. Laughter trailed through the house and onto the terrace, where lights were threaded through the balustrades and candles in lanterns lit the pathways, until everything became pleasantly blurred with champagne and music. Just after midnight, Olivia pulled him onto the dance floor and moulded her body against his as they moved gently together to the music. He felt her hands snake beneath his jacket and he lifted her chin up with his right hand so her eyes met his. The look they exchanged said it all and he bent and whispered into her ear.

'Now can we go and check out the bedroom? We've got a lot of catching up to do.'

3

The first rays of dawn peeking their way through the fine
muslin curtains that dressed the window woke Olivia. Jago's
arm was thrown across her, and her tanned legs were
intertwined with his on top of the crisp cotton sheets. He'd let
out a low whistle of appreciation when they first entered the
room, but his admiration of the soft furnishings had come to
an abrupt halt when Olivia had slipped her arms round his
waist and kissed him. After that they'd both lost rational
thought.

They'd left the wooden shutters open to allow the warm
night air to circulate and Olivia, reluctant to disturb Jago,
looked around the room from the comfort of the massive bed.

Although she hadn't been directly involved in the design
and decoration of the fifteen luxury en-suite bedrooms, she
knew from Lucinda that each room had its own unique
identity and feel. Kyra and Ellie had excelled themselves.

All the rooms had breathtaking sea or countryside views,
which the decor of each took its lead from, and were named
after a Falmouth packet ship. Jago and Olivia were in the sea-

facing Hampden Room, which according to the room information was the ship Joseph Braithwaite had regularly sailed to Lisbon, his most profitable route. Olivia smiled as she recalled how Lucinda had researched all the names in her typical meticulous way. She really was the queen of planning. Everything she did was carried out with the efficiency of a carefully crafted military campaign, and nothing was left to chance. Surprises were definitely not allowed.

The en-suite bathroom was beautifully indulgent too, with a roll-top bath and separate walk-in shower. Only those interested, or in the know, would appreciate that the baths were all reclaimed and restored, that there were efficient sanitary fittings to reduce water consumption without compromising pressure, and that the hotel's water was harvested and recycled for use elsewhere. Olivia liked the fact Ruan was determined not to lecture guests about the hotel's environmental credentials, but rather just prove that luxury and protecting the environment were not mutually exclusive.

Now she was awake, Olivia itched to get out into the early morning air. She'd always been an early riser and was used to setting off on her morning run with the first rays of light. In the heat of the past few weeks, she'd been going out even earlier. She liked being by herself in nature while everyone else was still asleep, and letting the breeze blow away her mental cobwebs. But as she turned to wake Jago with a kiss, his arms tightened round her as he shifted in his sleep and she snuggled into the crook of his arm, resting her head against his broad chest and listening to the strong, rhythmic beat of his heart.

Asleep, his face was unlined and untroubled and he looked like his old self. But she knew something was bothering him. She also knew he would only tell her when he was ready. He just needed time and space and there was plenty of that available now. She'd felt tense herself for the past three days, as if waiting for something to happen, but had put that down to the launch. Now that had been successful, could she relax a little? Although she and Rocky had other projects on their books, after the crazy months working flat out at Peneglos Hall, they had made sure to give themselves some lighter weeks over the summer.

'Morning.' Jago's deep voice broke into her thoughts. 'What are you worrying about?'

'I'm not worrying!' Olivia kissed him. 'Just thinking about our plans for the summer.'

'Let's get today out of the way first.' His hand lazily stroked up and down her arm. 'I presume there's an itinerary, knowing Lucinda?'

''Fraid so. She wants everyone to have a leisurely breakfast and then meet at the swimming pond at about eleven o'clock.'

Jago sighed. 'I still don't understand why they went to all the expense of building a swimming pond when there's a perfectly good cove at the bottom of the valley.'

Olivia sat up and clasped her knees to her chest. 'The steps down to the cove are eroding and it'll cost a fortune to restore them. Lucinda is adamant that the swimming pond is more cost-effective as it can be used almost all year round and is far more environmentally friendly than a conventional swimming pool.'

He didn't look convinced. 'And have you been to admire it?'

'Not yet.' Olivia looked shamefaced. 'You know it's not really my thing.' There was a silence while she thought about her phobia of water, caused by her older brother's drowning when they were young. She'd made a real effort to overcome it last summer, with lots of patience and help from Jago. But she hadn't been swimming at all in the last few months while he'd been in London.

He ran his hand down her back. 'Well, I'm sure Lucinda will understand if we give it a miss.'

'No!' Olivia knelt up in the bed, her dark eyes shining. 'Why don't we check it out now? Before everyone else is up.' She caught hold of his hands. 'We'll have it all to ourselves and it's got to be the perfect place for me to give it another go.'

Jago pulled her back down beside him and nuzzled her neck. 'It's not even six o'clock yet. Can't we just stay here instead?'

'I think you need to exercise a different set of muscles and a swim will be perfect.' She jumped out of bed and pulled on her navy and white one-piece. 'You did bring your trunks?'

From the look on Jago's face, she knew she'd won this argument. When she was determined about something, there was no stopping her.

'In my bag.'

She fished them out and threw them to him, before heading to the door. 'Come on,' she called over her shoulder. 'What's stopping you?'

---

They wandered hand in hand across the terrace, the sun warming their bodies through the white bath robes supplied by the Hall. They both took deep breaths of sea air and listened to the second dawn chorus. Olivia held her face to the sun like a flower, any worries about Jago being distant at the party momentarily quashed.

They followed a path from the terrace through the lawns and on to another oasis of lush green plants, in the middle of which lay what looked like a subtropical lagoon surrounded by tall umbrella palms, tree ferns, bamboos, reeds and bullrushes. Large natural boulders were interspersed with sedums, verbenas, geraniums and buddleia. Floating boardwalks ran off a sun deck surrounded with bold agapanthus at the far end of the pond and through the crystal-clear water to the other. Amidst the birdsong, brightly coloured dragonflies hovered and darted in front of them and damselflies skimmed the surface of the water. Jago turned to Olivia, with a smile on his face.

'This is incredible! Didn't Ruan once tell me it used to be an old cattle pond?'

She laughed. 'That's what he likes to believe. Apparently, it was just an old stagnant and redundant pond which had silted up over the years. But it's the perfect location for something like this. Near enough to the house for easy access, but far enough away to be able to imagine you are in a tropical paradise.'

'Well, it certainly beats the turquoise rectangles most hotels have. And I suppose it ticks a lot of green boxes?'

She shrugged. 'You'd better ask Ruan if you want all the technical details, but basically the pond is split into two zones. You swim in the larger one and in the other one the water is filtered somehow by plants and stuff.' She pointed out the shallower planted area at the far end, which was obscured by more subtropical plants on the banks. 'It doesn't use loads of energy to heat and circulate the water or harsh chemicals like chlorine. Lucinda raves about how clean and clear the water is and how wonderful it makes your skin feel.'

'Are you sure you want to try it?' He threw his bathrobe onto the low deep seating area, built in local granite and set within the oak decking, and hurried into the shallow waters of the pond, still conscious of the fading scars that criss-crossed his torso, caused by a knife attack some years before.

'Come on in!' he called. 'It's not even that cold!'

Her stomach clenched. Perhaps she hadn't come as far as she thought. 'You go on!' She placed her own robe down on the seats and paddled into the shallow waters, enjoying the cool water lapping around her ankles and the warmth of the sun on her bare shoulders.

'You're right! It's fantastic in here,' Jago called from halfway up the pond. 'No waves or currents, you'll be fine.'

Olivia smiled at his encouragement. She'd always enjoyed swimming as a child. Then Aidan had died in a horrific accident off a beach in Thailand and she'd been unable to save him. As a result, she hadn't swum in the sea, or anywhere else, for nearly twenty-five years.

Jago swam expertly down the pond and caught her in his arms. 'I'm so proud of you.' He twirled her around in the water and then held her close and kissed her. 'You're going to be back being the little fish George always told me about.'

She kissed him back. 'It really does feel like the perfect place to try.'

'Well, I'm going to explore the other end, where the plants are,' Jago announced. 'Fancy a race?'

'You're on!'

Olivia took a deep breath and plunged in head first. The shock of the chilly water took her breath for a split second before she powered through the water after Jago, muscle memory immediately coming into play with a delightful sense of her entire body stretching and working in a way that was so different from running. They raced through the water, Jago slightly ahead, due to his enthusiasm rather than any style, and Olivia was breathless when she stopped, totally out of practice. She paused while she recovered her breath, but when she eventually turned to Jago, he pulled her roughly away.

'Turn round and go back to the other end.' His voice was harsh.

'What's the matter?' She blinked the water out of her eyes.

'Just go, Olivia!'

'No!' She pushed past him. 'What is it?' She reared backwards in horror.

There, caught among the plants in the regeneration zone was a limp body dressed in waiting-staff uniform. Olivia shook the water out of her eyes, but she knew she recognised the body. It was the waitress who had dropped her tray at the party the night before.

# 4

'I just can't believe it was you two who had the misfortune of finding another dead body, my lovely!' The look that passed across Olivia's face made Cassie chide herself for her tactless words. 'But I suppose it's good you've been allowed to come home to wait for the police to take your statements. Let's just hope they get here soon and we can all get back to normal.'

They were sitting under the pergola in the garden at Tresillian, picking at the lunch she'd quickly prepared for them. The afternoon was hot and sunny and they were all glad of the shade and sweet scents provided by the clematis, honeysuckle and grapevines sprawling over the wooden structure.

'They tried to keep it low-key, but the sirens and flashing lights were a bit of a giveaway to the other guests. And I don't think the poor young copper who was first on the scene had ever seen a dead body before.' Jago put his hand on Olivia's knee and Cassie smiled at the easy affection between them. 'It all went downhill after that and I think it was decided it would be better to keep us out of the way. Took them long enough to get the okay from their higher powers though.'

Cassie was watching Olivia closely. She'd changed into shorts and vest top as soon as she got back home, but when a light breeze had blown up from the creek she'd added a hoodie in an attempt to get warm. She was still visibly shivering in spite of the hot sun, her knees drawn up to her chin, and she was keeping out of the conversation. This wasn't the confident, sassy Olivia whom she'd known for the last seven years, who faced life full on, ran a successful renovation and restoration business with Rocky and was a founding trustee of the nearby Penbartha Goods Shed Trust. She was a shadow of her usual self. Whatever she had seen that morning had obviously brought back some unwanted, upsetting memories. And, as usual, Cassie wanted to make everything better.

When Cassie had applied for the job as housekeeper and gardener seven years ago, she had instantly fallen under the spell of Tresillian House, the garden and all the family, including Olivia. After George's sudden death the previous year, Cassie had willingly taken over a more maternal role even though there was only a ten-year age gap between them. From the chats they'd shared when walking, gardening or just enjoying a late kitchen supper together, Cassie knew how much Olivia was looking forward to a peaceful summer, with the huge contract at Peneglos Hall successfully completed and Jago coming home for three months. There seemed to be something else bothering her too, but she knew Olivia well enough not to pry. What they needed now was the police to confirm that the poor waitress had drowned in a tragic accident and, awful as that would be, they could try to get back to their plans for the summer.

Zennor hovered on her back legs at Olivia's feet and

whined until she scooped the little dog up and buried her face in her white fur. Mylor immediately looked up from his favourite spot in the shade, wandered over and sat on his mistress's feet, determined not to be left out. Cassie smiled. That would do Olivia good, she thought. She adored those dogs and they always seemed able to read her needs better than any human. They usually went everywhere together, and last night being a rare night apart, they had happily spent it with Cassie, taking up more than their fair share of her bed. But the rapturous reception they had given Olivia when she returned home left no doubt as to who occupied the prime spot in their hearts.

Shouts and laughter from the creek broke the silence and Cassie looked across the lawn, neatly mowed into green velvety swirls and stripes, as a group of kayakers and paddleboarders raced each other down the smooth stretch of water. Holidaymakers, she thought as their noisy splashing disturbed a group of sunbathing oystercatchers, who flew crossly over to the other bank to seek refuge. Another soft breeze wafted enticing scents from the huge terracotta pots of scarlet bougainvillea towards them and she made a mental note to check if they needed watering.

Footsteps crunched on the gravel from the other side of the house, announcing the arrival of visitors, and Cassie noticed how Olivia instantly tensed. The dogs rushed off in a volley of barking, which stopped as quickly as it started and was immediately replaced by ecstatic whining.

'Well, that doesn't sound like a welcome for the police,' Cassie commented as she got to her feet to investigate. Zennor and Mylor ran backwards and forwards, tails wagging furiously, followed by a slightly subdued Rocky and Kitten. Rocky went straight to his old friend and squeezed her shoulder. Any hopes that last night's incident wouldn't be mentioned were quickly dashed when Jago got straight to the point.

'I take it you've heard the news then?'

'What do you expect in a place like this? It was probably all over the jungle drums before you'd finished making the 999 call!' Kitten exclaimed. 'We didn't even stay at the Hall last night, but have had loads of texts and messages about it.' She turned to Olivia, oblivious to her distress. 'Blimey, Olive, what is it with you and finding dead bodies?'

'Kitten!' Cassie hissed. 'Some poor girl has drowned and Olivia and Jago had the misfortune to find her. Stop being so thoughtless with your flippant remarks!'

Kitten subsided. 'Sorry, Mum.' She peered more closely at Olivia. 'Sorry, Olive. That was in totally poor taste now I think about it. Sorry.'

Cassie shook her head, and marched into the kitchen, so furious with her daughter she didn't dare speak to her. *When will that girl learn to think before she opens her mouth? And why did she have to bring up the subject of dead bodies?* She'd always been headstrong and outspoken, the complete opposite of Cassie, and far more like her father who had disappeared pretty much as soon as he'd learnt of his impending fatherhood and hadn't been seen since. She'd been living in Manchester then, as a student horticulturalist, and was too ashamed to admit her lack of judgement when it came to men. So rather than going home to her parents in Newlyn, she'd led them to believe he was still on the scene and stuck it out in the North West, retrained as a nurse and brought Kitten up alone.

Cassie sighed as she arranged more bread rolls and cheese on plates and took a bowl of salad out of the fridge. After an easy childhood, the soft and sweet little Kitten had turned into a feline tornado and spent her adolescence and early adulthood rebelling against everything and fighting for all the things she believed in. Which were many. Her fads and phases usually passed, but her most passionate and longstanding one, to protect the environment and all that entailed, looked like it was here to stay.

Thank God Kitten had decided to study at Falmouth University and pointed out, in her outspoken way, that it was time to admit her father wasn't coming back so Cassie might as well move home to Cornwall. Homeless and jobless, she had answered an advert in *The Lady* and the rest was history. The beautiful coach house in the gardens, restored by Olivia as one of her earlier projects, came with the job and Cassie was in heaven.

She gazed around the main house's kitchen, which merged into an orangery that extended across the whole width of the back of the house and had the most incredible views over the garden to the creek. She'd loved George and Mollie, who had treated her more like a daughter than an employee, and she adored Olivia who, as their ward and goddaughter, had come as part of their family unit, even though she was working away from home a lot at the time. Some may have wondered what would happen to her after Mollie and George died, but she'd quickly been assured that her future was secure at Tresillian and always would be.

She poured some home-made elderflower pressé into a jug and topped it up with fresh ice and water and gathered more glasses from the cabinet. She breathed out, her anger at her daughter easing and she was ready to face her again. Cassie loaded everything on to a tray and walked back outside, calm and smiling. At least since Kitten had been with Rocky she'd calmed down a bit, particularly appearance wise. She now looked less jumble and more vintage as her style had progressed from grungy to creative and eye-catching in a good way. And despite the ten-year age difference, Cassie thought Rocky was the solid, uncomplicated influence her daughter needed. She was happy Kitten was having better success with her choice of men than she ever had.

Cassie's eyes were on Olivia as she set the tray down on the large garden table. At least she was joining in now. She and Rocky were discussing some of the conversations they'd had the night before and making tentative plans for the following week's jobs. Cassie poured two glasses of elderflower water, handed one to Rocky and told him to help himself to food. He smiled at her and nodded towards Kitten. She took the hint and sat by her daughter.

'How are things at the Hall?'

Kitten rolled her eyes. 'Pretty much as you'd imagine. Lucinda's in a right state. Mainly about the waitress dying, but also about what it might mean for the Hall's opening date. Ruan's being stoical and Dylan's gone walkabout.'

Cassie immediately thought of Dylan, the quiet, reclusive gardener at the Hall and one of the few people she regarded as a genuine friend.

'Has he?'

'I thought he might have told you.'

After George's death, Cassie had found herself with more time on her hands and the guilt caused by her involvement with Martin had made her withdraw more into herself. Kitten and Olivia suggested she shared her knowledge and experience with Dylan and the volunteer gardeners at Peneglos Hall. Ruan and Lucinda had welcomed her onto their team with open arms and a generous budget and so for the last sixteen months she had cleared borders, weeded beds, and pruned and nurtured the more exotic plants that she'd slowly uncovered. Dylan had shared with her the piles of gardeners' journals and records he'd been given by Charles and while he concentrated on reviving the kitchen garden,

Cassie was given free range elsewhere. The gardens had slowly helped her heal, and she was fitter and stronger because of it.

'I don't pry. We talk about the gardens. Nothing else. I have no idea how his mind works. All I do know is he doesn't like being around people. He probably took off last night before the party.' She gave her daughter a sharp look and Kitten looked away. Perhaps she'd learnt to read her mother's mood after all these years and finally realised she gave all men a wide berth.

The distinctive sound of wheels crunching on the drive caused another volley of barking from the dogs and the mood under the pergola plummeted. Rocky and Kitten bade everyone a hasty farewell and, as they disappeared round one side of the house, another two figures appeared from the other.

'Hi, everybody. Long time no see!' The taller of the two men strode towards them, arm outstretched, and shook their hands in turn. 'Let me introduce my new DS, Sam O'Driscoll.'

While the stockier man was busy shaking hands Cassie noticed that DI Ross Trenow, who had investigated last year's murders at Penbartha Station, was looking tanned, refreshed and surprisingly pleased to see everyone. Mylor was busy thumping his tail with delight at seeing his old friend, and Zennor was rolling on her back, legs akimbo as he bent and scratched her tummy. Cassie shook her head in despair. She'd be happy to never see him again.

'Is DS Burridge no longer with us?' There was no mistaking the hope in Olivia's voice.

Trenow grimaced. 'Turned out Cornwall wasn't exciting enough for him, so he got himself a transfer to the Metropolitan Police and Sam's come down here on a kind of job swap. He's got a lot more tact and experience so let's just say the Met's loss is our gain.'

Cassie relaxed a little. Burridge had disliked everyone, particularly Olivia, whom he'd been only too willing to believe was guilty of murder. She stole a quick look at Sam O'Driscoll and relaxed a little more. He was the complete opposite of Burridge. Older, broader, calmer, with a face whose lines suggested he had seen most things before. He appeared completely comfortable in his shirtsleeves, his tie in a loose knot. Burridge would have been in a full three-piece suit, even in these temperatures. *Tuss!*

'Can I get you both a drink?'

The police officers exchanged a nod. 'Anything cold would be great, thanks, Cassie. Sam will help you while I have a chat with these two.'

Cassie took the hint and led the sergeant into the kitchen. He perched on one of the tall stools at the island and gazed around him, his admiration clear from his good-natured observations. She concentrated on quartering more lemons and plucking mint leaves from the jam jar on the counter and decided to let the policeman get his questions over with.

O'Driscoll followed her gaze across to the terrace. 'How are they doing?'

'I think Jago is okay. I'm more concerned about Olivia.' Cassie added water from the fridge cooler to a glass jug.

'It's probably brought back all sorts of memories.'

Cassie narrowed her eyes. Had he and Trenow been talking? 'Yes, but I think they're more to do with her brother's death.' The blank look that crossed the policeman's face gave her some satisfaction. 'He drowned in the sea in Thailand twenty-five years ago. Olivia was there.'

'Oh, sorry. I didn't know that.' He looked outside again. 'Poor girl.'

'Yes. But I suppose you and the inspector were talking about her finding Libby Walsh's body at Penbartha Station last year?' Cassie surprised herself with her direct question.

O'Driscoll nodded. 'That sounded like a pretty dreadful business.'

A wave of memories crashed through Cassie's mind, accompanied by a surge of guilt for the part she'd unwittingly played in Martin's deceit which had led to the murders.

'It was. But just as Olivia had absolutely nothing to do with any of those murders last year, I can assure you she had nothing to do with this poor girl's death.' Her voice rose. 'She and Jago were simply in the wrong place at the wrong time and I'd be grateful if you'd leave her alone and go and bother someone else.'

*Wow! Where had that come from?* Cassie took a deep breath and buried her face in the fridge for a moment to cool herself down. When she turned back to O'Driscoll he was watching her with a puzzled expression on his face.

'Okay. Shall we start again? I'm not here to ask questions about Olivia. I was just being polite.' He tried another smile. 'I understand you work in the gardens at Peneglos Hall?'

'That's right. On a part-time basis.'

'And when were you last there?'

Cassie blinked. 'Yesterday morning. Making sure everything in the garden was in order for the party.'

'Did you do any work round the swimming pond?'

Cassie shook her head. 'Not yesterday. I planned all the planting some while ago and it pretty much looks after itself now. The pond itself is Ruan and Lucinda's baby and they have a company come in to check that the filtration system is working properly.'

'Do you know the name of the maintenance company?' He pulled his notebook out.

'No, sorry. You'll have to ask Ruan.'

'And what about the other people who work in the garden?'

Cassie folded her arms tightly across her chest. 'They're mostly volunteers – retired or suchlike – who appreciate what we're doing with the gardens and want to help out.'

'Do you have a list of names?'

Cassie pursed her lips. 'Not personally, but I think there's a list on the shed wall. You'll have to ask Ruan.'

O'Driscoll flicked over a page in his notebook. 'I already have. The only one we haven't been able to contact is Dylan Bonnar.'

'He's a bit of a loner and probably took himself off somewhere to avoid all the people wandering around last night. Which is neither bad nor suspicious, is it?'

'Not at all. We're just trying to find out if anyone saw anything last night or earlier this morning.' She could feel his cool hazel eyes watching her closely and she turned away from their intense gaze.

'None of the volunteers were there last night, sergeant. Or this morning. They do have their own lives to lead.'

'I appreciate that. But we have to check or we wouldn't be doing our job properly.'

Cassie felt hot tears burning at the back of her eyelids. He was so bloody calm and here she was acting like an emotional wreck and probably just making matters worse for everyone. She needed to pull herself together.

'I'm sorry, sergeant. I'm not being deliberately obstructive. I just don't get involved in other people's business. If you ask

Inspector Trenow about what happened last year, you'll understand why.'

'No worries. These are just routine questions.' He paused. 'Is it okay for me to call you Cassie?' He carried on when she nodded. 'We're not accusing anyone of anything.'

O'Driscoll's lived-in face crumpled into a smile and he reached out a hand to touch her arm, but she shied away. She would not be taken in by the charms of another Londoner. Ever again. Not even one who wore delicious cologne that smelled of sandalwood, cedar and citrus.

'We're just trying to find out if anyone knew or saw the dead girl after the party. We haven't even established her identity yet.' He scratched the back of his neck.

Cassie's eyes filled again as she thought of the poor drowned girl whose family were probably wondering where she was this morning and she quickly grabbed the tray, turned to go outside and then stopped. Jago and Olivia sat rigidly, their backs straight and their faces tight. It didn't take a body language expert to tell Cassie they were unhappy with Trenow's line of questioning. The policeman didn't look much happier. Mylor was tense, watching the conversation closely, his ears twitching, and Zennor jumped up onto Olivia's lap and nuzzled into her neck.

'What's going on out there?' she demanded. 'What's he saying to them? Olivia looks upset.'

O'Driscoll took the tray from her and ushered her back into the orangery. 'Nothing to worry about. It's routine to interview the witnesses who were first at the crime scene.'

Cassie stared at him wide-eyed. 'Who says it's a crime scene? The poor girl just drowned, didn't she?'

'We're not sure yet. We have no idea who she was and we're not ruling out the possibility that she may already have been dead when she entered the water.'

# 5

'I didn't expect to see you in here this morning.' Kitten appeared as if by magic at Olivia's table in the Waiting Rooms café. 'Have you been in touch with Lucinda and Ruan?'

Olivia blinked, not expecting to be under siege before she'd even sat down. She was just enjoying the delicious aroma of fresh coffee mingling with the sweet scent of freshly baked bread and cakes, when Kitten pounced.

'It's only Tuesday and I haven't had a minute.' She pulled her thoughts away from her current project's most recent drawings that needed annotating and the upcoming Skype call with her New York office she hadn't yet prepared for and looked around at the busy café, almost full of local dog walkers, some holidaymakers and a group of middle-aged ramblers tucking in to ham and cheese toasties. 'I am trying to juggle at least three jobs at the minute. And I've just had a meeting with Bea Mathers, as per your request.'

Kitten ignored the rebuke, her attention now on another of her passions. 'Oh yes, of course!' Her eyes narrowed. 'I didn't see you in there.'

'Well, I promise I was.' Olivia held her gaze.

'Isn't Bea fabulous? How did it go?'

Olivia followed Kitten's eyes to the adjoining station master's house. After the success of the café when it opened, and the demand for an area in which village groups could meet in private, it had been agreed to knock through to extend the space. In typical Olivia and Rocky style, they had combined artistry and function by installing double sliding pocket doors of frosted glass and then commissioned a local artist to etch a detailed outline of the old Victorian station on the panes. The arrangement created a unique design statement, at the same time dividing and creating different zones and allowing natural light throughout while retaining privacy. The annex had been a huge success.

Through the doors Olivia could still see the group of people she'd spent the last hour with, sitting around the table surrounded by baskets of coloured threads, buttons, fabric offcuts, needles and scissors, their heads down and concentrating on their task, while a low hum of chat and laughter filled the air. Mrs Chynoweth, the retired village postmistress and her godmother's best friend, was still at the far side of the table, deep in conversation with a much younger woman, who Olivia now knew was busy embroidering tractor motifs onto a pair of children's ripped jeans.

'It went well, I think. Bea's certainly dedicated to the whole concept of sustainable fashion. And from the number of locals in there this morning for the Sew Social session, all wanting to repair or alter their existing clothes, I'd say there's a real demand for her services. And she seems to be a good teacher.'

Kitten sat down opposite her and signalled to her assistant behind the counter to bring two coffees over. 'I think she's great and I really like what she says about learning to recycle our clothes and breaking the habit of buying new.'

Olivia smiled. 'Yes, I was rather glad I was wearing one of Mollie's old shirts.' She looked down at the vintage Liberty shirt she wore loose over a vest and a pair of old cut-off jeans.

Kitten laughed. 'So, what's the next step?'

'Well, Bea feels the space that's available in the Engine Shed is ideal for all her equipment and everything else she needs, and she's fully on board with our mission statement, so I'll get a contract drawn up and report back to the board with my recommendation to offer her a tenancy at the next meeting.'

'Fantastic! Bea's just the sort of person we need.' Kitten leant forward, her eyes shining with a familiar zeal. 'Did she tell you all those awful facts about fast fashion? Textile production creates more greenhouse gas emissions than all international flights and maritime shipping combined, every year. Not to mention the half a million tonnes of microplastics that end up in the oceans from plastic-based textiles.'

'Yes, she did.' Olivia spoke firmly, making it clear she had no intention of going down that particular rabbit hole with Kitten just at the moment. 'And I agree with everything she said, but I can only do my bit. I'm more than happy to support other people's commitment to the environment, but I can't cry their tears for them, only my own.'

Kitten looked at her sharply, opened her mouth and then shut it again. The arrival of their drinks distracted her briefly and Olivia sipped at her cappuccino, her mind automatically drifting back to Tresillian where she'd left Jago in bed. He'd tossed and turned until the early hours every night since they'd discovered the body, so each morning she'd left him to sleep while she'd gone for a run.

There was definitely something bothering him. She'd known it from the first moment she'd seen his face at the Peneglos Hall party, but he was still completely in denial. And despite his protestations that he was perfectly okay, Olivia wasn't convinced. And she was worried. For the first time in their relationship, she was doubting almost every word he said.

'Earth to Olivia!' Kitten's impatient tone snapped Olivia out of her worries and she focused her attention on her friend. 'Can we get back to my original question about Ruan and Lucinda, please? Has anybody said anything to you about the *accident* in the swimming pond?'

Olivia heard the emphasis on the word accident.

'Only the police.' She didn't mention the fact she and Jago had deliberately avoided most people, and the inevitable conversations that would follow, since the weekend.

'Did the police suggest it was anything more than an accident?' Kitten's whisper rose.

'Not to me, they didn't. Trenow was asking us lots of questions, but not making any suggestions, as far as I can recall.'

'That's got to be a good sign, hasn't it?' Kitten perked up. 'Lucinda's in a right state as it is. She's so upset about the waitress drowning; she's even blaming herself for not making sure she'd got into the taxi.'

Olivia felt a rush of sympathy for her client. 'I'm sorry, that must be a horrible thing to have on your conscience. Even though she has nothing to feel guilty about.'

Kitten fiddled with her teaspoon. 'I think she wants to talk to you.'

Olivia swallowed. 'Why me?'

'Oh, come on, Olive.' Kitten's cat-like amber eyes flashed.

'You of all people should understand the implications of having a dead body found on your business premises...' She trailed off.

Heat flooded Olivia's face. She did not need reminding of the nightmare that had followed her discovery of Libby Walsh's body in the Weighbridge Hut. A nightmare that had only been solved with the help of Jago. And now here she was, full circle. Would Jago be prepared to go out on such a limb for her again? Given his current mood, she doubted it.

Kitten seemed to read her mind. 'What's Jago got to say about it all?'

'Not much,' Olivia muttered. 'He's got a lot on his mind at the moment.'

'He certainly didn't look too happy at the party. Even before the waitress fainted.' Kitten looked at her more closely. 'Do *you* think the waitress recognised him from somewhere?'

'No, I don't!' Olivia snapped, fanning herself frantically with the menu. 'Please, Kitten. You're really not helping.'

Kitten tilted her head to one side, a look of genuine concern settling on her feline features. 'I'm so sorry, Olive. I know how much you were looking forward to Jago coming home after all that time apart. Is there anything I can do to help? Do you want to talk about it?'

'No!' Olivia's reply was instinctive. 'I mean, I appreciate your concern, but Jago and I just need to get used to being together again, that's all. It's been a bit full-on since he got back, but we'll work it out.'

Kitten didn't look convinced. 'Olive, I just want to...'

'Kitten!' The girl behind the counter called for help. 'I need you over here. Now!'

She rose, reluctantly, and went to the rescue. Olivia gave a huge sigh of relief and looked again into the annex at the group of happy, smiling faces gathered there. Despite her own worries, a small thrill ran through her. This was what the Penbartha Station Trust was all about. Helping people to help the planet was at the core of what they all stood for. If only everything else in life could be so straightforward.

6

Jago wasn't feeling the joys of midsummer he'd hoped for as he walked into the village. He had already been struggling to accept the outcome of his latest trial, but discovering the dead body of the waitress had sent his thoughts firing off in all sorts of random directions.

A slight breeze was just about managing to keep the heat at a pleasant level, and he relished taking in deep breaths of fresh Cornish air, letting it fill his lungs in a way it never did in London. Memories of his last Old Bailey trial were still playing on a loop inside his head and before he knew it, he'd skirted the village playing field and hopped across the stepping stones at the head of the creek. He then walked up the hill onto the village's main street, following the mouth-watering smells that were coming out of the Bakehouse's open front doors.

As usual, there was a queue outside and Jago took a quick look at the building next door, which had recently been incorporated into the bakery and was now being fitted out as a delicatessen. The Bakehouse had proved such a success that its owners, Frazer and Willow Jardine, had bought the adjacent property in order to extend both their business premises and their living quarters above, and it looked to Jago as though everything was going according to schedule. As the queue moved and he stepped inside he could see it was as busy as ever and the counter displays of breads, rolls and pasties, tussling for space on large slate trays among cakes, scones, pastries and biscuits were already emptying.

Two unfamiliar middle-aged women were serving behind the counter, supervised by a tall, blonde, heavily pregnant figure whose striking features creased into a welcoming smile when she saw Jago waiting patiently behind an elderly couple who were trying to choose between cream puffs and lemon drizzle cake.

'Jago!' She waddled round the display counter and tried to throw her arms around him without her bump getting in the way. 'How lovely to see you! It's been far too long since you were here. Frazer said you might drop by this morning!'

A rush of affection took Jago by surprise as he hugged her back and then held her at arm's length.

'You look wonderful, Willow. Positively blooming!'

'Don't!' Willow swatted him with the tea towel she was carrying. 'This heat is killing me. Trust me to be eight months pregnant in the middle of the first heatwave Cornwall's had for years! Everything is so swollen by the end of the day all I want to do is sit under the oak tree with my feet in a bucket of cold water. And I mean everything!'

Jago laughed, happy to hear there was no real note of complaint in Willow's tone.

'And I miss everything these days because I'm so wiped out by seven o'clock.' She looked at him sideways. 'That's why we didn't get to the party at the Hall on Friday.'

Jago managed not to flinch. 'Well, you didn't miss much, in

my opinion.' He peered through the glass panels in the back wall of the serving area, which exposed the kitchen of the bakery – a large, airy space; clean and modern; and lined with shiny stainless-steel surfaces, ovens and trolleys that gleamed in the bright light. 'Is Frazer about?'

Willow's lip quirked and she gave him a knowing look. 'Okay, Jago, I can take a hint. No more questions from me.' She handed him a carafe of iced water and two glasses. 'Frazer will be finished in a minute. Why don't you take this through to the garden and sit in the shade while you wait for him. You can even use my bucket for your feet if you like.'

He blew her a kiss and escaped into the garden. He sat at the large wooden table, carefully positioned in the shade, surrounded by raised beds full of colourful flowers he didn't recognise, and took a deep breath. What was it with the women in the village and their mind-reading abilities? He knew he needed to talk to someone, he just wasn't sure how much to say.

'Jago!' Frazer strode across the lawn, still dressed in the Bakehouse's distinctive uniform of black and white checked trousers, black tunic and white apron. He embraced his friend and pulled off his apron and tunic to reveal a white slim-fitting tee shirt. He wiped his face with his apron and took a huge gulp of water.

'Phew! Am I glad to see you. It's as hot as hell in that kitchen. Even with the new fans.'

'It's even hotter in London, believe me. In all sorts of ways,' Jago remarked and then winced. He didn't want to think about London, let alone talk about it. 'Your building work's coming on well, I see.' He nodded towards the upper floor of the two adjoining buildings. His ploy worked. Frazer couldn't resist talking about his empire expansion.

'I'm so glad I insisted on them finishing the flat first,' he confided. 'At least Willow can nest to her heart's content now. And I can get on with overseeing fitting out the deli side of the shop.'

'Rocky's not doing that, is he?'

Frazer sighed. 'No, he's far too busy. We were lucky he could get one of his teams to do the actual building work and the guy who's here now comes highly recommended.'

'Do you reckon you'll be finished before the baby arrives?'

He shrugged. 'If all goes to plan, yes. But if the bairn decides to put in an early appearance, who knows?' He shifted in his seat and turned his gaze on Jago. 'But I don't want to think about that just now. What's up? You're not your usual laid-back self.'

Jago swallowed. 'I'm not really sure. I just have a bad feeling about things...'

Frazer narrowed his eyes. 'You're a barrister, Jago, you deal in facts and logic. Not feelings.'

Jago winced again. His friend was right. It was what he had been constantly telling Olivia the previous year when she'd been listening to her instincts and gut feelings while he kept banging on about facts and the truth.

'Perhaps I've been spending too much time with Olivia and her ways are rubbing off on me?' he suggested weakly.

'Come off it.' Frazer frowned. 'You've not seen much of her at all in the last three or four months, so don't try that one with me.'

Jago shrugged but Frazer wasn't letting him off that easily.

'What's really going on? I know you and Olivia found another dead body on Saturday morning and that's enough to freak most people out. But we're not talking about most people, are we? We're talking James Trevithick KC.'

Jago shifted uncomfortably in his seat. This was a new side to Frazer. Gone was the amiable, laid-back baker and in his place was the eagle-eyed, driven and determined managing partner of an international accountancy firm, a role he had given up three years previously to save his marriage and his mind. The years fell away and Jago felt like a young, fresh-faced and wet-behind-the-ears barrister in court for the first time and being called out by an experienced, formidable judge over some rookie mistake. He decided to try and bluff his way out.

'I'm supposed to be on holiday. Can we talk about something else?'

Frazer glowered. 'Just cut the crap and tell me what the hell is going on. Life's too short to play games.'

'Okay then.' He took a deep breath. 'I'm beginning to seriously question my decision to go back to the London Bar.'

'What?' Frazer was stunned. 'Have the bright lights of the Old Bailey dimmed already?'

'For many reasons.' He didn't even try to keep the bitterness out of his voice. 'Only one of which might be because they can't afford to pay the electricity bills anymore.'

'What? You've lost me already.'

One of the bakery assistants came out to them with a tray of bread, antipasto, fruit and more water, and unwittingly broke the tension between the two men.

'Willow thought this might be welcome.'

Frazer grinned at his new apprentice. 'That woman knows me too well.' He handed a plate to Jago and the two men ate in silence.

Jago was glad of the time to collect his thoughts. As a young barrister, he hadn't gone into criminal justice for an easy life or to make his fortune. He'd wanted to see justice done, fairly and properly. And last year, after the murders at the station site, he'd decided the urge was still there and he wanted to go back. To make sure that murderers like Martin

Lambert and all the other criminals who made up his daily working life were tried fairly and received their due sentence. But, he reflected as he munched on a red onion and cheese roll, it hadn't proved to be as straightforward as he'd hoped.

Frazer pushed his empty plate to one side and turned his tawny gaze back on his friend. 'You were saying…'

Jago sighed. 'I'm not sure what I'm saying. This is the first time I've articulated it to someone outside the Bar. When you're caught up in something you don't really notice things the same way.'

'Try me.'

Jago spun his unused knife around. 'At first it was just the little things in the public areas of the courts that got me down. To be fair, many of them had already been there before I left. I just accepted that the carpets would be tatty, the walls dirty and scuffed, the furniture collapsing, the loos broken. Even the Old Bailey is surprisingly shabby when you look past all its marble splendour.'

'Doesn't exactly inspire confidence in the victims, does it?'

'Or the barristers,' Jago commented drily.

'And that's all down to good old government cuts, is it?'

Jago nodded. 'Completely.'

'Why do I get the feeling that you're not a man who cares deep down about the infrastructure and you're actually concerned about something much more important?'

Frazer's gaze pinned Jago to the spot and he wondered for a moment whether his friend was wasted as a baker. *Or does he just have his priorities right?*

'You've hit the nail on the head,' he agreed. 'I can tolerate poor standards in the court buildings. What I can't bear is the deterioration in standards of advocacy.'

Frazer grimaced. 'That's not good.'

'You have no idea how awful it can be.' Jago stared at his

friend. 'I knew that a lot of the old KCs had decided to hang up their wigs and robes and retire while their pensions were still decent. And they were the real characters, the backbone of the criminal justice system. The performers, the entertainers, with biting wit, scarily quick minds and matching tongues. I miss squaring up to them in court, the verbal sparring, the fun times I had being prosecuting counsel in the days when it was a fair fight.' He paused for a moment, lost in memories.

'And the new ones coming through aren't of the same calibre?'

'A lot of them aren't. It's when I'm sitting as a judge that I really notice how things have changed. More and more often I'm presiding over trials where one side or the other is being represented by a barrister who just isn't up to the job. Sometimes they don't have the experience, sometimes the knowledge, and in the most worrying cases they just haven't got the fundamental ability, Frazer. Believe me!'

'And is that down to government cuts, or a system that's churning out ill-prepared barristers, like every other profession these days – all highly qualified on paper but bloody useless in practice?'

'You tell me.' Jago looked around him. 'More and more often as a judge these days, I feel like I'm refereeing the legal equivalent of a football match between a premier league side and a third division team. Which is not the way the system is supposed to work. How can I possibly ensure a fair, clean match?'

Frazer just shook his head.

'On one occasion recently, which I'd really rather forget, the defendant became so exasperated with the appalling performance of his barrister that he sacked him on the second day of the trial and decided to have a go at representing himself.'

'That doesn't sound good.'

'Let's just say it didn't end well. And I'm absolutely convinced that justice wasn't done.' He closed his eyes as the memory of his last case flooded his mind. He couldn't bring himself to tell Frazer about it. That was the one that had ended badly and still haunted him. The sort of thing that just shouldn't happen in this day and age. And yet it had.

'It sounds to me like you need a holiday, mate. And a chance to forget all about work for a while.' As soon as the words left his lips, Fazer winced. 'Ah. I see your problem.'

Jago raised tired eyes. 'You do?'

'Absolutely.' Frazer drained the last of his water. 'But I don't understand why you won't talk to Olivia.'

'I just can't. She's got enough going on with running her own business, never mind still doing too much at the Goods Shed, Waiting Rooms and now the Engine Shed as well. I don't want to burden her with my problems.'

'Isn't that what relationships are all about? Sharing burdens?'

'Perhaps.' He grimaced. 'I just haven't got the bandwidth for it at the moment. Especially not with Gabe stirring the shit with everyone, the police included.'

Frazer did a double take. 'You've lost me again.'

'Are you telling me that you haven't heard that particular gem?'

Frazer gestured towards the bakery. 'You are aware of the antisocial hours I work, aren't you?'

'I envy you for that sometimes.' He paused. 'Gabe took great delight in telling Trenow it was when the waitress saw me that she dropped the tray she was carrying.'

'Really?'

'But I was also with Lucinda, Gabe and Lexie at the time.' Jago thought for a moment. 'And Lucinda just put it down to having a funny turn because of the heat. It was a bit later on that Gabe suggested she might have recognised me from court.'

Frazer pulled a face. 'From court? That's not very likely down here, is it? Especially out of your wig and robes, I wouldn't have thought... Did you recognise her?'

'Not at all.'

'But Gabe told Trenow he thought she might have recognised you?'

'I'm pretty sure it was him. He kept referring to my job. It was the first time I'd met him and he just seemed... I don't know... over-familiar?' His face hardened. 'And he was over-friendly with Olivia too, if you ask me.'

Frazer chuckled. 'Neither of those things was against the law, last time I looked.'

He shrugged. 'No. Like I said, it's just a feeling. You must know him much better than I do, so what do you think of him?'

'He seems fine. He's a chef, not a baker, so we don't have that much in common. He was happy to let us supply all the bread and baked goods for the party and for when they first open while he concentrates on the menu. So, I generally deal with Lexie. Who's great.'

'But when you have had dealings with him, what have you thought?' Jago persisted.

Frazer took a while to reply. 'Confident, successful. Works well with Lucinda. Haven't seen him with Ruan very often, but I have no reason to believe they are anything but a good team.'

'What's he like with Willow?'

'Charming, confident. Respectful, I guess.' He sighed.

'Look, have you considered that perhaps you two just got off on the wrong foot?'

Jago decided to let it go. 'Perhaps. I just hope for Ruan and Lucinda's sake that his careless words don't have too much of an adverse effect on their whole enterprise. Do you remember the stresses we all went through last year?' He watched Frazer's face carefully and saw that his own words had achieved the desired effect on the accountant.

'Oh shit! I hadn't thought of that. Too much going on here.' His face paled. 'Will they be able to open the Hall as planned?'

'Perhaps. I suppose it depends on how long it takes to do all the forensics at the scene.'

'Have you been in touch with Ruan and Lucinda?'

'No,' Jago admitted. 'Olivia and I decided to keep out of the way while the police are carrying out their initial enquiries.'

'And because you're pissed off that someone from the Hall told Trenow about the incident with the waitress at the party?'

'Perhaps.'

'How's Olivia taking it all?'

Jago gazed round the garden. 'She was sad and down about it at the weekend. It obviously brought back some pretty horrific memories. But we escaped over to the Roseland with the dogs yesterday and made some plans for the summer. She's been much better since.' He paused. 'I think she's hoping it was a tragic accident. Which is still awful in itself, but better than the alternative.'

'And what do you think?'

Jago looked away. 'I'd like to think the same…'

'But…?'

'But I'm a hardened criminal barrister who's used to dealing with less pleasant outcomes in life.'

'And?'

Jago decided to be truthful. He needed to talk this through with someone he could trust.

'Trenow didn't reveal much, but reading between the lines, they seem to think it was suspicious. And I have to agree.'

'Why?'

'I got to the body first and there were marks on her neck. Fingermarks, perhaps? I don't think Olivia saw them, and I certainly haven't told her about them.'

Frazer's pale Scottish skin paled even more. 'Bloody hell, Jago. Now you tell me! Were the police okay with you?'

'How do you mean?'

'About the marks on her neck?'

'Why wouldn't they be? I was with Olivia for the entire evening and all night. There's nothing to connect me with the girl at all.' He closed his eyes. 'We don't even know her name.'

'Isn't that the police's job to find out?' Frazer ran his hand through his sandy hair and shook his head in despair. 'Jesus! Are you absolutely sure this isn't in any way connected with what's been going on in London?'

Jago refused to look his friend in the eye. 'I really hope not, for all our sakes.'

# 7

'Hey, Cassie, Lexie thought you could do with some water in this heat. But it's taken me so long to find you in this jungle, I think the ice may have melted.'

The unfamiliar voice jolted Cassie out of her thoughts as she hacked away at yet another giant camellia in one of the huge, overgrown flowerbeds they had discovered in Peneglos Hall's sheltered valley. She pulled her straw sun hat back into place and wiped the perspiration and leaf dust from her face, before facing her visitor, pruning shears still in hand.

*Damn. It's Detective Sergeant O'Driscoll – just what I need!* The only thing she was pleased to see was the green recycled glass bottle of water he was holding out to her. She took it, wordlessly, and drank thirstily. Lexie had been right.

She remembered her manners. 'Thanks. What brings you down to this part of the garden?'

O'Driscoll gazed round him as he spoke. 'The boss wanted to see Ruan and Lucinda and I thought I'd take a look round the gardens while I'm waiting.'

She returned to her pruning, but he didn't take the hint. 'Keen gardener, are you, sergeant?'

O'Driscoll chuckled. 'Not really, I was more drawn to the sea. Am I bothering you?'

Cassie avoided the question. 'I can talk and prune at the same time.'

'That's a fantastic view from the top of the garden. Reminds me of home.' There was a slight pang in his voice as he spoke and Cassie pricked up her ears. She knew he was probably here to ask her lots of questions, so she decided to play for time and ask a few of her own – a trick she'd picked up from Olivia.

'Where's home?' She forced herself to sound interested even though she wasn't sure she wanted to know much at all about the man standing in front of her.

'I'm originally from County Wexford. I've been over here for years now, but that's still home in many ways.' He paused. 'And please call me Sam.'

Cassie ignored his invitation. 'I didn't think you sounded like a Londoner when Inspector Trenow said you'd come from the Met.'

He laughed easily. 'No. It took almost twenty years to lose my Irish brogue. And when I joined the Met ten years ago, I promised my mother I wouldn't pick up a London accent.'

She was busy doing swift calculations in her head and listening carefully to his deep, almost musical, voice at the same time. He was probably about her age, but his crumpled, battered face made him look older. She briefly wondered if he'd been a boxer – that would account for the obviously crooked nose and bashed-looking ears. Wasn't boxing a big thing in Ireland? She seemed to recall several Irish boxing champions. Then she remembered she wasn't interested in the personal business of other people anymore and asked a different question.

'What's County Wexford like? I've never been to Ireland.'

'Ah, you're missing a treat.' A huge smile broke over his face, showing surprisingly even, white teeth for a boxer. 'It's in the bottom right-hand corner of Ireland as you look at a map and is known as the "sunny South East" as it has the most sun and the least rain in the whole of the country.' As he spoke, a stronger lilt came into his voice. 'It's a grand place. Wild and beautiful and famous for miles and miles of golden beaches, castles, lighthouses and offshore islands full of wildflowers and puffins.'

She turned to him, more interested. 'Sounds familiar.'

'And Wexford town itself, which we're proud to say has been there since the Viking times, sits at the mouth of the river Slaney, overlooking the harbour. It was a massive fishing port in the past apparently, not so much today. Like everywhere else, I suppose.'

'Follow me.' Cassie clasped her pruning shears in one hand and her water bottle in the other and practically skipped along the steep path leading up from the lower garden, and past a clump of her favourite rhododendrons with pure white flowers and an intoxicating scent that blended magically with the sea air. Finally, she reached a clearing with a bench and the most amazing view. She waited patiently for O'Driscoll to join her, listening to him panting with exertion. She wasn't at all out of breath herself – how things had changed. She looked back at him, dressed in suit trousers, shirt, tie and formal shoes; more appropriate for an air-conditioned office than a Cornish garden in this weather. It was a good job the heatwave had hardened the paths from their usual boggy condition or he'd never have made it this far.

'Oh my...' O'Driscoll breathed heavily and sank down on the bench to take it all in.

Falmouth Bay spread out in front of them in all its summer beauty; a vast, sparkling expanse of blue water with the sun glittering like diamonds on its surface, blemished only by two trawlers making their slow, determined way to their destination.

Cassie remained standing, breathing in all the different scents that were enhanced by the sea air, and decided to make the most of his inability to speak. 'As you can see, we have a lighthouse and two castles, but I'm afraid they only date back to the time of Henry VIII. We do, however, have the third deepest harbour in the world.'

O'Driscoll's eyes twinkled. 'Well, I reckon you've trumped me there.' He shifted up the bench and gestured for Cassie to join him. She perched on the far edge, finished her water and they sat in silence for a while, gazing out at the ocean.

'This is a grand viewpoint. I don't reckon there's anywhere in Wexford you can see castles, a lighthouse and beaches all at the same time.'

Even though Cassie agreed with him about the view, she wasn't going to say so. 'Can you imagine what the bay must have been like all those years ago, when it was one of the busiest ports in the country? They reckon Falmouth was so busy in the 1800s that you could walk from one side of the harbour to the other just by stepping from boat to boat.'

They both gazed across at the almost empty bay, lost in their own thoughts.

'It's because of Falmouth's position and the role it played in maritime history that Peneglos Hall was built and we're sitting here today.' Cassie broke the silence, deciding that if she talked about facts, she could steer the conversation in a direction she preferred.

'You've lost me there, sorry.'

'Joseph Braithwaite, Ruan's ancestor, who owned and built Peneglos Hall, made his fortune from being a captain in the packet service, which was basically a nautical mail service that had to find new routes from Europe that avoided the English Channel during the wars with France.' She stole a sideways glance at O'Driscoll who seemed to be listening intently.

'How come they chose Falmouth?' He leant towards Cassie, bringing a pleasant scent of shower gel and his delicious cologne.

Momentarily distracted, she coughed.

'It was vital to choose a port that was a long way from the French coast to avoid being attacked or seized by enemy boats. Falmouth had everything they needed. A harbour that was well fortified by our two castles, that provided good shelter from the prevailing winds and weather and that offered the shortest sea route to Spain and Portugal and on from there to the Americas and the West Indies.'

O'Driscoll's gaze turned to the gardens. 'Ruan's ancestor must have made a tidy sum of money to afford all this.'

Cassie chuckled. 'Family legend has it that Joseph made most of his money from the more illegitimate side of things. It was just a part of life for lots of people round here back then. A bonus if you like.'

'Smuggling?'

'Of a sort, I suppose. The packet ships went to places like the West Indies and brought back cloth, cotton, tea, sugar, silks, coffee, cocoa and spirits that were worth a fortune in those days.'

'And where did they land it? Weren't customs officers a thing by then?'

'Yes, but a lot of them were in on the smuggling too. Even so, the packet ships would usually meet smaller boats further out in the bay, who would then bring the contraband into private quays and coves.' Cassie nodded down the hill in the direction of Peneglos's own cove. 'I don't think Joseph's choice to build a grand house on this particular spot, by a conveniently hidden cove was at all coincidental. He was an astute, if not very pleasant, businessman by all accounts and his career gave him the means to pursue his interests in retirement.'

'Such as?'

She waved her arm around the garden at the magnificent trees, ferns and bushes. 'Look around you.' She stood up and walked across to the nearest tree which towered above them with a huge thick trunk. 'By Joseph's time, nouveau-riche people like him were using their gardens to show off their wealth and importance. Believe me, plants and gardens were the swanky cars and watches of their time.'

'How so?' O'Driscoll pursed his lips and looked like the sort of person who wouldn't know the difference between a daffodil and a buttercup, Cassie decided.

'By Joseph's time, explorers known as plant hunters were setting out on dangerous missions all over the world to collect new specimens of plants and trees. Many of them set sail on packet ships from here and Joseph always made sure he kept a few of the specimens they brought back with them, as a kind of perk. Lots of other packet captains did the same and shared their spoils. This garden is full of treasures and every time we uncover another section we unearth more and more. The rhododendrons you passed on the way up are from stock said to have been among the first seeds brought to Cornwall from the Himalayas.'

'I was too busy concentrating on not passing out to notice any of the flora,' O'Driscoll observed drily. 'It's no wonder you're so fit and trim working in a place like this.'

Cassie felt a flush warm her face and turned away from his compliment. She still thought of herself as the plump woman in her forties who tried to cover her extra weight with baggy layers and linen scarves. She looked down at her lightly tanned legs in their dungaree shorts and sturdy boots and frowned. She would never be as fit and lithe as Olivia, but gardening had tightened her stomach muscles, strengthened her legs and she was in the best physical shape of her life without even noticing it, apart from having to regularly replace her worn out clothes with smaller sizes.

'It must have taken hundreds of years to establish a garden like this.' O'Driscoll's observation interrupted her thoughts. 'I think I'm too impatient to be a gardener.'

Cassie was pretty sure boxers weren't known for their patience. 'Obviously it takes time, but Joseph's love for horticulture travelled down the generations. And his money enabled his descendants to invest wisely in other successful local industries, like mining and shipping, so they were able to sponsor other plant hunting expeditions and get the pick of all the new seeds and plants that were being brought into the country.'

O'Driscoll looked round the garden again. 'Has Ruan inherited his ancestors' passion for horticulture?'

'Not really. He's more interested in the house and what he can do with that to help it pay for itself. And his experience in the hotel business makes him the ideal person to do just that. The gardens are a vital part of the estate and that's why they employ me, and our faithful army of volunteers.'

O'Driscoll turned towards her. 'So, do you oversee the whole garden?'

'Most of it. Apart from the kitchen garden.' As soon as her words were out, Cassie froze.

O'Driscoll looked straight at her. 'Who looks after that?'

Cassie thought quickly. 'Ruan's uncle, Charles, was a practical man who felt it was more important to feed people than just give them pretty plants to look at, and he spent his life restoring it to how it was before the First World War. The kitchen garden requires a special skill set.'

'So who looks after it now?' O'Driscoll repeated his question patiently.

The seconds ticked by, slowly, until Cassie couldn't bear it anymore.

'Dylan,' she muttered.

'Ah, Dylan.'

Cassie mentally kicked herself and glared at the policeman. *Is that what he'd been after all along? Information about Dylan?* Had she really fallen for the oldest trick in the book again? A bit of feigned interest and a handsome face? Well, she'd learnt the hard way and was never going to be so naïve again.

'Any idea where I'll find him?'

She shrugged, still glaring. 'None at all.'

'Well, could you point me in the direction of his shepherd's hut? Lucinda told us that he lives in one in the grounds.'

She shrugged again. 'No idea, sorry. It's a shepherd's hut. It's on wheels. And he moves it around. You'll have to ask Ruan.'

'I will.' A sheepish-looking O'Driscoll got to his feet, wincing. 'Well, thanks for the chat. It's been most informative and enlightening. I'll be sure to catch up with you again soon.'

8

'Why on earth is Lucinda calling me on the landline here?'
Olivia followed Alice through the open-plan ground-floor
area of the Goods Shed, her mind whirring with possibilities.
Various members glanced up from their desks, all with ready
smiles for Olivia.

'She tried your mobile, apparently, but it must have been
on silent. So, she called Kitten who said she'd seen you coming
in here with Rozy.' The Goods Shed administrator spoke in a
loud whisper over her shoulder. 'I explained you were in a
meeting but she insisted it was important.' Alice ushered
Olivia through the door of her office and then stopped, her
cheeks pink and her eyes bright with concern.

'She sounds distressed…' She turned quickly on her heel
and left the room.

'Lucinda?' Olivia put the phone to her ear and then moved
it away quickly as a high-pitched wail came down the line.
'Lucinda?'

There were muffled sounds of an exchange of words and
then she heard Ruan's slightly calmer voice.

'Olivia? I'm so sorry to bother you, but the police have been to see us with the results of the post-mortem and I'm afraid it's not good news…'

Olivia sank onto Alice's chair as images of the bloated face of the waitress flooded her mind.

'Olivia?' Ruan's anxious voice broke in to her memories. 'Are you okay?'

'Er, yes. I think so.' She pulled herself together. 'The poor girl.'

There was another scuffle in the background and Lucinda's voice came down the line.

'Olivia, you've got to help us. We need you!'

Warning bells went off in her head. 'Me? Aren't the police dealing with it? I don't see what I can do.'

'You can help us. Please? We don't know what to do and you've done this sort of thing before. Kitten told us you and Jago solved the murders at the Goods Shed last year way before the police had worked out what was going on.'

Olivia winced. The awfulness of that time had haunted her dreams for months and she was only just getting over them. No way did she want a repeat performance. Not now. Not ever. An image of the waitress's face and neck swam back into her mind along with a new memory. She swallowed hard.

'Let me track Jago down and we'll be right over.'

---

Thirty minutes later they met Ruan outside Peneglos Hall's grand entrance. With a quick nod of acknowledgement, he led them around the side of the kitchen, across a cobbled courtyard surrounded by half-renovated outbuildings and through another doorway to a small cottage. Jago raised a questioning eyebrow at Olivia as they followed Ruan through the open front door and she stood on tiptoes to whisper into his ear.

'This is the old gardener's cottage where Charles lived when the house became uninhabitable. It's where Ruan and Lucinda are living at the moment.'

Lucinda was in the sitting room, on an ancient settee with its back to the window. Her pale face was almost unrecognisable without a trace of make-up, apart from messy mascara trails under her red-rimmed eyes, and her carefully styled hair. Ruan didn't look much better as he sat down next to his partner and put a protective arm around her shoulders. The tension in the room was palpable. The only sound was Lucinda's sniffing into the sodden tissue she was clutching.

Olivia looked helplessly at Jago. He nodded and guided her to the opposite, smaller settee, where they both sat down, their knees touching.

Jago didn't bother with pleasantries. 'So, what did the police say?'

Fresh tears spilled down Lucinda's cheeks and she waved her handkerchief at Ruan, who spoke for them both. 'Not a lot really. Just that the post-mortem results showed she didn't drown. She was already dead when she went into the water.'

'Did they say anything about the cause of death?'

Ruan shuddered. 'They said something about her being strangled! We were both so shocked, we didn't really take it in.'

The image of the waitress's swollen face, that had been floating just out of reach in Olivia's mind, suddenly came into sharp focus and this time she could clearly see livid bruises on her neck. *Were they fingermarks?* She stiffened at the thought and then felt Jago's hand rest on her thigh.

'Do they know who she is?'

Ruan shook his head. 'All they would say is that they're working on it.'

A silence fell on the room, all four of them thinking about the dead girl. Lucinda started sobbing again, her eyes enormous in her white face.

'Olivia, you've got to help us. Not only is this poor nameless girl dead, we will be letting a whole host of other local people down if we don't open on time. Suppliers, staff, customers...' She caught her breath. 'And we'll all be out of business before we've even got started. We need your help – for their sakes as well as ours.'

The unpleasant reality of Lucinda's words punched Olivia in the stomach. An unopened hotel would mean the end of a much-needed lifeline for many local businesses, whose plans would die before ever being realised. She glanced at Jago's stern face and for almost the first time ever, could read his mind. She crossed her legs and cleared her throat.

'It's still early days. I think you need to give the police a chance.'

'Olivia's right,' Jago agreed. 'These things aren't sorted out overnight. The police have to follow due process. It can take time.'

'I'm not sure we've got time.' Ruan was sombre. 'The Hall's been haemorrhaging money. We've thrown almost everything we've got between us at it, and we can't cope with it anymore.' He waved his arm round the faded room. 'I can't really expect Lucie to live like this for much longer.'

Lucinda sniffed. 'I don't care about that. I've told you repeatedly. And I certainly don't care about it now that poor girl is dead. All I want is for the police to find out who murdered her, so we don't let all the people who are relying on us down.' She turned to Olivia. 'You know what it's like to have a fledgling business in danger of being blown off the rails before it's even properly started.'

Olivia stared at the anguished expression on Lucinda's face and saw her own internal emotions of a year ago mirrored there and all the worries she'd had for the Goods Shed and its members. In many ways she was still struggling to come to terms with her godfather's sudden death and the enormous responsibilities she'd inherited from him. Emotion suddenly choked her and her words wouldn't form. She could feel Jago's eyes on her and she turned helplessly to him.

'I don't think it would be a good idea for us to get involved.' He spoke firmly and authoritatively, just how Olivia imagined he would in court. 'Olivia could quite easily have died last year and I'm sure none of us would want her exposed to that sort of danger again.'

Olivia gulped. This was getting worse by the minute. She caught Ruan's eye and he jumped in.

'We're not asking you to get involved to that extent. Kitten says you got quite close to the detective who's in charge of this case. DI Trenow, isn't it? We were just wondering if you could have a word with him and find out if they're waiting to find out who the girl was before they say we're not a crime scene anymore and can get back on track. And if that's the case perhaps you can—'

'I'm not sure Trenow would appreciate us interfering,' Jago interrupted. 'And I'm also pretty sure he won't be willing to disclose confidential details about the case.'

'But Kitten said that last time—' Lucinda began.

'Last time we got lucky.' Jago tried to cut her off but Lucinda held her ground.

'Whether it was by luck, skill, or some other means, you got a result. And we need you, Olivia. Kitten says you're the best at talking to people, getting information out of them and figuring things out.'

Olivia glanced at Jago's face. A muscle was twitching in his cheek.

'We don't want to step on Trenow's toes,' Jago repeated.

Lucinda burst into tears. 'But they don't even know who the poor girl was! How long will it take the police to find out who murdered her if they don't even know her identity? Weeks probably if they have to rely on medical records, if not longer! By then it will be too late. People will have found other hotels and we'll all be ruined.'

Lucinda's words ended in a wail. Ruan tried to comfort her and Olivia's heart went out to both of them.

'We're asking you as a friend.' Olivia flinched. 'Just to speak to a few people who were at the party. The people behind the scenes probably, rather than the guests themselves. I think the police have done that. We need to find out who this poor girl was and people will talk to you far more openly than to the police. You know what the locals are like round here. I'm a rank outsider!'

Olivia was quiet. She had a point. The police had come up against the locals' resistance to outsiders before and their investigation had suffered for it.

'You can find out who she is. The police will take forever. But you can do it. We know you can...'

Olivia thought back to the party and the bar staff, waiters and waitresses, all busy passing around flutes of champagne and hors d'oevres. She'd recognised a few, but most of them were strangers.

'Where did you get the waiting staff from for the party?' Olivia asked without really thinking, but was immediately aware of Jago's glare.

Lucinda sat up straight. 'They came from an agency in

Falmouth that Willow Jardine recommended. Apparently, she's come across them quite a few times before at events the Bakehouse has helped cater for.'

Olivia made a mental note to talk to Willow.

'Does this mean you'll help?' Ruan's voice was hopeful.

Jago opened his mouth to speak, but Olivia jumped in.

'We need to discuss it more first, but I don't see why we can't talk to the police and see which way the land lies.'

———

'Why on earth did you offer to talk to the police?' Jago waited until they were back at Tresillian before he spoke for the first time. 'I really think we should keep out of this.'

Olivia walked over to one of the high stools at the kitchen island and sat down, her head throbbing from the morning's events. She felt the wet nudge of a nose against her calf and the lick of a warm tongue, and stretched her hand down to stroke Mylor's head. He let out a low whine of empathy.

'What's come over you?' he tried again. 'Where's the woman who refused to get involved until she had no choice last year? And after what happened then, I'd have thought you'd be even less likely to get involved, not more!'

'It's not about me. You must understand that. I was in the same position last year as Lucinda is now. The future of Peneglos Hall is dependent on the outcome of this police investigation, just like the future of the Goods Shed was last year.'

'Not quite.'

'What do you mean?'

Jago winced. 'No-one is suggesting that Lucinda was responsible for the waitress's death, are they? Not like...' His words petered off.

'What? Not like the police thought I'd murdered Libby last year?' Olivia was shocked. 'In my eyes, that makes it worse. Neither Lucinda or Ruan are accused or suspected of anything and yet they could still lose everything. And a lot of totally blameless people will go down with them. We need to help them get it sorted. And sorted properly.'

Jago's face hardened. 'It's not your problem, Olivia. Let someone else help them out.'

'Like who? You heard them. They haven't got anyone else to turn to. Only me. Us.'

'They've got the police. The experts. We don't know what we're getting ourselves involved with. It may not be just the local nutjob, like it was last time.' He stood up suddenly and walked out of the kitchen.

With a sinking feeling Olivia realised this was a side to Jago she had never seen before. Resolute. Determined. Unmovable. He'd become gradually more distant from her over the last few weeks, even over the phone. Less chatty, less involved, more remote. She hadn't really given it much thought at the time, being so busy with everything that was going on at Peneglos Hall and her other projects and had just assumed that was what he'd always been like in the past when dealing with a big trial. As usual, she'd pushed it to the back of her mind and got on with her work, thinking they would deal with it when he got home. Now he was home and she didn't know what to do.

She moved around the kitchen to pull the kettle onto the boiling plate of the Aga, gathered mugs, a teapot, teabags and milk, all the while sifting thoughts and memories through her mind. She fed the dogs, cutting up cooked chicken and adding kibble to their bowls. Finally, she made the pot of tea and then carried everything outside where Jago was sitting under the pergola, staring at his mobile. She stirred the pot noisily and placed a mug in front of him.

'I wish you'd tell me what's really the matter. You've been acting weirdly ever since you got back from London.'

Jago didn't look up. 'I was looking forward to spending a carefree summer with you. I thought that was what we agreed. Getting away from all the crime and shit I have to deal with on an everyday basis in London. But I walked into a real-life murder mystery evening that's threatening to go on and on.'

A harshness had crept into his voice that she hadn't heard before and she looked at him, cold fingers of dread suddenly squeezing her stomach. His handsome face was set hard, the blue eyes that reflected the colour of the creek behind him were dull and his full lips were pinched tight. He looked like he had the worries of the world on his shoulders.

'Are you sure that's all there is to this?' Olivia's voice was little more than a squeak. 'Did something happen in your last case that's upset you?'

There was a definite pause. 'No.'

'You don't talk much about your work in London.' She voiced a thought that had been bothering her for a while. 'Whereas I witter on and on about my projects and the Goods Shed and the Waiting Rooms…'

'And the village and the Bakehouse and the dogs…' A smile lifted the corner of Jago's mouth. 'It's no wonder I don't get a word in edgeways.'

Olivia was stung. 'I'm not that bad, am I? I just want you to be involved, even when you're away. I thought you liked hearing about everything that's going on?'

Jago reached out and caught hold of her hand. His deep chuckle would normally have broken the tension between them, but it sounded forced. 'I do. I love it. I love hearing about the everyday things. The nice things. The people I know and care about. I deal with murder and rape and a whole host of horrible things that so-called human beings do to each other all the time in London. I don't want to do it here.'

'I was only going to ask a few questions. Not investigate the actual murder.'

He shook his head and dropped her hand. 'Leave it to the police. You don't know what you could be getting yourself into.' He rubbed his chin impatiently. 'Remember what happened last time.'

Olivia pushed her chair back. 'Trust me, Jago. I will never, ever forget what happened last time. But this is different. I'll just be asking a few questions to find out who she was.'

Jago's jaw stiffened. 'I know you. You'll find out who she was and then you'll start thinking of her as a person and want to know more and more about her. Then you'll move on to thinking about motives. Why would someone want to kill her? Did she know something? Did someone need to silence her? Who? Why? Where? When? How? It will go on and on and you'll get sucked further and further in.' He looked at her, with a definite wariness in his eyes. 'Please, listen to me. For my sake as well as yours. Keep out of it and let the police do their job.'

'I understand what you're saying and I'm more than happy to let the police do their job. But Lucinda and Ruan, Willow and Fraser, not to mention loads of other suppliers, are going to find themselves in a whole lot of trouble if you and I both sit back and do nothing.'

# 9

'Cass, I really need to talk to you… in private…'

Jago had eventually tracked Cassie down to the outer courtyard at Peneglos Hall, where a group of retired women and a few men dressed in gardening gear were gathering and exchanging hearty greetings, seemingly oblivious to the heat of the morning.

Her head snapped up from the plans she was examining. 'What's up? Is Olivia okay?'

'Olivia's fine,' Jago reassured her quickly. That was typical of Cassie. Olivia was always up there with Kitten in the forefront of her thoughts, which was exactly why he was seeking her out now.

Relief replaced the worry that had flashed across her face, but then she frowned. 'Let me just sort these volunteers out. I'll be with you in a minute.'

Puzzled by her reaction, Jago whistled for Steren and clipped on her lead to stop her greeting each volunteer in turn with her usual Labrador enthusiasm. He then stood to one side and watched as Cassie spoke to them all, carefully explaining their duties for the morning and handing them the necessary gardening implements. For the first time he noticed how much she'd changed since working in the gardens at the Hall. Her cheeks were pinker, her eyes brighter and her soft, friendly features more animated. Her blonde hair had brightened in the sun and the best change, in Jago's opinion, as he listened to her talk, was that her whole demeanour was more focused and confident.

Cassie joined him as the volunteers headed off across the wildflower meadows to the overgrown woodland that provided the protective shelter belts for the exotic plants being slowly uncovered under her careful supervision. It would also give them much-needed shade from the relentless sun that beat down from a cloudless sky. She glanced at his face and led him to the volunteers' mess shed that nestled against the external eastern wall of the kitchen garden. Once inside, Jago leaned forward to kiss her, but she dropped to her knees to welcome Steren and unclip her lead so she could roll on to her back and have her tummy tickled.

'We don't usually see you over this way.' Cassie didn't look up, but there was a definite frostiness in her tone. 'Are you sure Olivia's okay?'

'Olivia's fine,' he repeated, not telling her they had gone to bed with their differences unresolved and spent the night on the far sides of the bed, with the dogs taking advantage of the space between them and making themselves comfortable. It was, he realised, their first proper disagreement since they'd been together, and he hated himself for it.

'So, what is it then? As you can see, I'm rather busy.' Cassie turned away from him and set out mugs, tea and coffee paraphernalia and what looked like a tin of home-made biscuits that were presumably for the volunteers' tea break.

His spirits fell. This wasn't the Cassie he knew. The caring, warm woman he knew seemed to have been replaced with a distant lookalike who didn't even offer him a cup of tea. He swallowed, unsure how to react.

'I've come to ask for your help.' He decided to be upfront.

Cassie's eyes narrowed. 'What with?'

'I'd like you to help me persuade Olivia not to get involved with what's going on here.' He swallowed again. 'And by that, I mean the death of the waitress.'

She tutted. 'As far as I'm aware, she's just trying to help Ruan and Lucinda. What's wrong with that?'

'I really don't think it's a good idea, Cass.'

'Why not?'

'She's only doing it because Kitten told Ruan and Lucinda that we solved last year's murders before the police did, and they want her to do the same for them so the Hall can open on schedule.' He couldn't keep the impatience out of his voice.

Cassie's cheeks turned pink at the implied criticism of her only child. 'Don't you think there's more to it than that?'

'They've probably worked out that Olivia can be a bit of a soft touch if you know what buttons to press.'

'And what buttons are those?' She gave him a stony look.

'Comparing their situation to hers last year. Bringing all those memories back and guilting her into helping them.'

'Don't you think there might be other, more personal reasons, why she wants to help?'

Jago caught his breath. 'Like what?'

'The poor girl drowned. I'm assuming that's what has hit Olivia so hard. All those years ago, Aidan drowned and Olivia nearly did too. I understand the effect that had on her.' Her gaze held his. 'I take it you do too.'

Jago nodded dumbly as her words sunk in, and she continued. 'She remembers it all vividly. And it will have given her a link to this girl that's difficult for her to ignore. She remembers how it affected her family and the life-changing effects it had on all of them. That's what will be troubling her. The police don't even know the girl's name so they can inform her family. They can't grieve for her or arrange her funeral or come to terms with her death. I'm sure all Olivia wants to do is try and find out who the poor girl is. For her family's sake.'

'It's certainly an interesting theory...' Jago petered off, adopting his often-used technique of letting the other person fill the resulting silence while he processed his thoughts.

But Cassie turned away again and filled an empty bowl with water, from which Steren drank noisily. Jago stared at her back. She really had changed. And if Cassie was right, he had a horrible feeling he was fighting a losing battle. Olivia was one of the most stubborn people he had ever met. And Cassie wasn't going to help him out.

'I think you're the one with the problem here, Jago. If Olivia feels she needs to do this – to help the girl and her family – I don't see why, or how, I can stop her.'

'She should leave it to the police. Trenow and his new sidekick have made it very clear they don't want us to speak about what happened to anyone who is at all connected to the party.'

'From what I recall, that didn't stop you last time.'

'That was different.'

'How?'

'I wasn't actively working at the Bar then. I wasn't bound by a professional code of conduct like I am now.'

Cassie raised an eyebrow. She might as well have said out loud that she didn't believe him.

'Now, can I ask you something?' She folded her arms.

'Of course.'

'Why are you so opposed to Olivia doing this?'

Jago refused to meet her eyes 'I'm just concerned that although it might start with her only trying to establish the girl's identity, it could quite easily open up a huge can of worms.'

'How?'

'You know what Olivia's like. She always approaches things from the complete opposite direction from everyone else. And while the police are concentrating on the most obvious line of enquiry, she'll be attacking it from the opposite angle and will quite possibly discover not only her identity, but the fact that this girl is just a small piece in a much bigger jigsaw of problems.'

Cassie lifted her chin. 'Are you sure you're not frightened that Olivia might discover something you'd rather was kept hidden?'

'Like what?' Jago felt a sudden uneasiness.

'Lucinda told me that Gabe was pretty sure the waitress recognised you and that's why she dropped the tray.'

*Bloody hell! Was there anyone that annoying bloke hadn't shared his theories with?*

'Well, I certainly didn't recognise her and I doubt very much any witness or victim or defendant from a trial in London would recognise me out of my wig and robes.' He kept his voice calm. 'And even if they did, it's not very likely that would put me in the frame for their murder, is it?'

Cassie's face reddened. 'Is there any chance she knew you from somewhere else?'

The penny dropped and he went very still. 'What are you suggesting?'

'You tell me.'

*Shit!* He tried to bite down on a sudden surge of anger and spoke clearly and slowly. 'Okay, I'll tell you, Cassie. I do not know that girl and I have never seen her before in my life. Is that good enough for you?'

'Have the police talked to you about it?'

'As a matter of fact, they have. And Trenow has told me I'm not a person of interest to them. I've given him the details of my last few trials and he's happy there's no connection whatsoever between me and the poor girl. Plus,' he paused, 'I have a cast iron alibi for the night it happened.'

'So did Martin. Or so we thought.'

Jago caught his breath and looked round the room helplessly. *What on earth was going on?* When his gaze fell on Cassie's face, it was very pink and her eyes were brimming with tears.

'What is it, Cass? Don't you trust me?' He made sure his voice was gentle.

'I thought I did.' She wouldn't meet his eyes. 'But then, I'm not a good judge of character, am I?'

'Yes, you are.' He put a tentative hand on her arm and was relieved when she didn't shrug it off. 'If we're talking about Martin, and I assume we are, you weren't the only person to be taken in by him. Not by a long shot.'

Cassie was quiet for a few minutes and then her whole body sagged in what was clearly relief and she rubbed at her damp eyes with a soil-encrusted tissue.

'It's made me doubt myself. Not all the time, but it doesn't take much for a throwaway comment to make me doubt everything I thought I knew and believed in.'

'And Gabe's put doubts into your mind about me?'

'He was probably just trying to be funny.' She sniffed. 'But I've been hearing so many different things from all sorts of people, I just don't know who to believe anymore.'

Jago thought back to the night of the party and his instant dislike of the chef and his over-familiar ways.

'I wouldn't take too much notice of what Gabe says, if I were you. I reckon he's a troublemaker.'

'He's been saying stuff…' She corrected herself. 'Suggesting stuff… About Dylan too.'

'Dylan?' Jago's ears pricked up and then he racked his brain. 'The guy who works here with you? Ruan's old school mate? Olivia gets on well with him, doesn't she?'

She nodded, but looked away, clearly trying to decide whether or not to confide in him.

'What sort of stuff?'

'Just making insinuations about how he disappeared that night and the whole of the next day. How he's a bit of a closed book. A loner. That sort of thing…' Cassie petered off, obviously realising she wasn't painting Dylan in a particularly good light.

'Who's he being saying these things to?'

'Anyone who'll listen here at the Hall. Although because he's Ruan's best friend, he doesn't go on so much to him. I think he prefers dripping his poison into more impressionable ears. Like Lucinda's. Or Lexie's. Or any attractive woman's, come to think of it. I'm sure it won't be long before he has a quiet word with Olivia.'

Jago bristled. 'So does this guy fancy himself as an amateur detective or something? Or does he just like shit-stirring?'

Cassie blushed. 'The latter probably.'

'And are you concerned about Dylan?' Jago smiled gently at her. He remembered Olivia telling him that he was another of Cassie's lame ducks, as she laughingly described them, including herself in their number, whom she chose to mother.

'I don't believe he had anything to do with the waitress's

murder, if that's what you mean,' Cassie replied quickly. 'He's a gentle soul. And an easy target for someone like Gabe. He's quiet, reserved and prefers his own company. Not loud and showy. But if some people hear suggestions for long enough about someone who's a bit different, they may just start to believe them.'

'How do you mean?'

Cassie shook herself and ignored his question. 'Perhaps if Olivia discovers the waitress's identity, it will give the police something to focus on. That would be a good thing. Wouldn't it?'

Jago's heart sank. There was no way she was going to back him in his pleas not to get involved if there was hope for people she cared about. He was going to have to think of another approach. He let out a sigh and whistled for Steren.

'Right, I'll leave you to it. I'm glad we sorted some things out anyway.' This time when he went to kiss her, she threw her arms around him and hugged him tightly.

'It's not you, Jago, it's me. And my trust issues. As long as you look after Olivia and treat her well, I won't have a problem with you again. It's been wonderful to watch her settle down so well in Penbartha over the past twelve months. I don't think I've ever seen her so happy—'

The rest of her sentence was drowned out by the sudden arrival of Steren, claws scrabbling frantically on the wooden floor and her mouth full of what looked suspiciously like a sandwich, hotly pursued by a khaki-coloured cross between a human and a scarecrow. What struck Jago most forcibly was the khaki scarecrow's reaction to his dog's bad behaviour. Rather than being justifiably annoyed, from what Jago could see behind the long hair and straggly beard, the figure had a huge smile on his face.

'Steren! Drop!'

Steren glanced at her master with big brown eyes, skidded to a halt and swallowed the sandwich in one noisy gulp.

Jago closed his eyes for a moment, hoping that when he opened them his dog wouldn't really have done what he'd just witnessed.

Cassie chose that moment to intervene. 'Jago, this is Dylan Bonnar.'

# 10

A sudden rush of planning queries prevented Olivia from pursuing her investigation into the waitress's identity for a couple of days. She was tired and grumpy and feeling guilty she wasn't spending the time with Jago she'd promised. But she was also slightly annoyed that she was just expected to drop everything when he returned from London. Her job didn't work like that. She was at the mercy of various people's schedules, especially, it seemed, those of planning and conservation officers.

She'd just escaped from a particularly painful telephone conversation with Angus Webster, the planning department's conservation officer, about a listed building consent application she'd recently submitted, when there was a tap on the door and Jago appeared.

'Dad's just rung and asked me to go over to the farm and help with the silaging.' He looked out of the window, carefully avoiding her eyes. 'They're a man down on the tractors and he's asked me to fill in.'

'Really?' She was still smarting from his previous night's

regurgitation of all the reasons why she shouldn't get involved with the waitress's death, and didn't manage to keep the disbelief out of her voice. It all sounded a bit too convenient.

'Yes, really. Ted's broken his arm.' Jago's voice was sharp enough to send all three dogs scampering to their baskets in the corner. 'C'mon, Olivia, it's only for a day or two.'

Olivia's heart began to race and she eyed him warily. He'd never used that tone with her before. 'Would you like me to come too? I can bring my work with me.'

'There's no point.' He bent to pat the dogs to show them there were no hard feelings. 'We'll be out in the fields all hours of daylight and Mum will be too busy with the calves to entertain you.'

Olivia stared at him. *Is there going to be any apologetic gesture?* She waited. *Obviously not.* 'Okay, but can we talk before you go? Let's not part on bad terms. We need to sort this out.'

'Not now.' He glanced at his watch. 'I need to get going. You know how quickly the weather can change.'

'I doubt you ever dropped everything to rush to Launceston and help with the silaging when you were in London. Do you even remember how to drive a tractor?' Olivia could have bitten her tongue as soon as the words left her lips.

Jago just looked at her, his face impassive, closed off. 'Don't make this into something it isn't, Olivia. I'm a farmer's son and my dad needs help.'

She got to her feet and moved towards him, but he turned away whistling to Steren, and then called over his shoulder as he left the room, 'We'll talk when I get back.'

---

Olivia sat behind her desk. Worry about Jago had swept all other thoughts from her mind and her usual displacement activities had failed. She stretched her arms above her head, trying to ease the tension from her shoulders and decided to head out across the gardens with the dogs to seek refuge in her default sanctuary: Mollie's krowji.

The krowji was tucked into a corner of Tresillian's own walled kitchen garden, protecting the precious herbs and vegetables from the pernicious sea winds that blew up the garden from the creek. A modern contemporary structure, with cedar cladding now silvered with time and weather, and a sedum roof had replaced Mollie's original wooden cabin ten years previously. At this time of year, the raised beds were filled by Cassie with carefully curated combinations of herbs and medicinal plants and flowers tumbling out of the beds and across the paths. There they would jostle for space with their companion plants of runner beans, tomatoes, courgettes, carrots and peppers, all carefully chosen by Mollie, drawing on her vast understanding of the chemistry of plants to help each other grow and thrive.

If Olivia loved the herb garden, it was in the krowji itself that she felt closest to her godmother with its tantalising air full of earthy smells and exotic scents that she would forever associate with Mollie. Leaving the dogs to investigate whatever new smells had appeared in the garden overnight, Olivia instinctively bowed her head to the plaque of the sun god, Belenus, and thanked him for the wonderful job he was doing and went inside.

She always felt as though she was stepping back in time into an old apothecary's workroom and a thrill ran through her body as her senses engaged with her surroundings. She closed her eyes for a moment, breathing in all the different smells held within the room – the floral scents with an underlying tone of citrus and the fresh green properties of herbs, alongside the more earthy scents of soil and compost. She smiled at a sudden memory of Mollie telling her she came here to think and listen to the wisdom and peace that she always found in nature. And it was the place where she, Olivia, came to recharge and gather focus. Just spending a few moments in the krowji would take her away from the dark places in her head and make her feel better. Mollie's magic always worked.

For a while Olivia just sat, listening to the water feature tinkling outside through the open window, thinking about her godmother and Jago. Would she, whose philosophies had always been based on love and respect for all life, have supported Olivia in her quest to discover the identity of the murdered waitress and thereby at least allow her family to grieve for her? Yes, she would, Olivia decided. But how on earth was she going to go about it without upsetting Jago? Should she get a list of the guests from Lucinda and talk to some of them about what had happened that evening? Or should she talk to some of the other staff that were working there that night? Would they have more of an idea who the girl was?

A strong waft of lavender, mixed with rosemary and oregano, warned her of the fact that someone was walking through the kitchen garden. Mollie used to call it her early warning system as people always brushed against the aromatic herbs as they wandered down the narrow paths between the beds. As she stood up to see who it was, Inspector Trenow appeared, brandishing a tray with tea and home-made biscuits.

'Hi, Olivia, this is beginning to feel like old times! I just bumped into Kitten who asked me to bring this through.' Familiar with the building, he took the tray into the cooler, shadier end of the krowji and set it on the workbench, before pouring them both a mug.

Olivia smiled, a little nervously, automatically searching her conscience for any misdemeanours she may have committed recently. Policemen always had that effect on her. Even Trenow. Then, with a lurch, her mind shifted to Jago. *Is he the real reason Trenow is here?* She held her breath.

'Here you go.' He handed her a mug and sat himself down on one of the chairs before taking a large gulp of tea. He helped himself to two of Cassie's biscuits and practically swallowed them whole. 'Ooh, I'd forgotten how good these are.' He took another one off the plate. 'I'm not here to cause you trouble.'

'Or Jago?' Her words came out in a rush of breath.

'Nor Jago,' Trenow confirmed.

Olivia pulled herself together. 'That's good to know.'

Trenow looked at her more closely. 'I came to see how you're doing. After finding the body.'

'Really?' She couldn't keep the scepticism out of her voice. 'Well, it's not the best way to start the day, is it?'

'No.' Trenow shook his head. 'And I suppose it brought some unwanted memories back.'

Olivia seized on his words. 'It has, yes.' She shuddered. 'But, although we found this poor girl, at least none of us knew her this time. And I'm hoping that none of us know her murderer either.'

Trenow leant forward. It was a move Olivia recognised now, so she was prepared for the next question. 'Are you sure none of you knew her?'

She glanced quickly at his face but, as usual, it gave nothing away. 'Well, I certainly didn't know her. And I can only speak for myself. Presumably you've asked everyone else who was at the party the same question?' She stopped abruptly. 'Not that I'm interfering in your enquiry or anything.'

Trenow chuckled. 'Heaven forbid! We've got extra officers taking statements from everyone who was at the party – but it's taking forever to pin everyone down. And we're still processing and analysing them all so we can arrange background checks on anyone who seems of interest...'

The way his voice trailed off suggested they hadn't made much progress on that front, but there was one question she had to ask.

'What about Jago?' Olivia bit her lip.

Trenow raised his palms in a gesture of peace. 'He's not a person of interest, if that's what you mean.'

'Did Gabe tell you he thought the waitress must have recognised Jago and that's why she dropped the tray.' Her voice wavered. She could almost taste blood.

'Oh yes. Several times.' Trenow frowned. 'But I've had a long conversation with Jago and discussed all his recent cases. I have no reason to doubt anything he's told me.'

'I don't know anything about any of his recent cases. He doesn't talk about them anymore.' Olivia inspected her fingernails for potting compost.

The detective topped up his tea. 'He's doing increasingly unpleasant cases and trials now. You can't blame him for wanting to keep all that completely separate from his life here, can you?' He waved his arm around. 'He told me that this place is paradise in comparison to what he deals with every day in London.'

'Apart from finding the occasional dead body,' Olivia muttered darkly. 'Do you talk to your wife about your work?'

Trenow shook his head quickly. 'Certainly not. I try to leave all the nasty stuff at the nick and not take it home.'

Olivia brightened a little. 'So, it's not just me then?'

'No.' Trenow smiled at her. 'But talking of Gabe...'

'What about him?'

'What's your experience of him?'

She thought for a moment. 'I hardly know him. He's the chef, so I've not had much to do with him.'

'Jago doesn't seem to like him.'

'He only met him for the first time at the party, so I don't see why not.' Realisation dawned. 'Oh. Because he said that about the waitress?'

'Among other things.'

'What other things?'

Trenow coughed. 'He thought he was rather over-familiar with you.'

'When?' Colour tinged Olivia's cheeks.

'At the party.'

'He was just playing a role.' She exhaled slowly. 'The typical, flamboyant Italian chef. There was nothing more to it than that. As I said, I hardly know the guy. I work for Ruan and Lucinda.'

Trenow smiled and Olivia thought she had probably just played right into his hands.

'Ah, Ruan and Lucinda.'

The hairs on the back of her neck prickled and she picked at her nails again. *I can deal with this. At least he's moved on from Jago.* When she looked up Trenow was watching her.

'You've known them for a while now. I'd like to know what you think about them.'

She cocked her head to one side. 'Is this in an official capacity, inspector?'

It was Trenow's turn to redden. 'Not at all. It's completely off the record. I thought it might help to get your take on things up there.'

'I feel a bit uneasy talking about the people I work for.'

'Fair enough. Are they friends?'

She thought for a moment. 'They're clients first and foremost, really, but the nature of my job means I've spent a lot of time with them. Kitten knows them both far better than I do. Perhaps you could ask her?'

Trenow winced and Olivia hid a smile. Kitten's opinion of the police wasn't entirely favourable and she did nothing to hide it.

'Kitten's calmed down a lot,' Olivia informed him, glad to be on happier ground now Trenow seemed satisfied that Jago was not under any suspicion. 'I don't think she's been involved in any environmental protests all year. And she certainly hasn't been arrested. I made sure it was one of the conditions of her employment at the Waiting Rooms.'

Trenow grimaced. 'O'Driscoll's spoken to Cassie, but she seems to be playing her cards close to her chest as well.'

'I am not playing my cards close to my chest!' Olivia protested.

'Aren't you? I'm not too worried about Cassie. Let's just say she's a work in progress as far as O'Driscoll is concerned.' He laughed. 'I think my new DS has taken a bit of a shine to her. I've never seen him look so perky. He's over there now.'

'Good luck to him on that one!' she retorted. 'Cassie learnt her lesson the hard way with Martin last year and is very definitely no longer susceptible to the charms of younger men.'

'I wouldn't say O'Driscoll is younger than Cassie,' Trenow observed mildly. 'And I don't consider him to be charming at all.'

Olivia thought about the policeman with the lived-in face and glared. 'Perhaps not. But I'd still rather he didn't harass Cass, if you don't mind.'

Trenow sighed. 'And here we are, up against the perennial

problem of the locals all sticking together, and being no help to us at all.'

She stared at him with her mouth open. 'I recall you telling me off last year about getting too involved!'

'There is a happy medium!' he retorted.

Olivia hid her smile. Rather perversely, she enjoyed getting under Trenow's skin, and it took her mind off Jago and his recent out-of-character behaviour. 'Okay, okay. I'm not being obstructive about Lucinda and Ruan. They're both passionate advocates for sustainable tourism and have turned Peneglos Hall into an amazing eco-friendly hotel, with loads of plans for the future. They've both invested everything they've got – time and money wise – to achieve their dream and for that reason alone they have the most to lose if the opening of the Hall is prevented or postponed by this death.'

Trenow nodded. 'I know they're business partners, but are they a couple too?'

'Of course they are!' She shook her head in disbelief at his lack of emotional intelligence. 'Why on earth would you think they weren't?' Trenow shrugged and she carried on. 'Anyway, I thought you guys usually assumed that victims are killed by people they know. Yet you seem to be saying that neither the hosts nor any of the guests knew this girl.'

'You're right that we normally look at family and friends first yes, but until we establish her identity it's hard to know where to start.'

Her ears pricked up. 'Are you really no further forward on that?'

'No.' He met her gaze and held it. 'We're having all sorts of tests done, but until something comes up on a missing person register that could be a match, we have nothing to compare them with.'

'Well, at the risk of teaching my grandmother to suck eggs,

isn't the obvious first step to ask the other staff who were there on the night? They must have talked to her, known her name?'

'You'd have thought so.'

'Do I sense a "but"?'

Trenow's heavy sigh seemed heartfelt. 'Lucinda used an agency that came on recommendation from Willow Jardine. It's a place called Fal Staff, on one of the side streets in Falmouth. And the woman who owns it...' He fished his notebook out of his pocket. '...Mina Hughes, was not exactly forthcoming.'

'In what way?'

'In every way.' Trenow frowned. 'Once again, everyone in this part of the county seems to have taken a vow of silence when it comes to the police.'

'Even when one of her employees has been murdered?'

'She denied knowing anything about her. Said she must have got the job through one of the other girls.'

'What other girls? Did she have their details so you could talk to them?'

'That's where it all went downhill.' Trenow pulled a face. 'And where she clammed up. Apparently, she doesn't keep any paper records of her casual staff. For data protection reasons.'

'That old chestnut?'

'And a load of rubbish. If you ask me, Mrs Hughes is not as assiduous as she could be with tax and National Insurance and the like. And seemed to be more bothered about data protection than the fact someone has been murdered.'

'You reckon?' A plan was beginning to form in Olivia's mind.

'Yes, I do. I feel like putting in a call to HMRC. That'll show her what happens when you refuse to co-operate with a murder investigation.'

'That's not going to help, is it? Perhaps she'll think about it and get back in touch. People always feel insecure and anxious when the police turn up on their doorstep. I know I do.' She gave him a look. 'Why don't you give it a few days?'

'I might. Just because we've reached a bit of a dead end doesn't mean that we're giving up.' Trenow looked at her sideways. 'I've probably said more than I should have done. You do realise this chat is completely off the record, don't you?'

Olivia held his look. 'Oh, absolutely,' she replied and crossed her fingers behind her back.

# 11

'All this waitress business is putting Ruan and Lucinda under so much pressure, I'm not sure how much more they can put up with. The sooner Olive gets to the bottom of it, the better. I've never seen Lucinda so stressed!'

Cassie frowned at Kitten who, in her usual fashion, had not given her the chance to reply before segueing into an entirely different conversation about some tourists who had been in the Waiting Rooms café the day before, revelling in the hot weather and being completely unaware that the planet was burning because of the overuse of fossil fuels, until she had pointed it out to them. It was one of her favourite topics at the moment, so Cassie zoned out for a while and stretched her legs in front of her, guiltily enjoying the sensation of the sun warming her skin. They were having a rare morning off together, sitting on the sunny balcony of the coach house.

A sudden movement in the trees caught Cassie's eye and she turned her head, seeking the familiar form of the heron who nested every year in the tall trees that lined the bank. Her eyes soon detected the tall, noble figure stalking through the shallows with long, deliberate strides, his slender neck and orange dagger beak poised for spearing his prey. Cassie smiled. She liked to think of her heron as a lucky omen.

'And I can't believe that Ruan's now going back on his word and wants to use the estate cottages for holiday lets rather than for locals.'

Kitten's irate tone pulled her attention back to her daughter and she sat up straight. 'What did you say, my lovely?'

'According to Rocky, they've had a change of plan.' Kitten finished her mug of coffee and refilled it from the cafetière.

Cassie's mood plummeted. So much for the magical properties of Mr Heron. 'But I thought they were totally on board with the idea of supporting local people who can only afford to rent?' Affordable housing in Cornwall was a perennial problem and Cassie remembered how thrilled Dylan had been when Ruan decided that all the estate workers cottages on Peneglos land, which had been empty for years, would be renovated and let long term to locals. She knew how lucky she was, being able to live in the coach house as part of her job. Such positions were few and far between.

'They were. But there's been a change of plan. Presumably because of what's happened. Ruan and Lucinda reckon they might struggle to let them to locals, given the connection, but holidaymakers won't know, or care.'

'Ridiculous!' Cassie couldn't keep the disappointment out of her voice. 'I'm sure if you're that desperate for a roof over your head, you might not be too fussy. It's hardly like she was murdered in one of the cottages.'

Kitten shrugged. 'They've come up with a very convincing business plan that shows it's the best way forward. Rocky's hoping they might change their minds, because they're now asking for a much higher specification on all the fittings, so they can charge more for the lets, and it's messing his schedule up.' She drained her mug and turned troubled amber eyes to her mother. 'I feel a bit let down actually. I really thought Lucinda was on the same page as us when it came to Peneglos Hall supporting the community, but she reckons she can't get Ruan to budge. Although, how they're going to pay for it all is anyone's guess. She's already in a major panic about the budget.' Without giving Cassie the chance to respond she jumped to her feet and smoothed out the long, drapey skirt of her strappy summer dress made from colourful vintage fabric.

'That dress looks lovely on you.' Cassie was used to Kitten's sudden conversation swings and simply admired her daughter's less-outlandish-than-usual outfit.

Kitten threw back her head and laughed. 'Bea Mathers from the Sew Social group helped me make it. She says I'm getting to be a real expert on the sewing machine, and she just happened to have a roll of this fabric she'd rescued from a salvage warehouse and a pattern she'd made herself. So, win–win!'

She gave her mother a dramatic twirl and then dropped a kiss on her head. 'I've got to dash or I'll be late for my doctor's appointment and I've already waited three weeks for it, which is appalling really when you think—' She grabbed her straw bag and wide-brimmed hat and was just about to head off into the house when a deep voice called up from the garden.

'Hello up there! Anyone at home?'

Cassie was glad that her daughter's incoming rant about the state of the National Health Service had been interrupted, but then O'Driscoll appeared on the lawn beneath them and her stomach dropped. Kitten stopped mid-sentence and turned to her mother.

'Isn't that Trenow's new sidekick? I've seen him at the

Bakehouse talking to Willow and I'd recognise that boxer's face anywhere.'

'Yes,' Cassie hissed. 'And I don't want to talk to him on my day off. Go down and tell him I'm ill or something will you?'

Kitten peered at her. 'But you're not ill. Why don't you want to talk to him?' A look of realisation crossed her face and Cassie cursed herself for being so transparent. 'Mum, you can't go through the rest of your life avoiding men. I know he's a cop, but he's nothing like that idiot Burridge from what I've heard. What's he going to do to you?'

Cassie felt her cheeks warm. 'He tries to wheedle information out of me.'

'Really? Or is he just asking questions to try and find out what happened to the waitress? The sooner they find out who she was and who's responsible for her death, the sooner we can all get back on track.' Kitten's eyes narrowed. 'You don't have to bring Dylan into it, if he's who you're worried about. There are lots of other people to talk about.'

Cassie shook her head, and felt sick. 'He only seems to be interested in Dylan.'

Kitten waved her concern away. 'That's because Dylan's being elusive. As usual. If he'd just speak to the police willingly, I'm sure they'd soon cross him off their suspect list. Perhaps you could suggest it to him?'

Cassie felt a rush of relief at her daughter's words. If Kitten believed Dylan was innocent, perhaps O'Driscoll would too. Her face must have been full of worry because Kitten gave her a big hug. 'And for now, why don't you find out what the police think they know and pass the info on to Olive, as she'll probably solve this case way before they do?' She dropped a kiss on Cassie's cheek. 'C'mon, Mum. I've got to dash, but I'll show him up on my way out. And I'll call you later.'

By the time O'Driscoll appeared in the kitchen, Cassie had pulled a comb through her hair, changed into a fresh tee shirt and shorts and was standing by the kettle, hating herself for making an effort.

'Morning, sergeant. Tea? Coffee?'

His deep chuckle rumbled around the room. 'I wish you'd call me Sam. Sergeant sounds very formal, given the circumstances.'

'Circumstances? What circumstances?' Her voice came out as a squeak.

O'Driscoll chuckled again. 'I'm not here to see you on official business. I dropped the boss off at the big house and thought I'd pop over and say hello.'

'Oh.' Cassie pointed at the cafetière and he nodded. She busied herself making a jug of decaf. She felt wired enough already and needed to be on her guard. 'I hope he's not harassing Olivia?'

'I doubt it.' O'Driscoll took the tray from her and indicated he would follow her on to the balcony. 'They seem to have a decent relationship and the boss certainly respects her opinion.'

Cassie frowned as she poured the coffee and offered him the plate of biscuits. He took two and munched on the first appreciatively. 'Mmm, these are as good as the boss promised. You're very protective of Olivia.'

Cassie looked at him out of the corner of her eye while he was admiring the view across the creek. In spite of the heat, he still managed to look unflustered in his smart trousers and cotton shirt. He had forsaken his tie and rolled up his sleeves today so didn't look quite as formal as usual.

He turned to look at her, pulling his sunglasses down from

his head to shade his eyes, and she scrabbled for her own pair that were lying on the table next to an open gardening book. *Two can play at that game.*

'You were saying?'

In spite of the sunglasses, Cassie could see a smile lifting his lip.

'No, I wasn't. You had just made an observation. I didn't say anything,' she pointed out, surprising herself with her confidence.

'Fair point.' O'Driscoll laughed easily. 'And you're right. It was nice to meet your daughter. Do you have any other children?'

'Good heavens no!' Cassie spoke instinctively and then tried to explain herself. 'Kitten's always been enough for me. I had her when I was twenty and I was a single mother. There was no way I could have gone through that again.' She sipped at her coffee, determined to pursue her new-found confidence. 'And what about you, sergeant? Do you have any children?'

There was a slight pause. 'Touché, Cassie. And no, I don't. Circumstances, you know...' His voice trailed off and he suddenly looked uncertain.

A part of Cassie felt awkward but she pressed on, suddenly aware she had the upper hand. 'Are you married?'

'Not anymore.'

The wistfulness in his voice spoke volumes, and Cassie remembered reading somewhere about the high divorce rates among the police. He was obviously still unhappy about it and she couldn't bring herself to pursue the point. She tried more neutral ground. 'You said the other day that you're thinking of buying somewhere down here?'

'Yes.' He seized on the subject change. 'I'm living in a rented apartment in Truro at the moment and I think it's time to buy somewhere. But there are so many lovely places to choose from.'

'House prices are way too high for most locals now.' Cassie spoke with feeling.

'Second-homers?'

'Yes. People with London salaries as opposed to low local wages. And local people deciding to let their homes on Airbnb rather than long term to locals. The pool of available housing stock just gets smaller and more expensive.' Cassie felt her mood drop. 'Just don't get Kitten on the subject. She gets proper testy about it.' *As does Dylan*, she thought to herself, but decided not to bring his name up.

'Thanks for the heads-up.' He softened his words with a smile. 'I've already sold my London house – which was a tiny terrace before you think I've got loads of cash to splash, so I'm just a regular buyer. But I do need to get some financial advice.'

Cassie brightened. 'Well then, I may be able to help you there, or rather give you the name of someone who can help. There's a new tenant at the Goods Shed who specialises in green financial advice.'

O'Driscoll's eyes widened. 'What on earth is that?'

Cassie laughed. 'I was a bit like that and it's far too complicated for me to explain and give it justice. But in a nutshell, it's about making sure that your bank and mortgage provider don't invest money in fossil fuels. You'd be surprised at how many of them do, and everyone now understands the massive part fossil fuels play in climate change.'

O'Driscoll looked confused and impressed in equal measure. 'So the idea is to get a mortgage with a provider who doesn't invest in that area?'

'Absolutely. There are plenty about.'

'And that really makes a difference?'

'More than going vegan, quitting flying and buying preloved clothes combined, apparently,' Cassie told him seriously and then smiled. 'As Kitten always says, if we feel strongly about something it makes sense to check that everything we do supports it. Especially round here.'

She sat back and peeped at O'Driscoll over the top of her sunglasses. 'Are you laughing at me, sergeant?'

'Not at all!' He rushed to placate her, leaning across to touch her arm, but she snatched it away. 'It's something I hadn't ever even thought about before and it's interesting stuff. The boss told me how passionate Kitten can become on certain subjects and I can see where she gets it from. Like mother like daughter.'

'Oh.' No-one had ever made that observation about her before and she mellowed a little. 'I suppose being so close to her is bound to rub off on me a bit.'

O'Driscoll removed his sunglasses, sat back and smiled. She noticed his face crumpled into laughter lines round his eyes quite naturally, like they were used to it.

'It's good that you're so close. And that you share the same beliefs and passions.'

'Yes, it is. Usually.'

'I bet you're never happier than when you've got your loved ones around you and are feeding them all up. A true Irish mammy!' He lapsed into a strong Irish accent which made her smile and to prove his point, he seized the remaining biscuit on the plate and swallowed it whole, his hazel eyes sparkling with mischief.

'Like you said earlier, I'm protective of Olivia and a lot of people around here. We're a community and we stick together and look out for each other. I'm not being deliberately obstructive. Just careful.'

His face grew serious. 'I understand. And I'm not trying to

trick you into saying anything you don't want to. That's not my style.'

Cassie suddenly remembered what Kitten had told her to do. 'How's the investigation going? Or can't I ask that?'

His eyes sparkled again. 'Oh, you can ask. And I can say without betraying any confidences at all that we're still struggling to identify the victim. I'm beginning to learn that it's not just Londoners who close ranks where the police are concerned. I don't know why I thought it would be any different here.' His mobile beeped and he pulled it out of his trouser pocket with a sigh. 'Time's up, I'm afraid. The boss wants me. I'll see myself out.' He stood up and walked across the balcony. By the time he turned before he disappeared inside, Cassie had been distracted by her heron.

'Bye, Cassie. See you soon.'

'Bye, Sam,' she replied without thinking, not taking her eyes off the large bird and then started to laugh. *Did my heron just wink at me?*

12

Olivia had no trouble locating the office of Fal Staff, thanks to a quick Google search. She felt unexpectedly nervous as she rang the entryphone. She'd been caught up in a lengthy, but positive, finance meeting with Callum Armstrong, the Goods Shed's treasurer, all morning and then gone through a list of admin stuff with Alice. It was only on her journey into Falmouth that she'd turned her thoughts to her chat with Trenow, and she was beginning to wonder if he'd set her up to do this for him all along. Now standing outside the office, she suddenly realised she had given far more thought to Trenow's potential duplicity than to what she was going to say and snatched her mobile out of her pocket, searching for inspiration. As if by magic, a message appeared from Alice and Olivia read it eagerly.

A disembodied voice spoke through the intercom and Olivia leant forward.

'Oh hi. I was wondering if I could talk to someone about hiring staff for an event I have coming up?'

'Have you got an appointment?'

Her heart sank. Was she going to fall at the first hurdle? 'No, sorry. I was just passing and thought I'd pop in on the off-chance. Would it be possible to talk to someone now?'

There was a heavy sigh. 'We try to stick to an appointment system here.'

A sudden thought struck her. 'I'm a good friend of Willow Jardine and I know you work together fairly often. I recognised your name on the door as I walked past. Willow talks very highly of you and I thought you'd be ideal.'

The next sigh wasn't quite so heavy. 'Very well then. As you're a friend of Willow's… I'll buzz you in. Just come up the stairs; we're on the first floor.'

Olivia took her time walking up the wooden staircase, pulling her various thoughts together. She sniffed appreciatively at the smell of polish in the air and then noticed the wood panelling covering the bottom third of the walls. Above were pristine white walls lined with various large artistic photographs of smiling waiting and catering staff, alongside more casual shots of them going about their duties in a variety of attractive locations.

A door opened as Olivia approached the top step and a woman in her fifties appeared. She was tall and slim and perfectly made up with unsmiling magenta-glossed lips and matching nails. Her platinum blonde hair was styled into a short, spiky pixie cut, which Olivia decided, as she held out her hand to the unfriendly woman, suited her personality perfectly. She looked immaculate and cool in a well-cut black sleeveless shift dress and red high heels, which made Olivia feel underdressed in her vibrant orange, floaty sundress and flat sandals, but relieved she'd forsaken her denim shorts for once.

'Hi, thank you for seeing me. I don't think I gave you my name. I'm Olivia Wells.'

The older woman hesitated before shaking Olivia's hand and then ushered her in. 'And I'm Mina Hughes. I haven't got long, I'm afraid. I have another appointment in half an hour.'

'That's fine. I'm just so grateful you could see me now.'

Olivia took the proffered chair and gazed admiringly around the room while Mina sat back down behind her desk. More stylish photographs graced the walls, along with the biggest indoor plant collection Olivia had ever seen. But there were no metal filing cabinets, whiteboards or any of the usual office equipment one would expect in a busy recruitment agency. Mina's antique oak desk took centre stage, with a slim computer, several paper files and a desk fan that was doing a poor job of wafting the mid-afternoon's oppressive air around the room.

There was a smaller, empty desk at the back of the room, next to what was presumably the kitchen. One wall was taken up by a huge bank of pre-war solid oak filing drawers, and the opposite wall was lined with four separate one-metre-wide frosted glass writing boards, three of which were filled with names. Olivia let her eyes linger on the names for a moment before she turned back to Mina who had started to fiddle with the papers on her desk.

'I love what you've done with your office,' she observed with a smile. 'And it certainly looks like you're busy!'

Mina nodded curtly, her wide luminous eyes watching Olivia closely. 'The summer is one of our busiest times of year. We have lots of events and many casual staff – particularly with the university students all looking for work.'

Olivia filed that piece of information away and turned her attention back to Mina, who was now drumming her red nails on the desk.

'You said you were interested in hiring staff for an event you have coming up?'

'Oh yes, sorry. We, I mean, the trustees of the Goods Shed in Penbartha, are thinking of holding a summer party for the members and their clients.' It was the first thing that popped into Olivia's mind, but now she'd verbalised it, she quite liked the idea. 'Are you familiar with the Goods Shed, Mina?'

The woman's thin lips relaxed a little. 'Only through Willow. She's mentioned you to me a few times.' She paused. 'How is she by the way? It can't be long until her baby is due.'

Olivia beamed. 'Oh, she's blooming! Literally. I've never known anyone look so good this late on in a pregnancy. I'm so excited for the birth – she's already asked me to be godmother!'

Mina's lips relaxed into a full smile. 'Willow will be a wonderful mother. She's so calm and kind. She must think a lot of you to ask you to be godmother.'

Olivia blushed. 'What a lovely thing to say, thank you.'

'Does she know the baby's gender? I forgot to ask her.'

'It's too late to tell from the scans now, apparently. And when it was possible to tell, baby Jardine had their legs firmly crossed, so they couldn't say.' Olivia smiled. 'So, it will be a lovely surprise for all of us.'

Mina looked horrified. 'Who wants a surprise after nine months of pregnancy and God knows how many hours of agonising labour?'

Olivia laughed. 'That sounds heartfelt! I've never looked at it like that.'

'I take it you don't have children.'

'Heavens no!' Olivia spoke automatically. 'But you do?'

Mina smiled again. 'Yes, I have three. All grown up now, but still very precious.' What had appeared to be cold, pale eyes now sparkled like sapphires with affection and Olivia found herself warming to her. 'I know for a fact that godmothers are very carefully chosen and important in

Danish culture – like Willow's. As they are in the Dutch culture – like mine.'

Olivia sat up straighter. She'd thought she'd detected a slight accent when she'd heard Mina's voice through the entryphone, but had dismissed the idea when she met her face to face and put it down to a Cornish twang.

An even bigger smile lit up Mina's whole face. 'You are surprised?'

'Impressed.' Olivia recovered herself. 'I am so bad at languages.'

Mina waved her words away. 'I have been here many years now and my husband is Cornish,' she explained. 'Some of us lose our accents quicker than others. I can hear a slight American twang in your voice.'

'Really? I thought I'd lost it completely.'

Mina nodded. 'I have an ear for these things. It comes in very useful at times...' She trailed off and then recovered herself. 'You have many other talents according to Willow. You're an architect, a successful businesswoman, a good friend...' She paused for a moment. 'And a promising amateur detective.'

'I'm sorry?'

Mina lowered her voice. 'Willow told me what happened to you last year. It sounded dreadful. And I'm very sorry you had to go through all that. Men can be so very cruel.'

The sympathy in the older woman's voice brought tears to Olivia's eyes. She sniffed her thanks and concentrated on a magnificent weeping fig that dominated the far corner of the room.

'I was actually talking to Willow yesterday and she suggested I get in contact with you.'

'She did?'

'Yes. I think I might need your help.'

Olivia swallowed. 'You do?'

'Perhaps.' Mina turned away for a moment to adjust the fan and then changed the subject. 'I think there's going to be a storm later.' Olivia followed her gaze out of the window. The sky was still cloudless as far as she could see but the air was definitely getting heavier. 'The drop in air pressure always gives me a headache and a dry mouth. I need to rehydrate before it gets worse. Would you like some water?'

'Please.' Olivia used the brief moment Mina was in the kitchen to gather her thoughts together. This conversation was not going the way she had expected, but she wasn't at all confident that Mina would confide in her when it came to the crunch. She ran through various ways to encourage her to open up and abandoned them all as hopeless. She looked around the room in despair and caught a glance of the open diary on the desk. There was one entry for today's date. It simply said *Esmé 4pm.* She checked her watch and groaned. It was 3.45. Was she running out of time?

'A policeman came to see me a few days ago. About the girl who died at Peneglos Hall.' Mina started talking as soon as she reappeared.

Olivia pressed her lips together and nodded.

'He wanted all the names of the staff who were there that night.' Mina sat down and looked away for a moment. 'I gave him a list of the ones I knew.'

'Did that include the name of the girl who died?'

A hint of panic flashed in Mina's eyes. 'No. I didn't know it.'

Olivia's heart sank. 'Is that usual?'

Mina took a long drink of her water and Olivia could practically hear her brain whirring as she did battle with her conscience. She put her glass on the desk and looked straight at Olivia.

'Can what I am going to tell you stay just between us? For now, at least?'

'I should think so.'

'I have certain regular waiting staff on my books. And then I have some students and locals who just want to work on a casual basis. Which suits everyone and saves on some paperwork.' Her gaze challenged Olivia, but she wasn't at all interested in the niceties of PAYE and National Insurance. Presumably encouraged by her reaction, Mina continued. 'Anyway, as we had been personally recommended by Willow for the party at Peneglos Hall, I arranged for our most experienced staff to attend. It was an important event for us and I hoped it would lead to more work, but two of the girls rang in sick at the last minute.'

Olivia kept her gaze on the other woman.

'So, I asked someone who often finds replacements for me at the last minute to help.'

'And did she?'

Sudden tears filled Mina's eyes and she nodded. 'I wish she hadn't now.'

'And one of those stand-ins was the girl who died?'

Mina pressed her hand to her throat. 'Yes.'

'Can we backtrack a little? What's the name of the person you asked to find the extra help?'

Mina rubbed her temples and looked away. 'Esmé.'

Olivia's eyes strayed to the desk diary and then back to Mina, who was looking more and more uncomfortable. 'And did Esmé tell you anything about the girls she recommended?'

Mina looked away. 'Just that they needed to earn some cash. And that they were good workers.'

'Didn't you need their names for your records?'

'It was a one-off, so no.'

'Did they make their own way to the Hall?'

'No. Esmé dropped them off. And then they usually get a lift or a taxi home at the end of the evening. She sorts that out for them too, so I don't have to.'

Olivia frowned. 'That seems very good of her. Why does she do that?'

Mina coughed and then leaned forward and spoke very quietly. 'Esmé is involved in all sorts of charities that help women who are down on their luck, escaping abusive relationships and situations like that...' She trailed off. 'Occasionally she asks me to get work for one or two of them on a no-names basis because they don't want anything to be traced back to them. They don't want to be found by whoever they're avoiding. I pay them in cash and keep everything off the records.'

The way she spoke made Olivia believe she was genuinely trying to help these women rather than simply avoid paying tax, and she felt a stirring of admiration for the woman.

'And you haven't mentioned any of this to the police?'

'Only that she was a casual member of staff and I had no information about her.'

'Did you tell them about Esmé?'

'Good God, no!' Mina looked horrified. 'Esmé has a real thing about the police and I don't want to get her into trouble. She was just doing the poor girl a favour.'

'I bet she feels bad about what happened.' Olivia spoke with feeling.

'She most certainly does. Not that it has anything to do with you!' A furious voice from the doorway made them both jump and whirl round in their seats.

'It's okay, Esmé.' Mina hurried across the room to placate the short, almost rectangular woman who was radiating hostility and anger. Mina lapsed into her native tongue and a passionate exchange of words took place in Dutch, none of which Olivia understood apart from the odd name, but the tone and the volume of the conversation made it quite clear that Esmé was not happy. It was also abundantly clear from Mina's placatory tone that Esmé was the more dominant party in the friendship. She was older, perhaps in her sixties, and very short, with a steel-grey, perfectly symmetrical chin-length bob and black, thick-framed glasses that obscured much of her round face. Like Mina's, her voice was virtually accentless, but deep and gravelly, presumably from years of smoking. And in every other way they were complete opposites too. Whereas Mina was tall, striking and memorable, Esmé was drab, grey and instantly forgettable. *Presumably ideal in her line of work.*

Olivia sat in awkward silence as the two women voiced their unhappiness with each other. Eventually, Mina turned to her, with a pleading look on her face.

'Olivia, this is Esmé. Please tell her we can trust you.'

She took a deep breath. 'I'm sorry to put you in this situation, Esmé, but I do hope you'll soon realise you can trust me.'

The other woman snorted and glared, the owlishness of her slate-grey eyes emphasised by the black glasses. Olivia flinched a little and then realised that Esmé was testing her. She quickly thought back to what Mina had told her about how she helped vulnerable women. That made her honourable in Olivia's eyes and she needed to prove she was a tough woman too. She lifted her chin and stared back. 'What can I say that will help you decide whether to trust me or not?'

The glare faded. 'I need to know whether you will share what you learn from us with the police.'

Olivia thought carefully. This could be make or break. 'The only thing I would ever share is the girl's name. As it stands at the moment, she doesn't belong to anyone. Her family and loved ones don't even know she's died. They need to be able to grieve for her, give her the funeral she deserves, not live the rest of their lives wondering why she hasn't been in touch and if something's happened to her. Surely, you can understand that?'

Esmé narrowed her eyes. 'Even just giving her name could lead to a whole lot of questions being asked.'

'Isn't it more important that she's reunited with her family and they get to see justice done?'

'It's not that simple.' Esmé glanced at Mina, who nodded. 'I don't know whether Mina has told you, but I was helping this girl find work to earn money so she could get back home to her family.'

Mina spoke up. 'I didn't know that. I just thought she was one of your usual girls.'

Esmé waved her words away. 'I try to tell you as little as possible. Then you don't have the answers to any questions you may be asked.' She turned back to Olivia. 'I know the statistics, Miss Wells. Half of all murdered women are killed by their partner or ex. I work with women who've escaped violent, controlling and abusive relationships and need to earn money to get themselves back on their feet, without being tracked down through formal employment records.'

'But that wasn't the case with this girl?'

'No. This was different. She wasn't escaping an abusive partner. And she wasn't English. There was something else going on, but I didn't get to know her well enough to learn her full story.'

Olivia closed her eyes briefly. Just as she was beginning to understand things, they all shifted. She decided to let this new information lie for a while and get the conversation back on familiar ground.

'Okay.' She swallowed. 'So, is it usual for these women to get work through Mina's agency?'

'Not usual no. I don't want to get Mina into any trouble.' She looked fondly at the other Dutch woman. 'She does employ some of my women who are no longer at risk, formally through the books. And sometimes we help each other out, but Mina's come too far to risk everything she's achieved with this business to become too involved with my work.'

'But on the evening of the party at Peneglos Hall, you were helping each other out?'

'Yes. Mina was desperate for help, so we looked really carefully at the guest list. It was mainly people from London and local suppliers. We had no reason to believe any of them would recognise her. We thought she'd be safe.'

The anguish in Esmé's voice was genuine and Olivia felt sorry for her. 'Who did she go with?'

'Bex, one of our regulars. I dropped them off, and Lucinda Hayes called a taxi when she had a funny turn. That's all Bex knows.'

'You said you'd found this girl work before?'

'Yes.'

'May I ask how?'

Esmé crossed her arms. 'My husband's business.'

Olivia felt she was going backwards. She glanced at Mina, who just nodded encouragingly and then elbowed Esmé surreptitiously in the side.

'He runs a holiday letting business.'

'It's not just any old holiday letting business,' Mina jumped in, proudly. 'It's an ethical holiday cottage company. It's still fairly small and ideal for what Esmé needs.'

Olivia's interest was piqued. 'How does that work?'

Mina opened her mouth, but Esmé silenced her with a

look. 'We started off with cottages that had never been owned or occupied by local people. We renovated derelict or disused buildings, and bought up old estate cottages that weren't used for labourers anymore and had fallen into disrepair.'

Olivia thought about the various dilapidated estate cottages at Peneglos Hall and made a mental note to talk to Ruan about using them.

'Of course, that was in the days when they were going cheap because no-one wanted them.' She pursed her lips, her feelings clear. 'We can't afford to do it now, since property prices down here have become so ridiculously high and people from upcountry are prepared to pay silly money for what's basically a pile of old stones in a bit of field.' She took a breath. 'So, now we allow some carefully chosen holiday homeowners to use our services, as long as they abide by our rules.'

'Which are?'

'They have to drop their prices in less popular months to ensure the cottages are occupied throughout the year, which guarantees a steady income stream of customers for the local shops and businesses.'

'I like it.' Olivia smiled. 'Does it work?'

'It most certainly does. We have some of the highest year-round occupancy rates of all the letting agencies in Cornwall. Which keeps our women in year-round employment as housekeepers and cleaners. It's ideal for victims of domestic violence as we make sure they have different shifts, in different cottages, so they can't have their routines traced.' Esmé's eyes flashed behind her heavy glasses and Olivia began to see a new side to her. 'It gets better. And this is the part I like best. All cottage owners on our books, us included, have to donate at least one week's rental during high season to a special fund that we use to support affordable housing in the county for the locals.'

'Do they agree to that?'

Esmé shrugged. 'If they don't, they can go to one of the many other, less ethical agencies around who don't have our high social standards.' Esmé's lip twitched. 'Let's just say our books are always full.'

'That's fantastic!' Olivia didn't try to hide how impressed she was. Esmé was obviously a woman who held lots of causes close to her heart. She resolved not to introduce her to Kitten as she'd never have peace again. 'And just the sort of thing we try and support at the Goods Shed.'

'I know it is.' Mina nodded. 'Which is why I hoped we could trust you with this. I think we share the same kind of values.'

Olivia was touched. 'Thank you.'

'I was worried that Mina had been influenced by a pretty face, but now I've met you, I agree with my sister-in-law that we should trust you.'

'You're related?'

The two Dutch women exchanged a glance, but it was Mina who replied. 'Yes. Esmé helped me escape a previous life in Amsterdam. She was living in Cornwall by then, but kept up her contacts there. She offered me refuge here, introduced me to her husband's younger brother, and the rest, as they say, is history. Esmé kept her maiden name, which is the tradition in the Netherlands but I took my husband's name because I wanted an entirely new start.' Mina shot Olivia a look, her eyebrows raised, but Olivia just nodded. She got the message.

'Right.' Olivia brushed away the tendrils of hair that had fallen over her face. 'I get there's a lot at stake here. For everyone. But we do need to know what the girl's name is.'

# 13

'That's not going to be easy,' said Esmé.

'Why not? Can't you just ask the contact she came through? Surely she'll understand how important it is for her family to know what's happened?'

Esmé gave a slight shake of her head. 'It's not that straightforward.'

'I don't understand.' Olivia didn't even try to keep the frustration out of her voice.

Esmé and Mina exchanged a look that she couldn't interpret, then Mina signalled she had an errand to run and left the office.

Esmé fixed Olivia with a challenging stare and cleared her throat. 'Okay, it's not just victims of domestic violence we help. Like I mentioned, I used to run a support agency in Amsterdam that helped women escape prostitution and other forms of exploitation. I eventually had to leave because I was interfering in certain business models and it became too dangerous.'

Olivia closed her eyes for a moment as the meaning of Esmé's words sank in. 'So you came to Cornwall to be safe?'

'When I first moved to the UK, I lived in London. But it was too busy and noisy. I came to Cornwall for my first holiday and fell in love with the place. Yes, I thought it was all cream teas and sandy beaches to begin with, but it wasn't long before I discovered that people have similar problems the world over. I started helping victims of domestic abuse and found them refuge and work. Which is how I met my husband.'

Esmé's face broke out into a smile and Olivia suddenly very much wanted to meet the man who had softened this formidable woman's heart. 'He opened my eyes to a whole host of issues here in the UK and there are plenty of people – men and women – being exploited here in all sorts of ways.'

'I had no idea.'

'Most people don't. But there are always those, usually men, who are willing to exploit the vulnerable. The homeless, people dependent on drugs and alcohol or with mental health issues. Even recently released prisoners. Anyone who just needs a bit more money to make ends meet. Then there are the kids with difficult family backgrounds, the runaways. All sorts of people who desperately need money to survive or to fund an addiction and aren't going to ask too many questions.' The contempt in Esmé's voice was crystal clear.

'And what sort of work do they end up doing?'

Esmé shrugged. 'You name it. Sex work, forced labour on farms and building sites, in hospitality, nail bars. Some end up in domestic servitude, the kids get forced into taking drugs into rural areas and dealing. Then there's forced begging, shoplifting. Shall I go on?'

Olivia shuddered. 'I get the picture. Is there really no way of escape for them?'

'You have to remember that these people are carefully targeted. They have an inherent distrust of the police and anyone in authority. And they're even more scared of their employers. Some of them might be here illegally from Europe or elsewhere. They're all in impossible situations.'

Olivia's eyes widened. 'Are you telling me this a big problem in Cornwall?'

'No, not yet, but it's getting worse.' Esmé's voice was sombre. 'To begin with, we dealt mainly with girls who were working in other parts of the UK and, with charities and groups and people like me, we were able to bring them down here to help them. Some of the other victims we help have just jumped on a train to get as far away from their exploiters as they can. And you can't get much further away than here.' Esmé pursed her lips and fell silent.

'And then what happens to them?'

'They're provided with support and a safe space. And helped to find work, if they want it.'

The face of the drowned waitress flooded Olivia's mind and she gulped. 'Do you know if the girl who died at Peneglos Hall was one of these victims?'

'I'm not sure.' Esmé frowned. 'Like I said, she was different.'

'In what way?'

'There was something about her. I've become good at recognising the facial features of the nationalities we usually deal with, and she was different. Quite distinctive-looking in a way. High, sharp cheekbones, thick shiny hair and large dark eyes. More of a mix between Eastern European and Mediterranean, not English. And she didn't look malnourished, or as though she'd been beaten, like a lot of them do. I thought she either hadn't been here long, or was one of the lucky ones.'

Olivia winced. 'So how did you get to know about her?'

'Through one of the support groups I'm involved in.'

'Is there any way you could contact the person who put the girl in touch with you?'

'I'll try. She's not the easiest person to get hold of, for obvious reasons.' The expression on her face was decidedly unhappy. 'Would you have to give the girl's name to the police?'

'She's been murdered, Esmé! We're too late to help her. But perhaps if we find out her name, and the police get hold of her family, it might lead to you helping a load more victims in the long run.'

'Hmmph. I'll do what I can. As long as my contacts aren't dragged into it. I just have a horrible feeling we might be opening up a particularly nasty Pandora's box and, as we say in Amsterdam, when you burn your butt, you have to sit on your blisters.'

---

'So, what do you make of all that?' Olivia finished recounting their conversation to Jago over dinner. She'd arrived back at Tresillian to find his car on the drive, the silage obviously harvested, the dogs in a frenzy of excitement and the kitchen in complete turmoil as he prepared one of her favourite dishes. The clouds had got progressively lower and heavier as she'd driven back from Falmouth, and the orangery looked beautiful lit by candles and fairy lights wound through the shutters.

Any hopes that Jago's efforts may have been a peace-seeking mission were soon dashed. His face matched the darkening sky that hung across the creek. A sudden gust of wind shook the trees in the garden and spots of rain began to fall against the windows.

'I thought you'd decided to leave well alone?'

Olivia bristled. 'No. You wanted me to come to that decision. But I can't. Not now I've come this close to finding out her name.'

'And then you'll just pass it on to Trenow and leave it all to him, will you?' His jaw tightened.

'That's the plan.' She wouldn't meet his gaze as the spitting rain got heavier against the windows and the wind rippled its way across the surface of the agitated creek. *There's going to be a hell of a storm. Inside and outside.*

'Come off it, I know you better than that. Now that Esmé, or whatever her name is, has told you all that stuff about the women she works with, there's no way you're going to walk away.'

'And can you remind me again what's so wrong with wanting to help other people?' She felt like she was beginning to sound like a broken record.

'There's nothing wrong with it in theory. I'm just worried about you stepping on dangerous people's toes.'

'How would I be doing that?'

'Olivia.' Jago pushed his hands through his hair until it was standing up in angry spikes, just as it had always done when she first met him and they clashed repeatedly. 'Get real. Most of the people Esmé is talking about are not unfortunate victims, who happen to be in the wrong place at the wrong time and just get randomly picked up by the local bad guy. They're victims of human trafficking.'

Olivia felt her face drain of colour. 'No! Esmé was quite clear that most of the women she helps are local victims of domestic violence, with the occasional person from upcountry. She said it was rare for them to help girls from abroad. That's what made the waitress stand out.'

He stood up and turned on the lights. The air outside had gone ominously still as the clouds pressed further and further downwards, blocking out what was left of the day's natural light.

'And how does Esmé know that for sure? Do you really think these girls are going to tell her the truth? They'll be too damned scared! I bet some of them have been trafficked here, from elsewhere in the UK or from overseas, with the specific intention of being exploited for money.' He turned and fixed her with an icy stare. 'And, believe me, we're not talking about lone wolves who are doing this kind of thing. We're talking large-scale organised crime. The big boys. Who don't like people interfering in their successful operations, like Esmé said happened to her in Amsterdam. Do you really want to mess with those sorts of people?'

He came to a stop at the other side of the table and placed his palms on it so he could get her full attention. Olivia moved away. There was a strange energy to Jago she hadn't felt before. He was rattled, more rattled than she'd ever known him to be.

There was a sudden huge clap of thunder and all the lights flickered. Mylor gave a frightened yelp, ran across the room from his basket and leapt onto Olivia's lap. In spite of his bravery when it came to fighting off men who were attacking his mistress, he was terrified of thunderstorms. Olivia pulled a shawl from the back of her chair and wrapped it tightly around him, murmuring soothing noises into his silky ears as she did so, even though her mind was racing. When both she and Mylor had calmed down slightly, she lifted her eyes to Jago's. For once, Jago's face, which was normally impossible to read, had his emotions written all over it, but he turned away before she could interpret them. Olivia felt a surge of panic wash through her.

She took a deep breath. 'Where's this all coming from? I'm talking about a single waitress in Cornwall and you've suddenly made a massive leap to human exploitation on an international scale. Are you sure you're not getting carried away by the high-profile cases you're hearing about in London?' She narrowed her eyes. 'Have you been involved in any? Is that why you're so stressed?'

He glared back. 'No, it isn't, but it's all over the media! Haven't you read about it?'

'Of course I have. But we're talking about women who have come to Cornwall to get away from their abusers, not an international trafficking ring!'

Jago swallowed and looked away, his lips set in a grim line and a muscle twitching in his cheek.

Olivia took a deep breath. 'Look, I know I've asked you this a dozen times already, but will you please tell me what's bothering you?'

'And I'm telling you for the final time that it's just work stuff and I don't want to bring any of it into our lives down here. I just want to forget all about it, and I wish you would too!'

His harsh tone of voice was back and Olivia was hurt as much by its return as by his abrupt confirmation that he was now deliberately keeping important things from her.

She tried one more time. 'You don't have to keep me in some kind of vacuum. You can share stuff with me, you know.'

He raised a disdainful eyebrow. 'I'm not very good at sharing my work life. Never have been. That's probably why Sarah buggered off when she did.'

For the first time ever, Olivia felt a flash of sympathy for his ex-girlfriend. And then felt guilty. There was another loud clap of thunder and the rain began to lash down against the windows. She clutched Mylor to her more tightly, but said nothing. Zennor and Steren didn't even twitch in their sleep.

Jago leant across the table and squeezed her hand. 'I'm sorry. I'm probably on edge because I've come home and found myself in an episode of *Midsomer Murders* when I was hoping to get away from crime for a bit. And you're right, I'm blowing it out of proportion. Let's forget all about it until Esmé gets back to you.'

His attempt at a chuckle would normally have broken the tension, but it sounded forced and his mouth was pinched tight. Olivia's heart sank. This was his opportunity to confide in her. Nothing he said could be as bad as her worst imaginings. She'd learnt to depend on his logical and unflappable calmness, but now he was anxious and distracted and it scared her.

A deafening clap of thunder rocked the house, as the storm set in, rain lashing, thunder rumbling and lightning tearing the sky to shreds over the creek. For a few moments the noise was too loud to be heard over and they sat in an uncomfortable silence, watching a spectacular battle of the elements playing out. Eventually the storm moved away, easing the tension in the atmosphere inside as well as out. Jago moved round the table to sit next to her, and took her hand in one of his, the other stroking a still quivering Mylor.

Olivia's mobile rang out and she grabbed it. It was Esmé. Olivia tightened her grip on the phone and listened carefully, feeling her pulse quicken with every word.

'Thanks, Esmé. I need to think about what to do next. Yes, I'll be careful what I say to the police … Yes, I realise that … Can you just spell the girl's name for me, so I'm sure I get it right?'

She scribbled the name down and then pushed the piece of paper across to Jago while she said her goodbyes.

'At least we have a name for her now…' Olivia's voice trailed off when she turned back to him. He'd stopped stroking Mylor and was holding the note at arm's length in front of him, as if it was poisonous. And there was a wariness in his eyes that she hadn't seen before.

'Agnes Toska.' Jago's voice was flat.

She gulped. 'It seems even worse now she has a name. It makes her more real.' She blew her nose. 'Oh, there was something else that might help.'

'What?' Jago dropped the piece of paper.

'Esmé's contact reckoned she'd recently come over from Albania.'

# 14

Jago woke the next morning to the sound of a door closing and the promise of another beautiful summer's day. Through the slats of the shutters he could see the sky was back to its perfect blue self, without even the slightest wisp of cloud. Olivia's side of the bed was empty and the dogs were nowhere to be seen or heard. They'd obviously gone off for their early morning run, which was a relief as it meant he wouldn't have to face her for a while. Had their relationship really come to that? He groaned and pummelled his pillow into a more comfortable shape and lay staring up at the ceiling.

He had barely slept. Mylor, still suffering the effects of the storm, had positioned himself firmly between them on the bed, wrapped in his shawl, and had vibrated quietly between them until the early hours. Occasionally their fingers would touch as they both reached out at the same time to comfort the distressed dog, but that had been the sum of their contact. Jago sighed. Until this past week they had spent every night they had together curled up, with Olivia moulded into his side. No wonder he never slept well when he was alone in London.

London. That was the source of his problems. Or rather what had happened there recently. Images, voices, and a sense of anger mixed with another emotion he couldn't easily identify surged into his mind. At Olivia's mention of Albania all the random thoughts and feelings that had been swirling around his brain and body for the past week suddenly coalesced into one horrible but unassailable connection to the last trial he had presided over as a judge.

Edon Bregu, an Albanian career criminal, known to the National Crime Agency for his links to drug importation, money laundering and violence, had eventually been brought to court on a charge of grievous bodily harm, after stabbing a man three times outside a London wine bar. The NCA believed he was involved in far more serious crimes, but Bregu was a mastermind at covering his tracks. During his trial, various statements had been withdrawn and witnesses had not turned up at court, and after an extremely poor performance, the prosecuting counsel offered no evidence and the case collapsed. Jago, as the judge, had to instruct the jury to acquit, and then referred Bregu to the Director of Public Prosecutions for investigation and recommended that his residency in the UK be revoked. It had left a nasty taste in his mouth, not least because the only time Egon Bregu had taken his deep-set, menacing eyes off Jago throughout the whole trial was to stare at the few witnesses who had appeared for the prosecution. It was like he was memorising every inch of Jago's face, every word he uttered, every movement he made. Jago had met hundreds of criminals in his time, but none had ever got under his skin like this one. And more than once he had woken from a dream where Bregu's impassive face, with its neatly trimmed stubble and cropped hair that made him look more like a successful businessman than a hardened criminal, would break into the sneer that had crossed his face when Jago had been forced to acquit him.

The case had caused a huge furore among the judges and the press. Was this just the latest example of the accelerating decline of his profession that he'd been witnessing first-hand, or was it worse than that? Were the voluble and excitable jungle drums of the London Bar actually correct? Had the prosecuting barrister been threatened by Bregu's associates or had he, because of the decreasing level of pay for criminal barristers, taken a bribe? Either way, he had not been seen since, and according to the London Bar grapevine, had taken early retirement. Rumours and supposition were rife, barristers being the biggest gossips on the planet, and more than a few ribald comments had been made to Jago about watching his back. He'd tried to shrug them off, for the sake of bravado, but in his mind he was running through all sorts of scenarios, none of which had a pleasant outcome.

Jago thumped the pillow and glared at the ceiling. What the hell was he going to do now? As soon as he'd heard that the waitress was Albanian, Edon Bregu's face had flooded his mind and refused to move. What if those throwaway remarks by his colleagues were right? What if his contacts had traced Jago to Cornwall and were making their presence felt? Was that a ridiculous idea? Not if what Jago had learnt about the Albanian mafia was true. And did he dare take the risk? Not for him, but for those he loved?

Jago closed his eyes, saw the mocking face of Edon Bregu and propelled himself out of bed and into the shower.

The shower didn't have the necessary effect and just as Olivia often used her running as a distraction technique, he needed something physical to take his mind off his worries. Pulling on shorts and a sports vest, he ran down the stairs, out of the kitchen and across the garden to the old stone quay where he kept his kayak and paddleboard. He looked at them briefly, considering which would better suit his current mood. Paddleboarding was more peaceful and conducive to thinking things through. But he didn't want to think. He wanted to forget everything and get his heart pumping so fast he could only concentrate on his breathing. The kayak it would be.

For the next hour Jago kayaked down the creek and up the Carrick Roads like a man possessed, his arms and heart pumping. Every muscle in his upper body ached and his leg and abdominal muscles hurt. *Good.* When he pulled up alongside Tresillian's stone quay, physically exhausted, he sat for a moment, relishing the feelings of an outdoor workout and the sun on his face. It beat being in the gym hands down. To put off facing reality for a little longer, he deliberately flipped his kayak and let the shock of the cold water clear his mind.

'Feeling better?' Olivia's voice carried across the water.

Jago pushed his kayak onto the quay and climbed up next to it.

'I saw you powering back down the creek, looking like you were rocket-propelled!' There was a tentative smile on her face, and Jago felt a twinge of guilt. He looked at her sitting at the edge of the quay, in what had always been Mollie's favourite spot, and he noticed how rigidly she held herself. He could even see the tension in her neck now she had pulled her hair into a loose bun on top of her head. His mood was obviously affecting her too. He caught the towel she threw him and rubbed himself down.

'I needed that.' He smiled at her and saw her shoulders relax. At the sound of his voice all three dogs raced each other across the lawn to greet him, tails wagging furiously. Jago bent down to fuss them, all now clamouring for his attention, and wished his worries were as easily forgotten as Mylor's.

'Fancy some breakfast? We swung by the Bakehouse on the way back home and picked up some of your favourites.'

He felt another stab of guilt, and forced himself to smile. 'That would be fab. I've worked up quite an appetite.'

'Me too.' Olivia slipped her arm round his waist and he pulled her into his side as they walked to the house. 'We can have breakfast and then I've got a meeting with Alice at eleven, sorry.'

'That's okay.' He dropped a kiss on her head. 'How's Willow doing?'

'Fine. But she's so huge and uncomfortable. I can't think of anything worse than being heavily pregnant in this weather.' She shuddered dramatically and he laughed. 'She says she's done in by ten o'clock in the morning.'

'I bet she is.' He stood back to let her walk through the doorway first. 'Any other news?' As soon as the words left his mouth, he could have bitten his tongue. But Olivia was one step ahead of him.

'Oh, you know, just the usual girly chat.' She carried on through to the kitchen and they made breakfast together and chatted about inconsequential things, steadfastly ignoring the elephant in the room.

Jago watched as she regaled him with a funny tale about one of Kitten's latest campaigns. She was a natural but gentle mimic; her face was animated, her eyes bright and she was waving her arms around energetically in just the same way Kitten did to illustrate whatever point she was making.

A sudden surge of love swept through him and he caught his breath. How could he ever put this woman in any sort of danger? He'd seen her nearly die before, and it had scared him more than he'd ever admitted to himself. Had she not survived that fateful day at the harbour, what would have happened to the Goods Shed, the Waiting Rooms café, Tresillian? Who would have looked after Mylor and Zennor with as much love as she did? And what would he have done without her?

Could he persuade her to go to London with him and keep her out of harm that way? Unlikely. Olivia was the most obstinate person he knew and there was no way she would agree to leaving Penbartha without knowing the reason why. And he wasn't prepared to tell her until he was sure of his facts. To do that he needed to talk to someone who knew more about this area of law than he did, and find out whether the Albanian people smuggling gangs had infiltrated the South West yet, or whether the nationality of the dead waitress was just a coincidence.

In the meantime, perhaps the best thing to do was put some distance between him and Olivia and keep her at arm's length. That way, anyone who might be intending to do him harm and may have followed him to Cornwall wouldn't know she meant anything to him. Yes, that was it. If keeping away from her was the price he had to pay to keep her safe, then so be it. Even if it would nearly kill him in the process. But how on earth was he going to explain his absence to Olivia?

'Hey, are you okay?' Olivia's question catapulted him out of his thoughts.

'Yes, yes.' He ran his hand across his face and then looked at his watch. 'So, what's your meeting with Alice about?'

'She's drawn up the contract for a new tenant to lease one of the spaces in the Engine Shed and she wants us both there to go through the fine print.'

Jago frowned. 'I sometimes think they take your good nature for granted. Is dealing with that sort of thing really within your remit?'

Olivia sighed. 'Not really. It's Callum's now he's chair, but he's busy so Alice has asked me to do it as vice chair. And it's really no problem.' She looked at him more closely. 'You don't mind, do you? Did you have plans for us today?'

'No, it's fine. I should probably go and check in at the Signal Box anyway.'

Olivia's face crumpled. 'I'm sorry. I keep forgetting that you're on holiday and I'm supposed to be keeping more of my time free so we can do stuff together.'

'Don't worry about it. You take as long as you need. We've got the rest of the summer ahead of us.' Jago hid his wince as Olivia threw her arms around him and kissed his cheek.

'If I go now, I might be able to wrap the whole thing up and be back in time for lunch. Why don't you book a table at the Smuggler's Rest and we can get away from Penbartha for the rest of the day?' She turned her wide smile on him and he felt like a little bit of him died inside. Could he really go ahead with his plan to leave her?

---

Jago finished reloading the dishwasher, musing as usual if Olivia would ever learn to do it properly, while weighing up the pros and cons of going back to London. A fleeting thought made him wonder if he dare postpone it for a day or two, to give him more time with her. Just as he'd decided he could probably afford to do that, the door to the orangery opened and Trenow appeared. Jago's heart froze.

'Who are you looking for? If it's Olivia, she's at the Goods Shed.'

'You'll do.' Trenow sat down heavily at the table. 'Is the kettle on, by any chance?'

Jago sighed and pulled the kettle on to the Aga's hotplate. He kept his back to the policeman as he made the tea, still thinking of his plans, and then carried everything over to the table.

'I'm guessing this isn't a social call?'

Trenow shook his head, waiting for the tea to be sufficiently brewed before he spoke.

Jago took pity on him and added two croissants to the plate in front of him. 'Don't you police ever eat at home?'

Trenow mumbled something about being up since dawn through a mouthful of croissant, butter and jam and Jago signalled for him to finish his food while his mind switched to wondering what this visit was all about.

As soon as Trenow had finished eating and was making a start on his cup of tea, Jago got to the point. 'I take it this visit is prompted by Olivia's phone call about Agnes Toska?'

'Partly. The name was useful. There wasn't a lot of other information to help, but at least we know where to direct our efforts now. We've got the relevant liaison people working on it, and then we can hopefully inform her family.'

'So, do you reckon there are many Albanians working down here?' Jago kept his voice light.

Trenow grimaced. 'Let's just say she's the first one I've come across in my role as a police officer. I don't think Cornwall features highly in the Albanian TikTok videos as the place to come and make their fortune.' He drained his mug and poured himself another. 'Despite the politicians' best efforts, the Calais to Dover route is still the most popular with people smugglers and illegal migrants. And the poor buggers have to get to Calais overland. I'm sure London is much more likely to be their dream destination. The last thing they're going to want to do after that journey is trog all the way down here.'

'So you're not aware of any Albanians or other

nationalities working illegally down here?' Jago pressed for more information.

Trenow shook his head. 'There's been some raids on illegal cannabis farms further north in the county, and they tend to be run by Albanians these days, but nothing on a large scale. And we definitely haven't seen a rise in gangs or violence, which the Albanians are most known for. You should ask O'Driscoll about it. He's got a few tales about stuff he's seen that would make your hair curl.'

Jago didn't doubt it, and was slightly mollified by Trenow's reassurances. 'You said this visit was only partly to do with Olivia's information about the waitress?'

'Oh yes.' Trenow's face darkened. 'Have you heard from anyone at Peneglos Hall this morning?'

Jago shook his head. 'Olivia and I have both been busy. I haven't even looked at my mobile today.'

'So you haven't heard the news?'

'No.' Jago's heart beat faster.

'Look, it will be on the local news soon, so I'm not talking out of turn. I got a phone call at about seven o'clock this morning. From Ruan Braithwaite.' Trenow paused, but Jago remained silent. 'Apparently, Dylan Bonnar was walking along the shore at the cove at the bottom of the Hall's gardens at six o'clock this morning…'

'And…?'

'He found another body.'

Jago's stomach clenched. 'No.'

'I'm afraid so. Young—'

'Female?'

'No, actually. Male this time. Looked as though he'd been washed up in the storm.'

'Oh.' Jago released the breath he'd been holding. 'Anything else to go on?'

Trenow nodded. 'There was one identifying feature, but it means nothing to me.'

'Go on…'

'He had a tattoo.'

'What sort of tattoo?'

'It was a double-headed black eagle. Does that ring any bells for you? Jago, are you okay?'

Jago closed his eyes and concentrated on his breathing. It was a while before he lifted his eyes back to Trenow.

'For fuck's sake, Ross. It's the national emblem of Albania.'

---

Less than an hour later, Jago finished scribbling an inadequate note to Olivia and loaded his stuff into his car. 'C'mon, Steren. You're going to Launceston for a little holiday.' Zennor and Mylor looked sad and confused about why they weren't going with their friend, and Steren whined pathetically as she realised she was being parted from them.

'C'mon, old girl. It's for the best. I don't want to leave any more than you do. But if we want any chance of coming back here, we need to do this. If two dead bodies, both linked to Albania, exactly a week apart isn't a message, I don't know what is.' Jago spoke to his Labrador as he coaxed her into her car crate, anxious to be gone before Olivia returned from the Goods Shed. But the dog was not to be comforted and the pitiful howls that filled the car cut through Jago's heart as sharp as a shard of glass as he drove away.

# 15

'If you're looking for Cassie, she and Kitten have gone out for the morning.' Dylan's deep voice came from within the large granite store set into the external wall of the kitchen garden at Peneglos Hall.

'Oh, right. Sorry to bother you... I'd forgotten...' Olivia swallowed hard and turned on her heel, eager to get away before her voice cracked any more. The words of Jago's note were engraved on her heart and she couldn't think of anything else.

'Hey, wait!' Dylan called after her and she thought quickly. Could she get her emotions under control in time to face him, or should she just pretend she hadn't heard him and go home? The dogs, however, had different ideas and rushed off into the shed to find their friend.

Damn, it was too late. Taking several deep breaths, she dashed away the tears with a hand and fixed a smile on her face before she followed them. The shy smile she glimpsed on Dylan's face beneath his shaggy beard as he looked up from fussing Mylor and Zennor made her eyes sting again.

'You okay?' He scrambled to his feet but she held her arm out to stop him getting closer. He took the hint and stood still.

'Don't be nice to me, Dylan, please… not today.'

'Okay. Much as it goes against my kind nature.' He waved towards his shed. 'Do you fancy a cold drink? I need a break and you'd actually be doing me a favour.'

Olivia glanced into the cool shed and suddenly felt hot and tired. She could do worse than spend a few minutes with this gentle soul who never asked personal questions and didn't need to be entertained with constant chatter.

'Water would be lovely, thank you.'

'Water I can do. Straight from the spring, with not a chemical in sight. Back in a sec.'

Olivia settled herself on a three-legged milking stool while the dogs set off with Dylan, sniffing appreciatively at the mingling smells of earth, oil and the tantalising herbs that were strewn over the floor, an old trick Mollie had also used to keep unwanted insects away. Then she looked around. It was immediately obvious that this was far more than just a tool shed for Dylan. The walls were lined with rows of old wooden-handled gardening tools with highly polished metal work: spades, forks, rakes, hoes and other equipment she didn't recognise. One wall unit held terracotta pots of all sizes, watering cans, balls of string and neatly labelled tins of seeds. Huge charts hung on the opposite walls, documenting the planting, growing and harvesting of everything in the kitchen garden. It was laid out like a military campaign and Olivia, having never seen anything like it before, moved across to look at it in more detail.

She was so engrossed in examining the plans and enjoying the vibration of the bees in the climbing rose that arched over the doorway, she didn't even notice Dylan had returned until he handed her a chunky glass of water.

She turned to him in surprise. As usual, he blended in with his earthy surroundings, wearing scruffy khaki trousers and a pebble-coloured tee shirt with a slogan so faded she couldn't read it. For once, his long, unkempt hair was gathered into a topknot, which made him look younger and less scary, Olivia decided.

'Hey, I've never known anyone move around as silently as you.'

Dylan shrugged, gave one of his shy smiles and signalled that she sat back down on the stool. Then he dropped to the floor beside her in an easy cross-legged position. 'I decided we deserved ice.' He swirled the cubes in his glass. 'So I went to the kitchens.'

Olivia took a long drink. 'Thanks.' She looked around. 'Where are Mylor and Zennor?'

'Lexie asked if she could keep them for a while.' He picked up one of the old forks he'd been in the process of oiling and looked around for his rag. 'Some of these forks are as old as the house and gardens. I found this special oil recipe in one of the old gardener's journals and they're all coming up a treat.' He dipped the rag in the solution and began polishing the tines, his arm muscles, toned by years of outdoor life, making easy work of it. 'I think Lexie was glad of the distraction.'

Olivia frowned. 'From what? I thought things had calmed down.' She could feel Dylan's eyes scrutinising her and an old, but familiar, feeling of dread washed through her. 'What's happened now?'

Dylan went back to his task and didn't look up as he nodded towards the gardens. 'I thought that was why you're here. Didn't you see all the vehicles out the front?'

'No, I came down the rear drive as usual.' A sudden image of Jago's note flashed through her mind again and she pushed it away. 'What vehicles?'

Dylan stopped oiling the fork. 'Sorry. We've been talking at cross-purposes.' His gaze held hers. 'Another body has been found. I mean, I found a body early yesterday morning, washed up in the cove.'

Olivia's mouth went dry and her heart began to thump. 'Who?'

'A man this time. No ID on him. The police and forensics were crawling all over the place yesterday. Some have come back today and Lexie's been providing refreshments for them all.'

She tried to keep in the small, strangled noise that had formed in her throat, but Dylan, with his bat-like ears must have heard it as he cocked his head on one side.

'You okay?'

'Not really, no.' She let out a shaky breath. 'I sometimes feel like I'm stalked by death.'

'No, you're not. It's just a horrible coincidence.'

Despite the shockwaves reverberating through her mind, Olivia felt the cogs of her brain beginning to turn. 'You said you found the body?'

He nodded. 'Not the nicest start to the morning.'

'Tell me about it.' Olivia's comment was heartfelt. 'Are you okay?'

'I am now. Thanks for asking.'

Olivia's mind went back to the waitress's – no – Agnes's death and Trenow's interest in Dylan's whereabouts that night. 'Were the police okay with you?'

'Eventually. Reluctantly. It seems I can't win, whether I'm here or not.'

'It's a shame you hadn't gone back to wherever you were on the night of the party,' Olivia commented, wondering whether he'd take the bait.

Dylan looked at her for a long moment and seemed to

come to a decision. 'I was at a summer solstice celebration in West Penwith that night. It was just a weekend thing.'

Olivia felt the beginnings of a smile tug at her mouth. 'Ooh, Mollie always said they do the best celebrations there. I went a couple of times. Did you stay up all night waiting for the fires to die down?'

A matching smile transformed Dylan's tired face. 'We did. And gathered herbs in the morning dew. It was magical. Almost perfect.'

Olivia hadn't thought about all the fun and laughter she'd shared with George and Mollie at midsummer for ages, and she felt suddenly choked with emotion. After she'd swallowed a couple of times, she looked up to see Dylan watching her closely, his hazel eyes sparkling. She realised why she always felt comfortable in his presence. He had the same sense of peace and calm that had radiated from Mollie.

'I think I would have liked Mollie,' he stated quietly.

Olivia started, taken aback. *Can this half-feral man read my mind?*

'It's okay, Cassie talks about her a lot. She sounds like my kind of woman. Happiest with her herbs and plants.'

Olivia felt another surge of longing for her godmother. She would have known what to say to Jago. Again, Dylan must have sensed her sadness as he stood up swiftly and pointed outside.

'Why don't I show you around the kitchen garden? It's coming on nicely now.'

'Really?' Olivia scrambled to her feet, glad of the distraction. 'I thought entrance to the kitchen garden was by invitation only?'

'It is. And I'm inviting you. Let's go the long way so I can check the walls are all sound.' He headed off and called back to her. 'Unless you want it in writing?'

'No, I'm coming.' She caught up with him. 'It's just that Cassie has always said—'

'Cassie respects my space. The kitchen garden is my domain and she knows I like working alone. She's happy working on the woodland and more formal gardens with her trusty team of volunteers.' They walked side by side along a neat gravelled path that followed the circumference of the wall.

'And they've done the most amazing job.' Olivia couldn't help a note of defensiveness creep into her voice.

'They have indeed!' Dylan's voice was gentle. 'Cassie is perfect for these gardens. From what she's told me, Mollie regaled her with stories of the plant hunters who brought back wonderful plants from all over the world. And when she found out the Braithwaites' links with them meant lots of the species are here in the gardens, she was on a one-woman mission to find and restore as many of them as she could. I reckon she's been through Uncle Charles's archives word by word.'

Olivia smiled. 'I wouldn't be surprised if she has. His archives sound like a treasure trove of information, and she's loving every minute of it.' Olivia paused and realised Dylan's words had sparked her curiosity. 'You must have known him well to call him Uncle Charles.'

Dylan coloured. 'Does it sound a bit presumptuous? It's just that I spent so much time here with Ruan when we were teenagers that it was easier to call him uncle than Mr Braithwaite and there's no way I could have been so familiar to call him Charles. He wasn't that kind of man.' He looked away. 'But he was much nicer than most of his ancestors by all accounts.'

Olivia smiled. 'They certainly sound like an interesting bunch from what Cassie's told me.'

'You're probably right. I hope they became more law-abiding by Uncle Charles's time. But you don't get to establish a garden like this by abiding by the rules. People like Joseph Braithwaite, who built this place, wanted to flaunt their wealth by showing off their plant collections rather than masterpieces and antiques. And even Charles's grandfather, at the end of the nineteenth century, wasn't averse to flouting the import restrictions on things like tree ferns from Australia by arranging for them to be quietly brought into the cove here rather than the port at Falmouth.'

'Who would have thought trees and plants would have been the penis-extensions of past centuries in some circles?'

Dylan chuckled and nodded towards the line of giant redwoods that lined an avenue in the distance, tall and straight evergreen trees with deeply grooved, reddish-brown bark and distinctive drooping branches of grey-green leaves, towering above the adjacent oaks, beeches and sweet chestnuts

'You have to admit they're pretty impressive?'

Olivia nodded. 'How old are they?'

'Well, legend has it that these came from one of the first batches of cones that were sent over from San Francisco by our very own local plant hunter.'

Olivia searched her memory for a name. 'One of the Lobb brothers?'

'I see Mollie taught you well.' Dylan was impressed. 'William Lobb, the older one. They were both outdoors boys and unusually for the time, found work in local landowners' gardens rather than down the mines. Family legend has it that they hung around Falmouth harbour and got to know the local packet ship captains, and it was them who gave them the taste for travel.'

'Is that another of Joseph Braithwaite's claims to fame?'

'I don't think any of the Braithwaite dynasty lets facts get in the way of a good story.' Dylan ran his hand down a section of wall. 'Another family legend reckons that when he retired in 1820, he'd made the equivalent of five million pounds by smuggling all sorts of exotic goods on his ship and selling them on the black market.'

'Wow! No wonder he was able to build such a fabulous house.'

'And he, and then subsequent Braithwaites, probably used some of the money to finance some of the plant hunting expeditions themselves, so they could be the first families to have the finest collections in their gardens. They all took it very seriously, by all accounts. You don't build a garden that boasts original plants from over forty countries overnight.'

Olivia's gaze took in the gardens. 'Were they really just following fashion?'

'I think they might have been to start with. Joseph at least. I don't think he was a very nice man. He needed to flaunt his wealth and probably cleaned up his dirty money in the process. People didn't ask you where your cash came from in those days. And having established themselves as horticultural experts they just ran with it and enjoyed the fame and money that came with it. Gardens reflected a family's position in society.'

'Kitten always says that gardens like these were built on the back of colonialism and the expansion of the British Empire.'

Dylan bent to pull a weed out of the bottom of the wall and as he stood up a strong waft of rosemary drifted from his hair. 'Kitten's got a point. Plants were taken without permission or compensation and the plant hunters certainly didn't take into account their impact on local habitats, people or wildlife. Everyone has to live with those consequences today. And while this garden is full of these treasures, I believe it's our duty to look after them. Or rather Cassie's.'

'Is that why you prefer the kitchen garden. For moral reasons?'

'Maybe. I think Charles did too. Because his father and grandfather were really only interested in the exotics that were fashionable at the time and flourished especially well here, they left the kitchen gardens to the servants and hired gardeners. And of course, during the First World War they were completely abandoned. During the Second World War they were partially revived by the land army to provide food for the locals. When Charles came back from the war, he took it upon himself to restore the kitchen gardens and basically left the rest to look after themselves.'

'Was he the recluse everyone says he was? Ruan doesn't talk much about him and yet you seem to be very fond of him.'

'Well, he was always good to me. I enjoyed helping him in the kitchen garden during the holidays we spent here. And when Ruan took over the Hall, he said it made sense to get them to a standard where we can grow as much of the produce the hotel will use as possible. But Ruan's skipped the male Braithwaites' passion for gardens, so he asked me to help.' He paused. 'I saw how much good being in the garden did Charles over the years. I don't know what he went through during the war, or even afterwards, but I think the garden helped him cope with everything.'

'Mollie always said that gardening gives you hope for the future.' Olivia's voice caught in her throat.

'I like that. Nature certainly rewards your hard work, unlike a lot of things in life…' Dylan's voice faded away as they rounded the last wall of the rectangle and he opened one of the vast wooden doors and gestured her through.

Olivia stood open-mouthed. A long wooden glass house

stretched to the length of the shorter wall to her left and a bank of cold frames stood to the right, with all sorts of colourful produce spilling out on to the paths. And there in front of her, in all its abundant glory, was the most exquisite kitchen garden she had ever seen.

She reckoned it was over an acre in size, and split into six defined sections with large raised beds all edged with railway sleepers and bordered by more neat paths. Espalier apple and pear trees were trained up each of the long brick walls, with wide strips of free-standing fruit trees occupying the ground in front of them. Rather than the striped lawns she expected to see, the grass was full of beautiful wildflowers that buzzed and shimmered with insects.

'Oh wow!' She turned to Dylan who was smiling at her reaction.

'Glad you like it. It was a labour of love for Uncle Charles and I've been happy to continue it in his memory.'

'Can I have a tour?'

'Sure.' Dylan led her round the largest raised beds, pointing out the neat rows of vegetables that filled one, with black labels bearing the names of its contents in white chalk pen, then salad plants in another, herbs in another and the final two containing flowers for cutting and beautiful bedding plants.

'We try to keep to nineteenth-century varieties of all the fruit, veg and herbs where we can and we've used all the original planting designs, but we run the garden on a balance of traditional horticultural practices and modern organic principles because it's more sustainable and wildlife friendly.'

Olivia eyed the vegetable and salad beds, which were bursting with summer produce. 'You must be overrun with fruit and veg at the moment. What have you been doing with it all, as it's not needed for guests yet?'

'Lexie takes it to the local farmers' markets in Falmouth and Truro, we sell some at the gate with an honesty box and whatever's left over we give to food banks.' He cocked his head to one side. 'Speak of the devil'

Olivia looked around, confused. She hadn't seen or heard anything, but as her gaze reached the door on the far side of the garden, Lexie appeared, followed by Mylor and Zennor, who rushed down the central path, fortunately avoiding the raised beds, and greeted Olivia as if they hadn't seen her for twelve months.

'Hi, guys!' Lexie smiled as Olivia bent down to fuss her dogs. 'They've had a lovely time in the cool of the yard, but I've got a meeting with Alice and Toby at the Goods Shed in half an hour.'

'Oh yes, I forgot. The plants are all labelled and in trays in the far greenhouse.' Dylan turned to the sous-chef. 'D'you need a hand loading them in the back of your car?'

Lexie waved away his offer. 'I'll be good, thanks.' She glanced at Olivia and then Dylan. 'Should I be jealous that you're letting another woman into the kitchen garden?' She turned laughing eyes on her. 'He's very fussy, you know.'

Olivia looked at Dylan, just as a definite shade of pink rose up his tanned neck, but he turned away and addressed Lexie. 'You'd better get going, or those plants will be completely dead by the time you get to Penbartha and there won't be anything left to start a community garden.'

Lexie laughed and threw some remark, that Olivia couldn't catch over her shoulder as she hurried to the far corner of the enclosed garden.

'I take it you know about the community garden that Alice is planning for the Waiting Rooms and Goods Shed?'

Olivia shook her head. 'No, I don't actually, but it's good to see members acting on their own initiative and Alice being confident enough not to feel she has to run everything past me.' She perched on the edge of a railway sleeper and looked up at him, shading her eyes from the sun with her hand. 'Tell me about this community garden.'

Dylan shrugged. 'I think it might be something Lexie and Willow thought up between them, with a bit of help from one of Rocky's lads who's supposed to be working on the Bakehouse deli, but is currently constructing raised beds on the sunny side of the Goods Shed, Engine Shed and Waiting Rooms buildings. Apparently, the members have all clubbed together to buy the potting compost and Lexie asked me if we had any veg plants going spare.' He waved his hand towards the near rows. 'And I said they could have what they wanted.'

'Who'll look after them?'

'Everyone apparently. And then they'll all share the produce. It's an increasingly common thing among people who don't have gardens or the equipment themselves. They share the work and the rewards.'

'And Toby is?'

'One of Rocky's lads who has taken a bit of a shine to Lexie and let's just say, her wish is his command.'

Olivia watched his face closely. 'Does that bother you?'

Dylan frowned. 'Should it?'

'It's just that Lexie said…' Olivia began. 'I just thought…'

Understanding dawned and Dylan threw his head back, laughing. 'Good Lord no. Lexie's not my type – far too high-maintenance for me. We just work well together.' His face darkened. 'And being out here gets her away from Gabe and his…' Dylan's face froze and he turned his head slightly. 'Right, I'm off. I've enjoyed our chat.'

He headed off swiftly and noiselessly through a door Olivia hadn't even noticed. The noise of feet crunching on the gravel path behind her made her spin round. Trenow was heading towards her, looking hot and uncomfortable in his suit trousers and shirt. He'd taken off his tie and rolled up his sleeves, but still looked decidedly grumpy.

'Morning, Olivia. Fancy seeing you here!' He didn't sound particularly pleased about it.

Olivia bristled. 'Fancy. I was looking for Cassie.'

'Really? I was looking for Dylan Bonnar.'

'Really? Well, it looks as though we've both been disappointed then, doesn't it?' She glanced at her watch. 'I can't chat. I have an important meeting to get to.'

'So, you haven't seen Dylan?'

Olivia sighed. 'Like I said, I was looking for Cassie. I just thought she might be in here, but no.' She whistled to the dogs, who were paying no attention to the biscuit-less policeman. 'You know where I live if you need me.' And still holding her breath at such an uncharacteristic display of non-cooperation, she walked briskly away.

# 16

As Olivia drove home along the creek, she saw a team of tractors baling hay in the patchwork of fields on the opposite bank. The farmers were obviously making the most of the good weather to harvest their first cut of hay. And with this sunshine, it would be baked to perfection. Her thoughts automatically turned to Jago silaging and then to his note and her mood plummeted.

The police were no closer to finding Agnes's killer and Olivia didn't know what Jago was playing at. And now there was another unidentified victim. A curious mixture of loss, longing and frustration spread through Olivia, which by the time she'd parked up at Tresillian had been overtaken by a sense of annoyance and the niggling feeling that it was in her power to do something about it.

'Oh, sod it,' she muttered as she slammed the boot door closed after the dogs and ushered them into the cool of the house. They flopped down on the flagstones in the hall, and watched her lazily as she made her way up the stairs. By the time she came back down, five minutes later, they were snoozing happily. Zennor opened one eye and if she noticed that Olivia was in her running gear she pretended not to. It was too hot for dogs to be out in this heat anyway. She dropped a kiss on each shaggy head and promised to take them out later, when it was cooler. Zennor closed her eye and Mylor let out a gentle snore, already chasing rabbits in his sleep.

Olivia headed towards the coastal path, running at a steady pace that let her mind and body relax and her senses take in everything around her. The vibrant golden flowers of the gorse bushes and their tropical coconut scent mingled with the salty ocean air, and the harmonious calling of birdsong from the trees on the headland filtered everything else out. Within minutes she could feel the healing power the coastal paths always gave her.

As she began to relax and let her thoughts float across her mind, Jago's face appeared, centre stage, with his lop-sided smile that always melted her heart. A sudden sense of desolation mixed with anger swept through her and she instinctively stepped up her pace. What she needed was a hard, long steep run until the pain in her lungs and leg muscles was unbearable and her mind couldn't think of anything but breathing.

It was a distraction technique she'd used since the death of her brother. All these years later, she still ran every day. Sometimes she would drive over to the Atlantic coast to her favourite expanse of beach to stretch her legs, fill her lungs with fresh ocean air and let the dogs savage clumps of seaweed to their hearts' content. At other times she could be found pounding the woodland trails round the station, or the coastal paths that went on for miles and really put her legs to the test. Today was one of those days. She passed several groups of walkers as she sprinted up the steep incline towards her target – a lichen-covered wooden bench – where she often paused to admire the view and have a quick chat with Stanley Hazel, the man to whom the bench was dedicated.

'Afternoon, Stanley,' she whispered as she collapsed on to it, panting and watching the flotilla of classic sailing boats out at sea, their maroon sails barely moving. 'What do you reckon I should do? Forget about him, or go to London and have it out with him?' According to the bench, Stanley had been married to his much-loved Cathy for sixty-five years, so she had a pretty good idea what his reply would be.

Absent-mindedly, Olivia's fingers wrapped themselves round the smooth gemstone that always hung around her neck on a slim leather cord. It was one of her most precious possessions, given to her by Mollie before she'd moved to New York, because the dark brown stone with its amber flecks matched her eyes and possessed the qualities she needed most. It was known as the stone of strength, that absorbed negative energy and would help the wearer make the right decision whenever she reached a crossroads in her life. A memory of Jago confiding that Mollie had given him one too popped into her mind and how she'd taken it as a sign she could trust him. She automatically pulled the gemstone up to her lips and kissed it softly.

'Well, I've got plenty of negative energy that needs absorbing, Stanley,' she said to the bench, ignoring the startled looks she got from the walkers going past. 'And if this isn't a crossroad in my relationship with Jago, I don't know what is.'

She gazed back out to sea and watched the last boat sail round the orange buoy that marked the furthest point of the course before they headed back to shore, and knew it was time for her to head back too.

'Yeah, well, thanks for the chat, Stan. See you soon.' She

patted the bench affectionately, stretched her calf muscles and set off home, feeling much lighter.

---

She ran round the last corner of the lane approaching Tresillian House and slowed down to a gentle jog. As she turned into the drive, she heard the dogs barking inside the house and then a rustle in the bushes to the side of her. The hairs on the back of her neck stood up, all her senses on high alert. She raised her hands in a fighting stance and swivelled her hips to distribute her weight onto the balls of her feet. She was just about to execute a well-practised reverse spin kick when a familiar waft of rosemary greeted her nostrils and she dropped her arms.

'Dylan?' she hissed. 'What the…?'

More rustling came from a large clump of black bamboo and an arm shot out and yanked her through roughly. Surprise made her stumble and she fell to the ground on the other side of the bush. Before she could complain, Dylan was on his knees beside her, one hand clamped over her mouth, the other signalling her to be quiet. She lay like that, staring into his hazel eyes which, up close, had as many shades of brown and green in them as the gardens of Peneglos Hall, and contained absolutely no threat. She relaxed, indicating with her own eyes that he could remove his hand from her mouth. Which he did, but kept a finger to his lips.

Olivia listened carefully and could just make out footsteps crunching on the gravel, then a car door slam and an engine start up. Only when it had passed them on the drive and turned right on to the lane, did Dylan drop his hand from his lips and hold it out to help her to her feet.

'Ugh, you're really sweaty, Olivia.' He sounded disgusted, but his eyes danced with mirth.

'You'd be sweaty if you'd just done a five-mile run in this heat, rather than lurking in the bushes in my garden!' She brushed a mixture of soil, grass and bamboo leaves off her legs and then glared at him. 'Care to explain?'

'And yet you were still poised to take me down?' He grinned and then nodded towards the house. 'Can we go inside?'

'You were lucky I recognised the smell of your shampoo,' she commented over her shoulder as she led the way. 'Else you'd be in serious pain by now.'

Twenty minutes later they were sitting together in the shade of the pergola at the back of the house drinking tea, Olivia aching satisfyingly, and clean after a shower. The dogs, finally calm after giving Dylan a rapturous welcome, settled down at their feet.

'Now, explain please, Dylan. Why are you here? And why were you hiding from Trenow? It was his car, wasn't it?'

He regarded her with watchful eyes. 'Yes, it was. I came to see you, and he was already here, obviously looking for you. He then went over to Cassie's place, but she wasn't home either. He waited for about fifteen minutes and then you turned up. I didn't want you to get talking to him, so I risked life and limb by pulling you into the bamboo.' A slow smile crossed his face and Olivia couldn't stay cross with him.

'Well, I didn't want to talk to Trenow either, so thank you, I suppose,' she admitted. 'Just don't make a habit out of it. I can do without the adrenalin rushes, thanks.'

Dylan laughed, suddenly looking years younger and more

carefree. 'Oh, the thrill of danger, the taste of fear. Tell me about it.'

'Dylan, you never talk about your life before you came to live at Peneglos.'

His face hardened. 'There's nothing to tell. I've learnt that I don't have to put myself in confrontational situations in order to commit to a cause. I just want to live a quiet life now and be left alone. I'm an easy target for someone like Trenow and I'm fed up of answering his inane questions.'

'Oh, right.' Olivia took the hint and didn't ask any of her own. If Dylan had been an activist of some sort, that was up to him. Deep down, she admired people who had such strong convictions that they were prepared to put themselves in danger to fight for them. And by the look of Dylan, he'd done some pretty serious stuff. 'So, what did you want to talk to me about?'

A faint blush reddened what Olivia could see of his face under all the hair. 'I got the feeling you were upset about something when you came to see me at the Hall. But I also got the feeling you didn't want to talk about it then. I just wanted to check you're okay.'

Tears rushed into Olivia's eyes. Dylan was the last person she would expect to show such sensitivity. Then she thought again. Was he?

She sniffed. 'That's very kind of you, thanks.'

'So do you?'

'What?'

'Want to talk about it?' He ran his hand over his beard. 'Jeez, you're making this hard. I'm way out of my comfort zone. Do I take it that Jago's behind your current worries?'

Her heart started to thump. 'Has Cassie said something?'

'No.' He put his hands up in a sign of peace. 'Look, I watch and I notice things. I knew you were looking forward to seeing him again at the party, but afterwards you never seemed to be as happy as I thought you'd be. I know Gabe was insinuating that Jago knew the waitress, and stirring a whole load of shit, but things seemed to go downhill between you from then on.'

'Hmm.' The knot in Olivia's stomach tightened. She could see how it looked from where Dylan was standing.

Dylan's hazel eyes held hers. 'Do you want to talk about it?'

Olivia looked around. 'Let's go and sit down on the quay. We may get a breeze off the creek, if we're lucky.'

---

They sat, shoulder to shoulder, on Tresillian's quay, their backs against the stone balustrade that was covered in lichen and weathered by centuries of storms. They gazed out at the creek and breathed in the soothing cocktail of lavender, sweet peas, seawater and fresh air. It was the perfect spot to talk, hidden from the garden and invisible from the opposite bank, but with the most fantastic view up the creek and out to the Carrick Roads estuary.

The peaceful surroundings helped Olivia slowly relax and she began to tell Dylan about everything that had happened between her and Jago, from his appearance at the party, his reluctance to get involved in discovering the waitress's identity and his uncharacteristic behaviour, to his sudden disappearance after the second body had been found and the inadequate note he'd left behind. She spoke uninterrupted, suddenly relieved to talk to someone who didn't know Jago at all. She finished on a crescendo of emotion. 'We never used to keep secrets from each other, but it seems we do now. And I don't know if I want a relationship like that.'

Dylan chewed on a piece of grass for a while before he spoke.

'Look, I'm no expert, but here's what I think.' He paused. 'We all have our issues from things that have happened in the past. You, me, even someone as successful and driven as Jago probably has had things happen that still affect him. And although you may think you've both worked through these things together, they're bound to come back and bite you occasionally. Probably when you least expect it. So, perhaps something has happened to spook Jago. He's got a pretty big job – who knows what's going on with that – and yes, I know he could have spoken to you about it, but perhaps he doesn't want that part of his life to contaminate the time he spends with you.'

'He did say that,' Olivia admitted. 'But he helped me deal with my baggage and obviously doesn't think he needs my help with his. That hurts.'

'Give him time.' He turned to Olivia and smiled. 'I've only met the guy once, but even I can tell he's crazy about you. Trust me. And trust him.'

Olivia bit her lip. 'I'm trying to, but it's hard. I've fantasised so many times about running back to New York. About getting away from everything at the station site: the buildings, the people, the trustees' meetings, the regular finance meetings, the constant juggling, the endless to-do list I only ever get halfway through, not to mention my own business. I've lost count of the occasions when everything's going wrong, or it's pissed it down with rain for three solid weeks and I've dreamed about being a single New Yorker, with no cares about anyone else. But no! Have you seen me running away?'

'So why do you stay?'

'Because it's the right thing to do! But I don't want to do it without Jago.' Her voice cracked and the tears fell, silently at first and then in big, noisy unladylike sobs. Dylan handed her a surprisingly clean hankie and shuffled closer, placing his arm around her shoulder, waiting for the tears to subside.

'Is that really the only reason you're here? Because it's the right thing to do?' he eventually asked in his gentle voice. 'Because that's not the impression I get.'

Olivia sniffed. 'No. You're right. When I came here eighteen months ago, after George died, I thought I was a big-city girl and I needed to live in a place where you can get anything you want, whenever you want it. New York is a real 24/7 world. Everyone works ridiculously long hours, making lots of money to spend on meaningless things. And I guess I was just as bad. Life here in Penbartha was a whole new game, but I adapted and I realised I don't need the things I thought I did: the clothes, the make-up, the possessions. And I find it freeing.'

Dylan smiled. 'You're preaching to the converted.'

'I went from thinking I'd lost everything to realising I'd found everything I've ever wanted: community, my work, the countryside, the dogs, the ocean, and the closest thing to family I'll ever have. The first thing I do every morning is gaze out at this creek, and look for the birds, the wildlife, check the weather.' She looked around. 'I belong here. And I'm just so pissed off with Jago for not loving it as much as I do.'

'I reckon he knows exactly how you feel about this place. But if something's spooked him, I also reckon that he thinks by going back to London, he's protecting both you and the place you love so much. He's probably feeling pretty bad about leaving the way he did and it'll take him a while to work out what to do to put it right.'

She blew her nose into Dylan's hankie and pulled an apologetic face at him. 'So what do you suggest I do now?'

'Give him time, like I said. Cassie's always said how good you two are together. That you've got the type of relationship she's always dreamed of. Surely that's worth fighting for?'

Olivia nodded and then smiled. 'I reckon I know what it is you used to do.'

Dylan stiffened. 'You do?'

'A relationship counsellor! What sort of other man gives a woman the chance to talk about her feelings? Jago struggles to talk about his own feelings, let alone mine, and would rather talk about politics, or the weather, or how an air-fryer works.'

'I take that as a compliment then.' He nudged her and they both laughed.

'Well, here's another one. You're very good at it. Perhaps you should take it up. Another string to your bow?'

He shuddered. 'No thanks. Too much peopling.'

Olivia laughed at the mournful expression on his face and they sat in a contented silence, looking out over the creek. She tipped her face skywards to bask in the warm sun. How long would it be before this heatwave broke and they were plunged back into the relentless mizzle Cornwall was so famous for?

'I might be able to help you with something else though.' Dylan broke the silence.

Olivia turned to him; her interest piqued. 'Really? Like what?'

'Someone's got to sort out this mess, haven't they? And if not you and Jago, then who?' He faced her then. 'If you want to carry on looking into these murders, but don't want to go it alone, I might have some skills that will help.'

Olivia's mind began to race. 'I don't know, Jago warned me off.'

'What Jago doesn't know won't hurt him. And I'll make sure you're safe.' He got up from the quay. 'I'll be off then, Olli-o. You know where to find me if you change your mind.'

# 17

'Oh, Cass, thanks so much for agreeing to walk up to the woods with me. Ruan's busy on the phone and I've had a sudden yearning to be among trees. And I'll feel safer being with someone else,' Lucinda explained breathlessly as they left the valley and made their way up the steep path to the main arboretum, the area of garden furthest away from the cove.

As Lucinda paused for the third time to catch her breath, Cassie turned to look at the breathtaking view of the glittering ocean and sky merging into one. Sometimes she wondered how, as a born and bred Cornishwoman, she had survived for twenty years away from the ocean, and now she was back, she vowed never to leave again.

She tuned back into Lucinda's chat and patted her employer's arm gently. 'No worries, it's perfectly safe and the thought of being in the cool of the woods does appeal. As we're thinning the rhododendrons and camellias down in the valley, the sun's getting through more and it's very warm. I'm happy to leave the volunteers to it for a while.'

'I don't blame you. I would never have believed that Cornwall could be so hot if I wasn't here to feel it for myself.'

'Well, don't get used to it, my lovely,' Cassie warned. 'It doesn't happen very often, despite Kitten's warnings.'

'I'd better make the most of it then.' Lucinda flapped at her face with her hand, shaking her fringe out of her eyes. She didn't really have the complexion for the Cornish heatwave, Cassie reflected as they tromped up the hill, Lucinda panting heavily again. She was a classic English rose, and pale from all the time she spent working indoors. Now her face was scarlet from the exertion.

'Do you ever stop working?' Cassie asked, barely out of breath.

'Only if I'm forced to. Like now. But Ruan reckons the police will leave us alone soon, and then we'll have to make up for all the time we've lost and there will be *so* much to do!' Lucinda's enthusiasm and commitment to Ruan and Peneglos Hall was one of the many things that Cassie liked about her. 'Until then, I thought we could start formalising our plans for this side of the garden and at least be ahead of schedule on something.'

They reached the woodland area, and were immediately cocooned in a dark, cool oasis perfumed with woody and zesty scents from the fir, pine and spruce trees surrounding them. The two women simply stood, relishing the shade from the relentless sun.

Lucinda pointed to two tree stumps in a nearby clearing and they both sat down, still silent.

'Have you heard of forest bathing?'

Cassie smiled. 'Isn't that what we're doing?'

'Yes!' Lucinda struggled to her feet, a little of the old spark of excitement back in her eyes. 'We're doing exactly that! And isn't it wonderful? I feel calmer and more energised after just these few minutes than I have for ages.'

Cassie remained seated, enjoying the peace and cool, and her eyes wandered to the woodland floor which, now the bluebells had died back, was an amazing carpet of pink and white campions, sitting prettily among their hairy green foliage. She knew Lucinda well enough to expect that she had something important to say. She reminded her of Kitten in that respect. Her enthusiasms were infectious and unlike Kitten, who could sometimes put people's backs up with her forthright ways, Lucinda was very good at getting people on her side straight away. *Perhaps if the two girls spent more time together, some of Lucinda's ways might rub off on Kitten and smooth those edges.*

'Did you know that spending just two hours in woodland can help prevent the build-up of many modern stress-related illnesses and be beneficial for up to thirty days?' Lucinda turned shining eyes on Cassie, looking and sounding much more like her old self.

'Well, that would certainly explain why I've been feeling much happier and more peaceful since I've been working here.'

'Yes! It's because there are chemicals called phytoncides that are released by trees which boost our immune system for several days. Some health specialists are saying that forest bathing should be offered as a non-medical therapy for things like high blood pressure, stress and depression.'

Cassie waited.

'So, Ruan and I were talking this morning. If spending just a few hours in woodland is so good for you, how good would an entire holiday spent here be? We could offer eco-glamping pods for those guests who don't want the luxury of staying in the Hall or who have kids, and do off-grid holidays here based round forest bathing, star-gazing, foraging and bushcraft skills. Not to mention wild swimming if we ever get round to fixing those treacherous steps down to the cove. We could appeal to two completely different audiences.'

Cassie looked around, trying to imagine part of the arboretum filled with eco-glamping pods, and frowned.

Lucinda's face fell. 'Oh no! You think I'm being insensitive about the waitress dying, don't you?' She rushed to explain. 'I'm just so worried about Ruan – he's taking the deaths so much to heart and I don't want him to spiral into a depression about failing his ancestors by not bringing the Hall back to life. A lot of things are on hold up at the hotel until the police have finished their investigations and I thought this would give him something else to think about and research. I'm just trying to keep him looking forward, Cass.'

Cassie felt a stab of guilt. She'd been so busy worrying about Dylan she hadn't really thought about things from Ruan's viewpoint, but she couldn't fault Lucinda's loyalty to him and the Hall. *Of course she'd be trying to help Ruan through these difficult times.*

'I don't think you're being insensitive at all, now you've explained it.' Cassie chose her words carefully. 'You're a businesswoman, Lucinda, as well as Ruan's partner and I can see that you can't afford to take your foot off the pedal.' She thought for a moment. 'Have you thought about asking Dylan to help out with the bushcraft and foraging side of things?'

Lucinda bent to pick a white campion from the ground and held it to her nose. 'Ruan said that it was actually Dylan who suggested those activities for further down the line. I think they must have been in the Boy Scouts together or something. But I think I'll source a more conservative provider for now. We don't want to put too much pressure on Dylan, do we? Or frighten the guests?'

Cassie was just about to leap to Dylan's defence when there was a rustling in the trees and Ruan himself appeared. Closely followed by Sam O'Driscoll.

'I thought I'd find you here!' Ruan declared, handing them each a bottle of water. Cassie caught the look on Lucinda's face. 'I'm sorry, I know they're plastic but I found them in the fridge and thought we'd better use them up. I promise I'll recycle them properly.'

Cassie drank gratefully from hers and then watched, surprised, as Ruan shepherded Lucinda towards the edge of the clearing. 'We'll leave you to it, Cass. A national travel journalist has just called to chat to both of us and we arranged a Zoom for fifteen minutes' time.' He pulled a wry face at Lucinda. 'You might want to pull a brush through your hair first…'

Cassie and Sam exchanged looks as they heard Lucinda's famous belly laugh fade as they disappeared into the trees.

'Not going with them, sergeant?' She kept her voice light.

'I don't think I've got anything to say that would add to their expertise,' he shot back easily. 'I told Ruan they could get on and I'd make sure you got back to the Hall, or wherever else you want to go, safely.'

Cassie frowned. 'I'm quite capable of getting there myself…' She stopped mid-sentence, her heart quickening as she recalled Lucinda's similar fears. 'Do you know something I don't? Do you think the murderer is hanging about here somewhere?' She looked around quickly, from side to side, almost expecting someone to jump out at them.

'Not at all.' Sam rushed to placate her. 'And I'm sorry if I scared you. It was Ruan's suggestion that I come with him to find Lucinda. He's feeling protective towards everyone at the moment. This second body seems to have really rattled him.' His eyes met Cassie's. 'I don't think he can kid himself the waitress's death was just a random, but horrible event anymore.'

Cassie held his hazel gaze, seeing only concern in his eyes and felt herself shiver.

'No. None of us can. I try not to think about it. Olivia was saying the same...' She stopped herself mid-sentence, but it was too late. The bat-eared O'Driscoll picked up on it straight away.

'Is Olivia okay? I heard that Jago had to go back to London unexpectedly. Is that right?'

Cassie avoided his eyes. 'That's what she told me. He deals with some pretty serious cases in London. He's a clever guy and in demand.'

'And is she okay with that? Doesn't she ever get worried about him?'

'I think she accepts it goes with the territory.' Cassie was careful with her reply. 'And she's not a huge fan of London anymore, so she's happier being here, even without him. Her life is here. Who wouldn't rather be here than in a crime hotspot like London? It's so peaceful and beautiful, isn't it?'

'Bad things can happen in beautiful places as well as not-so-beautiful ones. As we've recently discovered.' A shadow crossed Sam's face and Cassie felt a spark of compassion for him. For the first time she wondered what else had made him swap his London life for a supposedly more peaceful one in Cornwall.

'Hey, don't look so scared. I'm here to protect you. Or the other way round.' Sam tried to lighten the mood and prove they were quite safe by settling himself on the tree stump vacated by Lucinda and looking around the clearing. 'Ruan was telling me about their plans for this place. Sounds very Robinson Crusoe. I can just imagine a load of teepees or yurts or whatever you call them dotted about in here.'

'Oh, I'm sure it will be a whole lot more glamorous and upmarket than that if Lucinda has anything to do with it. It will be off-grid eco-pods or top-of-the-range shepherd's huts, or whatever they decide will have the least impact on the woodland,' Cassie suggested, glad of the change in subject. She kept her thoughts that Dylan could be a valuable asset to any off-grid enterprise and her wish that Lucinda didn't always dismiss him so readily, to herself.

She forced a brighter expression onto her face and sat back down. 'Did you know that this woodland dates back to the nineteenth century and has conifer species from every single continent? It's quite the collection.'

'Those Braithwaites certainly got about,' Sam commented. 'Sounds to me like they were right megalomaniacs, always having to have the latest and best in everything the botanical world had to offer.'

Cassie laughed. 'You're probably right. Perhaps that's what it took to create such wonderful gardens in those days. They were certainly obsessive when it came to them. Although I wouldn't say it in front of Ruan.'

'No,' Sam agreed. 'And, luckily, he seems to have missed out on that gene and is fairly laid-back about most things as far as I can tell.'

'He's a thoroughly kind and decent man,' Cassie declared. 'And very good at his job. Peneglos Hall will soon be on the map as one of the best, if not the best, sustainable hotel in Cornwall. And that's all I'm going to say about anyone.' She gave Sam a determined look and his crumpled face crumpled even more into a smile as he got to his feet.

'Okay. So, let's talk some more about these trees.'

For someone who'd lived in London for so many years Sam was fairly knowledgeable about trees, Cassie decided as they wandered around the woodland areas of the garden together. He was like a small boy, pointing out the specimens he recognised and asking lots of questions about those he didn't. At the same time, he had a solidity to him that she found reassuring, given his earlier words.

It was a long time since Cassie had allowed herself to enjoy the company of a man. She sometimes wondered whether it was the skill sets most men brought with them that she really missed. But after being single for so long, Cassie was as good with a hammer, drill or screwdriver as most men she knew and, she reminded herself, she had Rocky for the more complicated jobs. Martin Lambert's totally feigned interest in her had made her wonder about the possibilities life might offer beyond singledom. But yet again, she'd been betrayed in the most awful way. *No*, she decided. *Men are more trouble than they are worth.*

'I think you should become an official guide here if they ever open these gardens to the public or offer to do the occasional tour.' Sam's words brought her back to reality and she realised she'd been operating on autopilot.

She felt herself redden. 'I don't think so. I don't know nearly enough. And besides…' Her words petered off

'I mean it. I could listen to you talking about the gardens for hours. You bring their stories to life.'

'You should have heard Mollie talking about them. She was captivating.'

Sam frowned. 'Mollie as in Tresillian House?'

Cassie could see him struggling to join the dots between all the people in the complicated Penbartha web and found herself telling him all about her old boss and friend. By the end of it she felt tears fill her eyes and then drip slowly down onto the bib of her dungaree shorts as she confessed how much she missed Mollie. Sam pulled a neatly ironed and folded cotton handkerchief out of his trouser pocket and handed it over, not at all embarrassed by a middle-aged woman crying in front of him. *Perhaps the police do special courses...*

She patted her eyes and blew her nose and then looked at him, hot with embarrassment. 'I'm sorry. I don't usually do that.' She waved his hankie at him. 'I'll wash it and get it back to you.'

Sam's face softened with kindness and compassion. 'No worries. I have plenty.' He edged closer and patted her shoulder awkwardly.

Cassie glanced sideways at him, pulled herself together and quickly changed the subject.

'Are you any closer to knowing who the man was who washed up in the cove?'

Sam sighed. 'Not yet. And that's a confidential police matter, by the way.'

'Have you run his DNA through your databases, or whatever you call them?' Cassie's sudden boldness surprised both of them, but they were glad to be back on neutral ground.

'You know I can't tell you that.' His mouth twitched in a small smile. 'What I can say is that we haven't had any matches on the UK sites.'

'Can't you use Interpol or something like that? See if he's connected in any way to the waitress that was killed?'

His lips twitched again. 'It's a confidential police matter and we shouldn't be talking about it.'

'So it's okay for you to ask me questions, but not the other way round?' Cassie realised she was enjoying teasing him.

A grin spread across his battered face and he gave a deep chuckle. 'I'm police, you're a member of the public. I ask the questions, and you answer them. That's how it works. Usually.'

'Seems a bit one-sided to me.' She felt her own face break into a smile. 'Given the circumstances.'

'Sorry, but that's the way it is. For now, at least.' He looked at his watch and sighed. 'Right, I've got to get back to the station. Do you want me to walk you down to the volunteers?'

'I can hear them, coming up the path by the middle pond. I'm sure I'll be fine.'

Sam smiled, his face relaxing into the grooves and creases. 'I'm sure you will.' He went off whistling up the path and then turned.

Cassie was still watching him, a mixture of unfamiliar emotions doing battle in her stomach.

'I'll drop by for that hanky sometime.'

# 18

Jago left his flat in Gray's Inn and hurried across South Square, past the porter's lodge where he nodded hello to Tom, feeling strangely assured that the burly young man would be watching his back the whole way to the main road. Tom and his fellow porters had always gone the extra mile to ensure his safety since the vicious attack that had left him fighting for his life four years ago.

Unable to shake off the discomfort memories of that time always caused him, Jago turned through the Inn's ancient gateway, right onto High Holborn and dashed across the road without waiting for the pedestrian lights. He took the first left down Chancery Lane and slipped into the passageway that led into Lincoln's Inn, letting out the breath he had been subconsciously holding. From there he hastened past Stone Buildings, through Old Square and into New Square, heading for the Great Hall and his destination. The terrace outside the Main Common Room was busy with members congregating at tables under smart white sun canopies, and Jago weaved his way through to the main door where he was immediately met by a smartly dressed waiter.

'May I help you, sir?'

Jago nodded. 'Thanks. I think my colleague, who's a member here, has booked a table, Bhasin Katri?'

'Ah yes, of course, sir. I'll show you to his usual table.'

As Jago followed, he noticed that the tables were all placed at discreet distances from each other and could imagine the sort of post-trial confidential conversations that went on here. It was already filling up with enough people and chatter to make any conversation private. He took the seat that faced the door and the window, a habit he'd adopted since his attack, ordered a sparkling water and sat back to wait.

He looked around him, his eyes immediately drawn to the impressive stone vaulted ceiling. The rear of the menu told him this vast space had been the original Victorian kitchen to the Great Hall, and had recently been renovated to its current incarnation as a contemporary restaurant and bar in a way that honoured and reflected its history and heritage. Jago could only begin to imagine the layers of centuries-old paint, dirt and kitchen soot that had been removed to reveal the original stonework.

*Olivia would like it here*, was his immediate thought. *If she ever speaks to me again, but I wouldn't blame her if she didn't.* He spotted his old friend walking towards him and was grateful for the distraction.

Bhasin Katri looked every bit the portrait of a distinguished, well-dressed King's Counsel, but had a slightly debonair air about him that made him different. He was tall, about Jago's height, slim and wore a beautifully tailored three-piece black suit with an emerald green lining, revealed as he unbuttoned his jacket, that exactly matched the shade of his tie. A perfectly tied black turban and rimless spectacles added to his gravitas. The only sign of any ageing was in his trimmed, greying beard, Jago noticed with a sigh, thinking of his own prematurely silver hair.

The two men shook hands formally, sat down and then Bhasin broke into a grin. 'Great to see you, Jim. It's been too long.'

The use of his old nickname took Jago by surprise. It was a long time since anyone had called him Jim. He'd been prepared to adopt the anglicised version of his first name to avoid the *Poldark* and country turnip jokes, but he'd forgotten how students shortened every name and still used them years down the line.

'It has.' He nodded his agreement. 'Life's been a bit crazy this year. I'm sitting more than anything else.'

'So I've heard. I had a catch-up with Alistair Browne the last time I was in front of him. He called me round to his chambers afterwards and we had a good chat. He knows we were mates at Bar School, so he always keeps me up to date with your news.' He grinned again. 'He was waxing lyrical about their last visit to your place in Cornwall...' The dark eyes narrowed. 'Oh no. Do I sense trouble in paradise?'

Jago was relieved to be able to ditch the small talk and get to the point. 'Nothing to do with Cornwall, or Olivia per se, but I do need to talk to you about something quite urgent, Baz, if you don't mind?'

'Not at all. I think I owe you a few favours anyway. Let's order food and then I'm all yours.' He scanned the menu and called the waiter over. 'I'll have the fish, please. And a bottle of sparkling water. Jim?'

Jago wasn't sure he could face any sort of food, but went for the easy option. 'I'll have the same, please.'

As soon as the waiter was out of earshot, he started to speak. 'Did you hear about my GBH trial that went tits up? Edon Bregu?'

Bhasin nodded. 'The Bar talked of little else for a week. But then something else took people's attention and it's old news now.'

'I'm not so sure.' And Jago told him about everything that had happened at Peneglos Hall since he returned there: the waitress's reaction to him, Gabe's comment, her drowning, Olivia's discovery of her identity and the second body being washed up a week later. Bhasin listened carefully, without interruption, Jago only pausing when the waiter brought their food. By the time he'd finished, the other barrister was tucking into his Atlantic cod.

'And you think this might be connected with your last trial? That Bregu is sending you warning messages?'

The way Bhasin stated the fact so simply made Jago feel slightly foolish.

'Well, it's a bit of a coincidence, isn't it? How many Albanians can there be in Cornwall who just happen to have died since I got back there, having overseen my first ever trial involving an Albanian criminal gang? And it's not me I'm worried about, it's Olivia. There is no way she should ever be caught up in anything I do here.'

Bhasin chewed his food thoughtfully and then placed his knife and fork carefully on either side of his plate.

'I agree wholeheartedly with that. But now I need to ask you a question.'

'Fire away.' Jago held his breath.

'Why are you talking to me about this? I don't do crime anymore. I'd have thought there are plenty of other people more qualified to help.'

Jago let out his breath in a whoosh. 'C'mon, Baz, you know

me. I never go down the obvious route. I don't want another criminal lawyer's opinion yet. I know the law as far as the criminal element is concerned. What I don't know enough about is the immigration side of things.'

A serene smile spread across Bhasin's face. 'Ah. You want me to reassure you that the Home Office will revoke Bregu's Leave to Remain, have him removed from the UK within four weeks and he will never darken our shores again?'

Jago had the grace to look embarrassed. 'Something like that.'

'Okay, so let's start at the beginning. Do you know his grounds for being here?'

He frowned. 'I think he may have married a girl from Bulgaria.'

'Ah, sounds likely.' Bhasin was matter-of-fact. 'It's not that long ago an Albanian gang was using TikTok to advertise marriages between irregular Albanian migrants and EU women for about £25,000 a time.'

Jago let out a low whistle. 'How on earth can they afford that much?'

'Well, people like Bregu can, because he'll be earning a lot of money illegally. Your average Albanian migrant can't. Most of them can't even afford the exorbitant fees of three to five grand that the gangs are charging their fellow countrymen to get them across the Channel. But they know they'll earn it back by working for the gangs once they're here.' He finished his main course and then sat back. 'The Albanians seem to have tied up all the migratory networks across Europe, Africa and the Balkans, so there isn't a lot of competition. They never quite managed to infiltrate the monopoly on the actual boat crossings though, so they have to do business with the Kurdish, Moroccan and Syrian gangs for that.'

'From what I've been reading, it seems that we're talking

about people smuggling rather than trafficking. The reports suggest that most migrants go into this with their eyes open, rather than under force or false pretences.'

Bhasin nodded. 'Globally, most refugees, those fleeing from danger, etc., are women and children and they're the ones you find in refugee camps around the world. The pictures we all saw of the boatloads of fit and healthy young Albanian men arriving on our beaches aren't entitled to refugee status. Both our government and theirs like to tell us that Albania's a safe country. Yes, wages may be low and the cost of living high, but it's not at war and it's a signatory to European conventions relating to human rights. A lot of those men come here, knowing they'll be able to get jobs working illegally for their fellow nationals, with no need for any documentation.'

'And yet we're still overwhelmed with asylum claims from them? That's crazy.'

'We were, because they know how to play the system and it's all part of the deal. As over ninety per cent of the small boat crossings are now intercepted, the smugglers advise them how to claim asylum as soon as they're picked up. They get sent by our authorities to a hostel, often disappear after a few days, pop along to the local Albanian coffee shop or barber and immediately find work to earn enough money to send home to their families.'

'What I don't understand is why they want to come here when they can easily travel overland to another EU country in Europe and disappear there.'

Bhasin waved at the waiter to order dessert and then spoke quietly. 'Some do. Italy and Greece have much larger numbers of Albanian migrants than us. But there's a popular perception among immigrants that it's easier to work in the UK without documentation than in any other EU country, and that our asylum system will allow anyone who reaches our shores to stay for very long periods, if not indefinitely, before anything is done about it. By which time a lot of them have disappeared into the ether altogether.' He looked solemn. 'It's all a bit embarrassing, really. The Home Office couldn't organise the proverbial in a brewery if they tried. I have friends who sit as judges in that jurisdiction who constantly refuse appeals, issue deportation and removal orders and the Home Office does nothing about it.'

'And what happens then?'

'Usually? Absolutely nothing. The Home Office is pretty useless at enforcing the judges' decisions.'

'That must be bloody frustrating. At least in my court, if I sentence someone to prison, they're taken there immediately.' Unless the case collapses, he reminded himself, in which case, there was nothing he could do, and he knew exactly how infuriated his immigration colleagues must feel.

'Yes, well, you're not alone in thinking that. But these poor buggers from Albania, are so desperate to improve life for themselves and their families that they're prepared to come here to work in cannabis factories and other shitty places in order to make money to send back home. And they're totally exploited by their own countrymen in both countries.'

'Who then get away with it, even when the immigrants are caught?'

'Afraid so.' Bhasin sighed. 'The current government plan is to make the UK less attractive to these people through the reputation that it's not a soft touch, and helping the Albanian government sort itself and their prison system out. That will hopefully put the smugglers out of business.'

'In an ideal world,' Jago mused. 'Meanwhile there will be

some bastards out there looking for routes to get into the UK in order to keep their business interests going.'

'Of course. And I don't think anywhere in the UK is immune to it. Even Cornwall. I'm sure I've heard of some cannabis farms being raided down there.'

Jago let his mind wander for a moment and didn't like where it was going.

'And the latest thing is for the men who are found running the places to claim they're victims themselves, even if it eventually turns out they're the ones doing the trafficking, and just happened to be in the wrong place at the wrong time and got caught.' Bhasin grimaced.

'So, what happens to them?'

'After the judge has made the decision to return them to Albania, or wherever they're from, they should be sent there. But the muppets at the Home Office don't often get round to doing that part of their job.'

'So, if the Home Office isn't returning or deporting convicted criminals, because of their inefficiencies, what chance is there of Edon Bregu being sent back?' Jago couldn't keep the despair out of his voice. 'It's things like this that make me want to jack the whole lot in and go back home to Cornwall for good.'

'And yet we keep going, my friend, Because it's the right thing to do. And if you want my opinion, I don't think you need to worry about Bregu. There's every chance that the referral you made after the trial will see him deported by Operation Nexus as a result of his character, conduct and associations, and it's ruled that his continuing presence in the UK is not conducive to the public good.'

'Really?' Jago perked up.

Bhasin nodded. 'Operation Nexus is getting better results, probably due more to the police involvement in the initiative than the Home Office. It's causing a lot of commotion among the Human Rights and Liberties groups, I might add. But they can't be wrong in every case and, as they say, it pays the mortgage.'

Jago decided the glint in his eye could be read in a number of ways. 'Do you think I need to be concerned that Bregu is mixed up in the stuff that's going on at home? In Cornwall.'

Bhasin shook his head. 'No, and I don't think he's a threat to you. You won't be high on his list of priorities. If he's referred to Nexus he'll go, and go quietly. Once he's deported, he'll be more concerned about lying low, keeping a close eye on his London business empire from a distance and worrying about which of his cronies he can trust. I hate to say this, Jim, but you're not worth getting his hands dirty for. Should anything happen to you or your loved ones, the authorities will be onto him. He won't want that sort of attention. It's not good for the sort of business he's in.'

'Thanks, I think.'

Bhasin laughed, his teeth white against his dark skin and silvering beard. 'My pleasure.' He sobered. 'But I don't think you're really that concerned about your own personal safety, are you? That's not the Jim Trevithick I know and admire. Are you worried that Bregu might try to get to you through Olivia?'

'Isn't that the way these bastards usually operate? He'd reckon that would be the easiest way to get to me?'

'Perhaps, but I think you're over-reacting. Which is totally understandable. And I do think you need to be concerned, or wary at least, about what's going on at that Hall place. It may be a coincidence that two Albanians have met with untimely ends there, but I'm not sure I believe in coincidences like that. I think you need to be talking to the local police to see if there's any more information. Use whatever resources you have available there and here to get to the bottom of this. And of course, there's the elephant in the room.'

'What elephant?'

'I know I'm not a crime expert anymore, but if I were you I'd start with finding out why that chef said what he did about you and the waitress.'

# 19

Olivia was kept busy for the next few days catching up with Alice at the Goods Shed and meeting some of her needier clients, but then she woke in the early hours of the morning with a start, drenched in sweat and clutching her neck. For the third night in a row, she'd dreamt about Martin strangling her. She could still feel his foul breath on her face, his relentless fingers trying to strangle the life out of her, and her struggle to breathe. She'd been sure she was going to die. Much-needed night-time rain was lashing against the window and she'd automatically reached out to Jago's side of the bed, which was empty of human life. Instead, it was occupied by two sleepy dogs whose warm damp noses nudged her hand and she suddenly felt overwhelmed by a crashing sense of loneliness, helplessness and fear.

It was 5am. To stop herself giving into tears, she dragged herself out of bed and pulled on her running shorts and top, left the dogs sleeping and let herself out of the back door and into the garden. The creek was choppy from another night storm whipping it up, but despite the rain still lashing down, it felt warm. She could see lighter sky over the ocean in the distance and decided to enjoy the feel of the rain against her face.

This time she ran at a steady pace, being careful not to slip on the wet lane, and headed towards the station site. Her slower strides allowed her brain to relax and subconscious thoughts to float through it without being registered. In the past, some of her best ideas had come to her this way and she let her mind filter through everything that had happened over the last couple of weeks. Before long a plan was forming. After Jago had left, she'd made the decision not to pursue any sort of investigation alone, but now she felt her recurrent dreams were telling her that these two innocent victims needed justice, and something was going on that had to be connected with Peneglos Hall. Her mind was made up. And whereas she still felt she wasn't equipped to investigate alone, there was something about Dylan that made her trust him and she was confident he had the skills to help. *And hadn't he said I only had to ask?*

Later that morning, Olivia found Dylan in the walled kitchen garden, picking tomatoes in the large glasshouse. His wooden trug was already filled with what looked to her like garden weeds.

He followed her gaze to the trug and gave her one of his crooked smiles. 'Lex and I have been foraging and I was just adding some basic garden veg to our finds. She's making soup.' He lowered his voice. 'She's a bit worried about her future here, so she decided to trial some foraged food recipes for the new menu. She's trying to keep positive. And although she knows quite a bit about woodland and hedgerow foraging, seaweed's a whole new ball game for her. So we were out wading up to our knees in the cove at seven o'clock this morning.'

Olivia's upper lip curled. 'Not sure I like the sound of seaweed soup. I'm not that adventurous.'

Dylan threw up his hands in mock horror. 'It's amazing! Right,' he picked up the trug with one hand and caught hold of Olivia's arm with the other, 'let's get this to Lex in the kitchen, grab a flask of the seaweed soup and we can talk over lunch in my hut.'

Twenty minutes later, having admired the delicious smells coming from the two vats bubbling away, they left the kitchen armed with a flask of soup and some freshly baked soda bread. Dylan led the way from the Hall, past the gardener's cottage and the courtyard where Rocky's men were busy, and down a long, hidden track until they eventually reached a patch of dense woodland. Completely distracted by the wonderful scents of damp moss, wet tree trunks and the resinous smell of the pine-needle-covered floor, all heightened by the night storm, Olivia followed. She was so busy breathing in deeply and filling her nose with the intoxicating air, she barely noticed the small clearing where Dylan finally came to a stop and pointed to his shepherd's hut.

Olivia's jaw dropped. It certainly wasn't the sort of shepherd's hut she was expecting. Its walls were constructed from modern corrugated steel cladding, and the three double-glazed windows and stable door were made of golden oak. Topped off by the iconic curved black roof, the hut blended in perfectly with its natural surroundings.

'Oh, Dylan. It's beautiful! I never dreamed it would be like this.' Her brow creased. 'I thought Cassie said you were living in an ancient clapped-out hut that hadn't been used since the 1950s?'

'Hmmph.' He frowned. 'I was. Quite happily too, as a matter of fact. It was where I lived in the summer, and when it got too wet and damp in the winter I'd move into the gardener's cottage with Uncle Charles. But after he died and Ruan and Lucinda moved in, that arrangement didn't work anymore. So as a surprise they had this built for me as an empty shell and I've fitted it out myself.'

Olivia smiled. 'How kind of them!'

Dylan shrugged and his face went a bit pink. 'It was, but the old one was usually parked further down the gardens, nearer the cove because I like listening to the ocean. The axel on this one doesn't allow it to be moved around much, so I can't really shift it from up here.' His hazel eyes met hers. 'Does that sound ungrateful?'

She felt sorry for him. 'Only a bit. I can understand wanting to hear the ocean, though.' She looked round the clearing. 'You're quite a long way from the cove up here, but what a setting! These woods are fabulous. And it fits in perfectly. Can I see inside?'

Dylan brightened and ushered her up the steps and into the hut.

It was a deceptively large, very masculine and functional space. There was a kitchen area on the left-hand side with reclaimed oak units and a small Belfast sink, a handmade table and two chairs to the side and a woodburning stove. To the other side of the central door was a small double bed, neatly made with what looked like an army surplus blanket. Her eyes swept the hut for personal touches but other than one tiny photo of two teenage lads she presumed were Dylan and Ruan on a small table alongside a jam jar of cut sweet peas, there weren't any. It looked to Olivia like a place you could quickly disappear from without leaving any trace.

'Heavens, Dylan. It's just perfect! And you fitted it all out yourself?'

He nodded. 'It gave me something to do over the winter months. Ruan was thinking of maybe offering some sort of off-grid holiday accommodation and asked me to fit this one out as a kind of prototype. Everything is as sustainable as possible, from the sheep's wool insulation to the floor, and everything else is made from reclaimed wood and copper pipes.'

'Ruan must have been thrilled!'

'He was. I've always loved working with wood and it turns out I'm pretty good at it.' His face reddened again round his beard. 'This place is perfect for off-grid living.'

Olivia jumped down the steps again and squinted up at the roof. 'Solar panels?'

'Yes. Because we're in a clearing I generate enough electricity to run lighting and power. I've got a compost toilet, wood at hand for the wood burner, and Calor gas if I need to use the hob. But I prefer to cook outside over the fire pit. And talking of which, we'd better have our soup.'

They sat outside, listening to the insects buzzing and the birds singing in the trees as they ate their soup. Olivia grudgingly admitted that despite looking like it had been skimmed off the top of a stagnant pond, it tasted much better than she'd feared.

'Ruan and Lucinda must be devastated to have to put a stop to all their plans for the time being.'

'Ruan's putting on a brave face, but Lucinda's pretty twitchy. I think she likes being in control and just can't cope with not being able to get on with everything that needs doing. I'm glad I'm living over here – away from all the drama.'

Dylan spoke with such feeling that Olivia turned to look at him. He'd never once bad-mouthed Lucinda in front of her, but it was clear he was concerned for Ruan.

'Is Ruan okay? I thought he and Lucinda were working well together?'

'Hmmm.' Dylan blew out loudly through pursed lips. 'Lucinda has some great plans for this place, and I can't fault her for that. But I'm not sure how their budget is doing. I know that stresses Ruan out and he also stresses about his responsibilities long term, to the Hall and the estate and everything. I'm a bit worried about him, actually.'

'Well, balancing a budget is always a nightmare where building is concerned.' Olivia sympathised. 'Let's just hope the police get to the bottom of it all soon and they can get on with opening.' She swallowed. 'And talking of which…'

Dylan settled back in his camping chair, stretching his legs out in front of him, then turned to Olivia with one eyebrow raised.

'You did say you might have some skills that could help,' she started slowly. 'If I decided to look into what's really going on here.' Her mouth suddenly went dry.

'I did, yes.'

'Did you mean it?' Olivia couldn't read the expression on his face and suddenly thought she might burst into tears.

'Of course I meant it. But why now? What's changed?'

'Nothing. It just feels personal,' she admitted. 'Jago and I found her and nobody knew her name. Then Gabe was making all those insinuations about Jago, which made him feel really bad. It's come between us and Jago's spooked in some way. I feel I need to sort it out if we have any chance of getting back together.'

'And you're sure that's what you want?'

'Yes. This situation is making everyone here miserable. And it's going to affect lots of people and local businesses if we don't sort it once and for all. I can't just sit back and do nothing anymore, but I know I can't do it on my own.' She turned beseechingly to him.

'So why the change of heart about letting me help?'

She looked away. 'You called me Olli-o,' she said in a small voice. 'The only other person who ever called me that was my brother. And I realised that's who you remind me of. I think he might have been like you if he hadn't...' Her voice trailed off.

Dylan pulled his chair closer to hers and nudged her with his shoulder, just like she remembered Aidan doing. 'I think I'd have liked a little sister like you.' He squeezed her hand gently with his own rough but warm one, and then let it go. 'I also think you'd have been a right pain in the backside, so I'm glad I missed out on that bit, and we can take it from here.'

'Thanks, I think.'

'Right.' Dylan scratched his beard thoughtfully and a faraway look crossed his face. 'I'll put my cards on the table too. I have a vested interest in this place, for obvious reasons.' He nodded towards his hut. 'And I want it sorted for Ruan's sake so he can relax and concentrate on what he's good at. So, let's go through what we know so far.'

'Well, as far as I can make out it all started when the waitress apparently recognised Jago and dropped her tray.'

'And who exactly was Jago with when the waitress apparently recognised him?'

Olivia chewed her lip. 'Gabe and Lexie. Ruan and Lucinda were there too.'

'Okay. We can rule Ruan and Lex out straight away.'

'Can we?'

'I'd trust Ruan with my life.' He held on to her gaze. 'Believe me.'

She nodded. 'What about Lexie?'

Dylan shook his head. 'I trust her too. Perhaps not with my life, but over this I do. I think she got in a bit over her head with Gabe to begin with, but she's past that now and gives him a wide berth.'

Olivia decided to file that particular nugget of information away and think about it later.

'So what about Gabe?'

Dylan's face darkened. 'I don't like the guy.'

'Why not?'

'He's got too much influence over Lucinda. I know they've known each other a long time, but sometimes you'd think it was him running the place rather than Ruan.'

Olivia admired Dylan for his loyalty to his friend. 'Do you trust Lucinda?'

'I don't know. Her efficiency and enthusiasm scare the life out of me in many ways. But Ruan knows her far better than me and although I was a bit gobsmacked when I first met her, I'm trying to trust his judgement.'

'Okay, tell me more about Gabe.'

'There's just something about him… can't put my finger on it… and then when I heard what he was suggesting about Jago…' He paused. 'Perhaps he was clutching at straws when he mentioned his job, and struck lucky with Jago's reaction. Then he was just stirring the pot when he insinuated it might have been someone Jago knew in a more personal way.'

Olivia's pulse quickened. 'That was just mean of him. Jago was horrified and I was embarrassed the way Gabe kept going on about it. He even mentioned it to the police, for God's sake. Why would he do that?'

'He's an alpha male. He likes being the centre of attention, the most handsome man in the room. You've seen the way he plays on being the Italian master chef. My guess is he felt threatened by Jago and it was an easy way to put him in an awkward situation.'

Olivia's scalp prickled as a thought occurred to her. 'Or was he deflecting attention from himself? And it was actually Gabe the waitress recognised?'

Dylan shrugged. 'Perhaps.'

Olivia sat up and then subsided back down again just as quickly. 'Trenow said everyone had a bona fide alibi for the rest of that night. Do you know who Gabe's was?'

A shadow clouded his face. 'Just between you and me, it was Lexie, allegedly. She says she had too much to drink and can't remember anything about it, but Gabe swears she was with him all night.'

Alarm bells started ringing in Olivia's ears, as a horrible sense of déjà vu hit her. 'Really? And I suppose Lexie was too embarrassed to tell the police that she couldn't remember a thing about it, so went along with his story?'

Dylan looked at her sideways. 'You don't sound surprised.'

'Let's just say I've heard that one before.' She proceeded to give him a brief summary of Martin's similar claims the previous year. Dylan's face looked like a thundercloud by the time she'd finished and he scratched his beard furiously.

'I'm so sorry, Olivia. It sounds like Gabe and Martin are cut from the same cloth.'

Olivia simply nodded and moved on. 'So, now it looks like we can probably disregard Gabe's alibi, is he your number one suspect?'

'At the moment, yes. But I don't have a lot of evidence to back it up. Apart from an even greater dislike of the guy now.'

She groaned. 'Oh, you men and the need for evidence!

What's wrong with good old intuition and imagination? You're as bad as Jago.'

He laughed. 'Thank you. Which is why you're a great architect and Jago is excellent at his job.'

Olivia pulled her face. 'Okay, what motive do you think Gabe had for killing the waitress?'

'Why do most people kill someone else? Love? Revenge? Hatred? Because they know something the killer doesn't want getting out?'

'Fair enough. But what makes you think Gabe is involved, rather than anyone else?'

'I keep finding him in all sorts of weird places in the garden, which I know isn't a crime in itself, but he doesn't strike me as the gardening type. And he asks a lot of questions about the tides because he reckons he's into sea swimming. But I swim at the cove most mornings and I've only seen him there once.' He paused. 'Saying it out loud doesn't help my case, does it?'

Olivia sighed.

'Then one day when I was working in the orchard, I heard him talking on his mobile. But I'm pretty sure he wasn't speaking English or Italian and when he saw me, he cut the call and rushed off.' He groaned. 'It all sounds really circumstantial and a bit pathetic, doesn't it? Perhaps I'm just looking for stuff because I don't like the guy.'

Olivia tucked a lock of hair behind her ear and stood up. 'You said your old hut was in a different part of the garden?'

'Yes. And if I'd been there either of those nights, I might have heard if anyone came up from the cove, or went back that way. The path went straight past it. I don't hear a thing up here.'

'Will you show me exactly where it was?'

Olivia followed Dylan as they zig-zagged through the gardens without using any of the main paths, and she realised this was how he probably moved around the grounds without being seen or heard. *Perhaps Gabe could do with taking some lessons from him in being more discreet.* Dylan walked ahead of her, silently, through the bushes, pointing out where someone had been before them, leaving broken stems and flattened plants and then suddenly froze.

He sank down to his knees in a swift movement, pulling Olivia down with him, his finger to his lips. A few seconds later they caught a brief flash of blue in the distance as someone rushed past on the main path that led up to the formal gardens. Olivia stiffened but Dylan shook his head, signalling for her to stay low down and silent. She waited, her leg cramping painfully beneath her, marvelling that Dylan could stay so still, fitting in with the landscape in his khaki green clothes, with only his quiet breathing giving him away.

Two men appeared from the bushes on the far side of the path, deep in conversation, but too far away to hear. Dylan pulled the binoculars hanging round his neck up to his eyes and focused them. As the men drew nearer, Olivia held her breath. Their voices reached them first and it sounded like they were arguing in a foreign language. The taller man stopped suddenly, gesticulating angrily. Olivia froze. She didn't recognise him. But when the slightly shorter man turned back, his own angry face was clear. Gabe.

They carried on arguing and by the time they moved on, Olivia's heart was thumping so hard she thought it would burst. Dylan made them wait a while longer before he got back to his feet, brushing the leaves from his clothes, and then pulled Olivia up.

'Right,' he whispered. 'Forget my old hut for now, I'm going to follow them. See where they go.'

'Who is he?'

'No idea, but I reckon it's the same guy I heard him talking to on the phone. It's definitely the same language.'

'Shall we call the police?'

'And tell them what? No, we need to get some evidence first. I'm sure Gabe's up to something. And it sounds like things are getting pretty tense between them.'

Olivia felt herself go pale. 'Be careful.'

He waved his binoculars at her. 'I'll keep my distance. Promise me something, Olli-o?' He started to walk away. 'If ever you can't get hold of me, or it looks like I've disappeared, promise me you'll go straight to Jago and tell him everything.'

# 20

Jago stood at the window of his top-floor flat gazing over the sun-filled glorious gardens of Gray's Inn, a small green oasis of history protected from the hustle and bustle of London. He'd been up early and hit the residents' gym hard, subconsciously reverting to the punishing schedule he'd adopted after his knife attack and religiously kept to when he was living in the city. Twenty minutes on the bike, twenty on the rowing machine, followed by one hundred sit-ups, another hundred press-ups and then some squats, deadlifts and bench presses. He was already noticing the difference in his body. A busy few days in Penbartha, with not much time for anything but the odd paddle on the creek had softened him up, and he needed to get back into what he thought of as a position of strength.

He'd done well trying not to think about Penbartha, because as soon as he did his mind immediately focused on Olivia. He hated himself for rushing away with only a pathetically inadequate note. What he really hated, he admitted as he watched a group of tourists being guided round the gardens on a walking tour of Legal and Illegal London, was the knowledge that Olivia, a proven ball-busting, fiercely independent woman would absolutely and fundamentally disagree with the idea that he was doing it to protect her. And so now he had to face the fact he may have overreacted and by not being completely honest, was at risk of losing her. He still wasn't convinced that she wasn't at risk in any way, because there was obviously something fishy going on at Peneglos Hall, but he was now determined to find out everything he could before going back home.

Jago checked his watch. He had a couple of hours before he was able to implement the next part of his plan. To prepare, he sat at his desk, uncapped his fountain pen and started making a list of everybody connected to Peneglos Hall in any way. He then went through the list, line by line, annotating each name with his own theories.

A buzzing from his mobile brought him out of his thoughts. He snatched it up from his desk and smiled as he read the text message.

*Judge has risen until 2.15pm for defence counsel to take instructions. Meet me in my Chambers in 10.*

Typical. No time wasted with pleasantries. Just as he liked it. Jago placed his papers into a file which he slipped into a briefcase. Then he changed into one of his lighter suits, so he would fit in with all the other barristers bustling about Gray's Inn at this time of day.

He followed the route of many a famous, infamous and colourful legal character across several ancient flag-stoned courtyards, and through The Walks until he arrived at his destination with three minutes to spare.

Frederick Chambers was housed, along with many others, in a long four-storey Georgian brick-built terrace with rows of perfectly proportioned and symmetrical six-paned double-sash windows and arched front doors. Each terrace was lined with iconic black railings and oozed history. He paused for a moment on the step before pushing the door open and walking into the reception area and back two hundred years.

All traditional barristers' chambers smelt the same, Jago reflected as he strode towards the desk, his eyes slowly adjusting from the brightness outside to the much dimmer interior. Whether it was the oak-panelled corridors lined with bookcases containing years and years of law reports bound in red, blue and gold leather, the thick but slightly ancient carpets on the floors, or some of the questionable original oil paintings on the walls, Jago could close his eyes and be in any chambers he knew. He found it surprisingly comforting.

'Can I help you, sir?' The receptionist's voice interrupted his musings.

'Oh yes, sorry, I was miles away.' Jago shook himself. 'I'm here to see Maeve Kelly. She's expecting me.'

The receptionist checked the computer screen in front of her. 'Ah yes. Ms Kelly has just returned from court. Would you like me to show you to her room?'

Jago gripped the handle of his briefcase more tightly. 'No, it's fine, thanks, I know my way.' He flashed a quick smile and headed off down the main corridor, past various doors to rooms on each side, some closed and silent, others open and from which came the sound of serious discussions, some with low laughter. He kept his head down. He knew quite a few of the barristers based in these chambers, and he did not want to get caught up in any meaningless chit-chat.

He let out a huge sigh of relief as he reached the last door on the right and saw that it was ajar. He knocked softly and a familiar voice called out.

'That you, Trevithick? You took your time.'

A large smile spread over his face and no sooner had he

walked through the door, he was met by a slight, titian-haired woman dressed in formal court wear who gave him such a strong hug, it almost hurt.

'Am I glad to see you – it's been far too long!' She stood back and held him at arm's length, her green eyes bright in her pale, freckled face as she looked him up and down. He stood there like a small boy being inspected by a critical, but adoring aunt, even though they were the same age.

'Looking good, James. All that work you're putting in at the gym, according to my spies, is obviously paying off.' She ignored his groan. 'And you're rocking the silver fox look.'

Jago laughed. 'We've been through this, Maeve. I'm not your type.'

The green eyes sparkled. 'Too bloody right you're not. You attract too much trouble.' She peered at his face. 'What have I said? Has something happened? I heard about your last trial collapsing, but your face tells me there's something else going on. Spit it out.'

Jago felt himself relaxing. He and Maeve went back a long way and she could read him like a book.

'Have you got time now?'

Maeve glanced at her watch. 'It's 11.45 and I'll have to leave at two to be back in court for 2.15, so that gives us over two hours. What the hell can take that long?' Her soft Dublin accent suddenly sounded stronger, more like when he had first met her. 'What the feck is going on, James? Sit down.' She walked back round to the other side of her large oak, double pedestal desk, picked up her mobile and tapped out a quick message before sitting down and fixing him with a hard stare.

Jago remembered from occasions he'd prosecuted jointly with her how fearsome Maeve could be with defendants and opponents, and sat down quickly. Just as he had done with Bhasin, he outlined everything that had happened at Peneglos

Hall while he was there: the waitress's reaction to him, Gabe's comment, her drowning, Olivia's discovery of her identity and the second body being washed up a week later. Then he finished up with Baz's theory that it was unlikely to be connected to the Bregu case.

Maeve was silent for a moment, and then drank from the water bottle sitting on her desk.

'I reckon Baz is right. He's the go-to person for this sort of thing, so he should know. Let's put Bregu to one side and get back to what's happened in the last week. Tell me about this hippy place where it's all going on.'

Subconsciously relieved that Maeve was taking his worries seriously, Jago started to laugh. 'It's not a hippy place. It's a top-of-the-range, eco-boutique hotel in a massive old Georgian house. Honestly, Maeve, it's stunning. All mod cons, no expense spared. You'd love it.'

'It wouldn't love my kids, believe me. They're feral. I can't take them anywhere I might want to return to.'

Jago chuckled. He knew she didn't mean it. 'Perhaps you could get away without them. Just you and Joey?'

Maeve shot him a stern look. 'Why would I want to go to a place where there's a murderer on the loose? Can we get back to basics, please?'

Jago opened his case and pulled his papers out. He was just about to start talking when there was a knock on the door.

'Come in, Monty,' Maeve said.

The door opened and a serious-looking, slightly built young man entered nervously, armed with a brown paper carrier bag, which he handed over to Maeve.

'Hope that's all okay, Maeve.' He turned to leave, but she called him back.

'Pull up a chair, Monty, and join us for lunch.' She started pulling napkins and thickly cut sandwiches out of the bag, along with glass bottles of water.

Surprised, Jago looked questioningly at Maeve. She nodded reassuringly and he relaxed. He trusted her judgement implicitly. If she trusted this Monty, then so would he.

'Monty, this is James Trevithick. James this is Monty Vaughan, my current pupil.'

If Harry Potter had become a barrister, he would look just like Monty Vaughan, Jago decided. Dark-haired and slight, with round, wire-rimmed glasses, Monty's earnest face turned bright red.

'*The* James Trevithick?' he said, totally in awe. 'The one you're always talking about?'

It was Maeve's turn to blush. Jago was amused and didn't bother to hide it.

'I do not talk about him all the time,' she reprimanded her pupil sharply. 'But when you spend as much time working together as Treasury Juniors as we did, you get to know someone very well.'

'God, those were the days.' Jago groaned. 'But I did spend an awful lot of time with her, so you have my sympathy, Monty. I know what she's like to work with and I admire your perseverance.'

Monty's blush deepened. 'Not at all. Maeve's a wonderful pupil supervisor. I'm learning so much.'

Jago looked at the pupil's earnest face and saw his own, twenty years younger, shining back at him. 'Well, if you want to get on in this crazy world of ours, go for it. Work bloody hard and never let go of your dream. That's what Maeve and I did. Don't be put off by folks who say Daddy has to be a High Court judge. My father's a dairy farmer who's only been to London about six times in his whole life. It's all down to you and how good you are at the job. You have to show talent, commitment and a willingness to learn.'

Maeve nodded. 'And you're about to learn some more. So, buckle up, Mr Vaughan, listen and take notes.' She turned to Jago. 'Right, let's start at the beginning. Tell us all about Peneglos Hall and the cast list of all the people who are involved there.'

Jago went through his list methodically and without emotion, just like he would in court, leaving nothing and no-one out. He was aware of Maeve's eagle eyes watching him closely, head on one side as she made occasional notes on the pad in front of her. In contrast, Monty was writing furiously. When he'd finished, he sat back and waited for Maeve to speak. She waved for him to hand over his list and then cast her sharp eyes over it, digesting information and firing out questions. Who was this person? Had Jago met them? What did he think of them? How were they involved in the Hall itself? This was Maeve in professional mode: analysing, chasing up questions, probing and probing. After a long discussion, she came to the same conclusion as Jago.

'I agree with you, James, something dodgy must be going on there, even without the rising body count.'

'Part of me wishes you'd dismissed the whole thing as a figment of my imagination,' Jago reflected. 'I'd have tried to agree with you and gone back to enjoying my summer holiday.'

'No you wouldn't,' Maeve retorted. 'You'd have been stressing it was linked to some big Albanian mafia gang you may or may not have upset in your last trial, and not relaxed for a minute. You'd have driven Olivia mad and ended up back here, single and miserable.'

She peered at him closely. 'A bit like you are now, actually. I'm with Bhasin on this one. You're far too small fry for the

Albanians to be bothered with. They'll be more concerned with protecting their business empire elsewhere. I agree it's a hell of a coincidence that the murder victims are from the same country, but we need to consider how they got to Cornwall in the first place. I think we can rule out they were on their holidays, but we need to double-check.' Maeve took a breath and then made sure that Monty was keeping up.

'James, you're as aware as I am that people tend to be murdered by people they know, and it's often because they'll either benefit in some way from the victim not being around, or the victim knows something the murderer doesn't want getting out.' She turned to Monty. 'I think we need to check out Ruan Braithwaite, Lucinda Hayes, Dylan Bonnar and Gabe Marotta. See what you can find out about them. Birthdays, families, education, work history and so on.' She paused. 'Especially Marotta, but leave him until last – for a treat. He sounds a right creep. You know the drill, Monty.'

Jago stared at the two barristers opposite, his mouth open. 'What's this? Are you running a side hustle as private investigators now?'

'Not at all.' Maeve frowned sharply. 'Monty's a bit of an expert in genealogy among all sorts of other useful things. There is nothing he can't find out from the internet. I don't ask too many questions… But it has proved to be invaluable in a number of cases.'

'Are you sure it's—'

Maeve cut him off, her accent suddenly stronger. 'Do you want our help or not, Trevithick? Do you want to get to the bottom of what's going on down there? And, most importantly of all, do you want to save your relationship with Olivia? Because from the look on your face every time I mention her name, I'd say that's the most important thing to you in all this.'

Jago nodded. He would never admit it to Maeve, but the way she pronounced Olivia's name in her musical Irish lilt, with the emphasis on the O, made him miss her even more.

'You're right.' He smiled at his friend and saw her face soften as she smiled back. 'As usual.'

Maeve glanced at her watch and signalled to Monty to get ready. 'Good to see you haven't forgotten. That makes me happy.'

She gathered her stuff together and adjusted her collar and bands. Jago walked with her to the door of her room.

'Thanks, Maeve.'

She hugged him tight and kissed his cheek. 'I'll be happy to work with you again, James. And as I always say to Joey, happy wife, happy life.'

Jago hugged her back. 'Joey is one lucky woman.' His mobile rang and he dragged it out of his pocket, and waved goodbye to his old friend.

'Jago?' It was Trenow, sounding stressed.

Jago's blood ran cold. 'What's happened?'

'It's Gabe Marotta. I thought you'd want to know. And it'll be all over the news later. He's been found in the gardens at the Hall, stabbed to death. But that's not all.'

Jago exhaled slowly.

'The hunting knife used has been found in Dylan Bonnar's shepherd's hut. And Dylan's disappeared.'

# 21

'Shoot me a text when you get to Paddington, and then let me know later how you get on with Jago.' Rocky's face was clouded with worry as he gave Olivia a quick hug when he dropped her at Truro railway station at six thirty in the morning. 'And try to keep calm.'

She took her overnight case from him and hoisted a tote bag over her shoulder, before turning to face her oldest friend. He looked tired, she decided. And stressed. The sooner this business was sorted out, the better for everyone.

'I promise. And please ask Cassie to be as vague as possible about where I've gone.'

Rocky pulled an anguished face. 'You know we aren't any good at all this secrecy.'

Olivia was flooded with a sudden rush of affection. 'And I hate putting you in this position, but Cassie will want to protect Dylan as much as I do, and what she doesn't know, she can't pass on.'

'Kitten seems to think he's very keen on her.'

'Everyone seems to think he's keen on her. It's whether

she's keen on him that matters.' Olivia's face crumpled. 'Why does this have to happen now? Just when things were looking up for her? She'll never forgive Sam if he tracks Dylan down before anyone else does.'

Rocky hugged her again. 'Look, Olive, we're doing all we can. You need to talk to Jago – and not just about what's going on at the Hall. Don't let your relationship be another casualty of that place.'

Rocky's words came back to her as her train made its way through the Cornish countryside and she shifted uncomfortably in her seat. There were so many casualties caused by what was going on at Peneglos Hall. Agnes Toska, the still-nameless man whose body had been washed up after the storm, and now, almost unbelievably, Gabe. Olivia refused to believe that Dylan had anything to do with his death, but if the police followed the evidence, it wouldn't be long before they came to the conclusion that he had. Then they just had to find him. Which, hopefully, would be much easier said than done.

And there were even more potential casualties. Unless this could all be tied up soon, the whole future of the Hall was at stake. If Ruan and Lucinda were unable to open on time, they were going to lose vital business. Their suppliers, customers and staff would all suffer too. Their professional reputation would be in tatters and heaven only knew what it was going to do to their personal relationship, which Olivia noticed was becoming increasingly strained. The ripples just spread out and out. Rocky was stressed about the workmen they still had on site there, if their bills would be paid, or whether they should just move on to the next job which was already behind schedule.

Olivia wriggled again and accepted a glass of water from

the on-board catering manager as she rolled her trolley down the aisle.

'Fabulous dress!' she commented as she filled the glass she had placed on a paper coaster in front of Olivia. 'I bet you didn't buy that in a chain store.'

Olivia smiled, happy to be distracted from her worries. This morning, she'd eschewed her summer work uniform of shorts, vest and preloved Liberty shirt from Mollie, in favour of a simple cream sundress Bea Mathers had made her as a thank-you for letting her become a tenant at the Engine Shed. It was loose-fitting with spaghetti straps, made from vintage cotton lace and Olivia loved the boho vibe it gave her. Bea had suggested she wore it with brown calf-length boots, but in view of the heatwave Olivia had chosen her most comfortable leather thongs.

'Thank you. And you're right, a friend made it for me.'

'Well, she's very talented and you're very lucky. It's right on trend and really suits you. Especially with your tan. Enjoy the rest of your journey.' She trundled off down the aisle, leaving Olivia to go back to her thoughts. She pulled her notebook out and began reading through the copious notes, diagrams and drawings that catalogued all the locations, events and people involved with Peneglos Hall. She added Gabe's name to the list of victims and then reluctantly added Dylan's to the list of suspects. After an hour of getting nowhere, she closed her notebook in despair. It was difficult enough to think that three people had died tragically in such a beautiful place, but to know someone had killed them deliberately made it really tough.

It was just like when Libby had died the year before. All the people she was listing and suspecting were people she knew and cared about, apart from Gabe, but even he didn't deserve to die the way he had. Her thoughts turned automatically to

Jago and she sighed. She was still confused and hurt by his note and sudden departure from Penbartha and needed to think about how she was going to approach seeing him again. Asking for his help wasn't going to be easy. Olivia squeezed her eyes shut to get rid of the image of his face and admitted to herself there was only one way she was going to get through the rest of this long journey; by distracting herself with work. This time it was her laptop she pulled from her tote bag. She dealt with her emails and then turned her attention to a particularly complicated set of schedules, spreadsheets and calculations for an upcoming renovation project.

Olivia's train arrived at Paddington right on time and she nipped into the ladies to freshen up after the long journey. She spritzed herself with perfume, applied more moisturiser and lip gloss and pulled her hair into a loose knot so she could feel the air on her neck. She frowned at herself in the mirror. Just the thought of seeing Jago made her stomach lurch and her pulse quicken. They really had to sort this out. Once and for all.

'C'mon, Wells.' She grimaced at her pale reflection. 'He's not your enemy. Man up!'

---

'Good afternoon, Miss Wells.' Tom greeted her at the porter's lodge and discreetly checked his watch for the correct time.

*Does this man ever sleep?*

Olivia smiled at him. 'Hi, Tom. I don't suppose you know if James is about?'

'I saw him going over to his chambers about twenty minutes ago. If you leave your case here, I'll bring it over to his residence later.'

'That's kind, thanks.' She handed over her wheeled case. 'Can you remind me how to get to his chambers, please? I always get lost.'

'Of course, ma'am.' He rattled off a list of directions accompanied by a lot of pointing. Olivia nodded and wandered off in the direction of his finger, momentarily rattled by being called ma'am. No matter how many times she asked him not to, Tom was incapable of addressing her in any way but the formal manner he used for all female members of the Inn.

Once at the wrought iron gates to the Inn's own large, private gardens, Olivia found her bearings. She stayed within the shade of the trees as she skirted the tired-looking lawns in front of the northern terrace of buildings. Dickens Court Chambers, her destination, was almost the last property in the row. She paused to admire the Georgian architecture, one of her favourite styles. Looking at the grand terrace of premises, with their long sash windows and black wrought iron railings, she doubted it had changed much in the last two hundred years.

'You're just putting it off, Wells. Pull yourself together,' Olivia spoke aloud, surprising a passer-by. She smiled awkwardly, pulled her shoulders back and skipped up the steps to One Bardell Buildings, trying to ignore her racing heart and the churning in her stomach.

She paused at the reception desk with a warm smile firmly in place. The clerk was someone she vaguely recognised.

'Mr Trevithick is in his room,' he informed her seriously. 'Is he expecting you?'

'Thank you.' She ignored his question and spoke with more confidence than she felt. 'I know the way.' And without giving the clerk the chance to speak again, she hefted her bag more firmly onto her shoulder and walked briskly down the thickly carpeted corridor.

Barristers' chambers scared Olivia, she realised as she turned the corner out of sight of the clerk and allowed herself to slow down. They always felt so grand and cerebral, full of intellectual minds and even more ego. She paused as she reached the open door to Jago's room and stood to one side, out of sight, listening to the lilting sound of a woman's voice. Olivia moved closer and caught sight of a slim, fierce-looking woman in a black suit, with red hair pulled sharply into a knot at the nape of her neck, sitting in one of the wing-backed chairs opposite the desk, deep in conversation. A second, more familiar, voice replied. Olivia's heart missed a beat and she dared to peer round the door.

And there he was, a more serious and intense version of the Jago she knew, with no hint of a Cornish burr in his neutral accent, perfectly at home in his professional habitat. He leant across his desk to look closer at the woman's iPad, and Olivia noticed the broadness of his shoulders in his white shirt. He looked harder, more muscular. He'd obviously been putting himself through punishing workouts in the gym to take his mind off his worries. *Well, I know all about that.*

Her stomach muscles contracted and she let go of the breath she'd been unconsciously holding. Jago looked up sharply, mid-sentence, his jaw tense and his eyes narrowed. Even from a distance she could see his face tighten as his gaze rested on her. She couldn't decide whether his expression was one of disapproval, anger, or something else. She met his eyes, now the colour of a stormy Cornish sea, and swallowed hard. Silence fell in the room.

'You must be Olivia.' The owner of the Irish voice twisted round in her chair; her voice full of curiosity mixed with amusement. 'What an unexpected pleasure! Come and join us.' She signalled to an empty seat.

Olivia scoured the woman's words for any hint of sarcasm and couldn't find any. In turn she tried to make her own voice friendly and light-hearted.

'It's okay, I'll come back later. I don't want to interrupt.' She turned to Jago, who was still staring at her. Her heart plummeted. 'I didn't realise Jag— I mean James, would be working...' Her voice trailed off and she turned away, feeling tears burning at her eyelids, unsure whether it was sadness or anger that was responsible for them.

As she neared the door, she heard a hiss and then Jago was at her side, reaching for her arm. The feel of him beside her unnerved her, but when she looked up at him, he was back in control and the only sign of emotion in his face was a twitch of one eyebrow.

'No, Olivia, please stay.' His voice didn't sound quite steady. 'You'll be interested in what we're talking about.'

Olivia doubted it, but said nothing.

'What James is trying, and failing, to say,' came the woman's voice behind them, 'is that we've been looking into that hotel set-up in Cornwall. And you may be interested in what we've learned.'

Olivia spun round, her mind spinning as well.

'Really?'

'Yes.' The woman stood up and walked towards her, hand outstretched in welcome. 'I'm Maeve Kelly and I've worked with James for years. Why don't we let him make us a cup of tea and sort out some lunch while we get to know each other?'

There was no mistaking the glare that Maeve sent in Jago's direction. Or the speed with which he picked up on it. She practically shooed him out of the door and then shepherded Olivia into the comfiest looking chair in the room. She pulled up another chair opposite and leant forward.

'Olivia, I know we've never met before, but James has told me a lot about you over the last year or so, and I feel I kind of know you. So I want to tell you something.'

Olivia stiffened. She didn't like the sound of this.

The older woman seemed to sense her discomfort and when she spoke next, her voice was softer.

'Please don't think James has been talking about you behind your back. He would never do that. I could just tell, from his sudden reappearance here and from how he's been acting, that something has been going on between the two of you. That was before he told me about the murders. I just want to ask you to give him the time and space to explain his actions.' She paused. 'Which I kind of guess is why you're here?'

Olivia nodded. 'I need his help.'

Maeve leant forward again and touched Olivia's hand. 'And you'll get it. From Monty and me too, now we've got our teeth into this weird little mystery that's going on down there.'

Olivia felt relief wash through her, although she wouldn't have described three murders as a little mystery. Perhaps it was in Maeve's world. 'Thanks.'

Maeve smiled. 'And before you ask, I'll tell you why I'm so keen on helping James out. Just for the sake of transparency.'

'Okay.' Olivia cocked her head to one side.

'James is one of the kindest, strongest, most generous guys at the London Bar. He and I go back a long way and he's always been there for me. As a friend. He is so not my type.' She laughed again and Olivia glimpsed the fun side of Maeve Kelly. 'And I want him to be happy. Everyone here loves him – even my own wife loves him – but I've never, ever seen him look at anyone the way he just looked at you. Ever.'

## 22

Jago could feel Olivia's stare from across the room. Her face was frowning through the tendrils of dark hair, her cheeks tinged with colour and her lips pursed. God, he'd missed her so much. And now here she was and he was overcome with the urge to gather her up in his arms, kiss her and assure her that everything was going to be alright. But he couldn't. She sat rigidly in the armchair, her eyes challenging him. Only her tell-tale swallow betrayed her inner struggles.

In spite of all his years at the London Bar, Jago felt suddenly helpless and turned to Maeve who was looking at him with a mixture of humour and exasperation. She gave an imperceptible nod, turned towards Olivia and took control.

'Right, I think we need you to bring us up to speed on what's been happening at Peneglos Hall since James has been here. Is that okay with you, Olivia?'

Olivia nodded and let Maeve guide her through all the recent events at the Hall: Dylan's theory about Gabe, how he'd regularly seen him in the gardens, Gabe's death and Dylan's subsequent disappearance. Maeve encouraged Olivia to speak freely and at length, only stopping her every now and then to ask a question, confirm something or add an astute observation of her own.

Jago stood by the window, listening carefully and remembering their times in court together and how good Maeve had always been with witnesses and juries alike. He'd often joked that people would be quite happy to listen to Maeve reading out a shopping list in her melodic soft accent. And it seemed to be working with Olivia too. Her reaction to the questions she was being asked showed that she had decided to trust Maeve and he was surprised at how relieved he felt.

'Right, so the last contact you had with the police in Cornwall was to be told that Gabe Marotta's body had been found, the murder weapon found in Dylan Bonnar's shepherd's hut and that he was nowhere to be found.'

Olivia nodded sharply. 'Yes, but I refuse to accept that Dylan had anything to do with Gabe's murder. He's obviously being framed for it and he's gone to ground while the police investigate it properly.' She shot a hostile look in Jago's direction as her voice rose. 'And I'm very aware that certain people may think that I've been in this position before, my judgement is poor and that I'm trying to defend an obviously guilty person.'

Shame sliced through Jago. He had to admit that the thought had gone through his mind. He hadn't understood Olivia when she'd insisted on defending Martin Lambert the previous year. In Jago's eyes, and subsequently proved, he was as guilty as hell. But he also knew Olivia had changed. Like Cassie, she was no longer quick to trust people, so was she right or had she been taken in by Dylan?

He zoned back into Olivia's words.

'But that business with Martin changed me; made me

question a lot of things, look at people differently, suspect everyone. And I hate it, but I still trust Dylan!'

'I can tell you do, but let's just deal with the facts, Olivia,' Maeve suggested gently, placing a calming hand over Olivia's. 'You could be right about Dylan being framed. And if he has been, the police should be looking for the person responsible for that.'

'Or will they just take the easy way out, hunt Dylan down and when they do finally find him, charge him with all three murders?'

'I don't think Trenow will do that.' Jago spoke up from his corner. 'He and I go back a long way and he's got bags of integrity.' He rummaged in his pocket and pulled out his ringing mobile. 'Speak of the devil. I'll take this outside.'

He stepped into the corridor, relieved to get away from Olivia's distress.

'Hi, Jago, I'll get straight to the point.'

'Good.'

'Is Olivia with you? Cassie's being very vague about her whereabouts, but I just want to know she's safe and out of harm's way. And I don't have to get a search party out for her too.'

Jago thought quickly. 'Yes, she is. Why? What's going on?'

'Has she heard anything from Dylan?'

'She says she hasn't.'

'Do you believe her?'

'Of course I do!'

'Okay, okay. Let's move on. In the light of our last conversation at Tresillian, when you got so antsy about the tattoo on the body of our drowned man...'

Jago's stomach clenched. 'The double-headed eagle?'

'Yup. You're not going to like this, but examination of Gabe Marotta's body revealed he had one too.'

'Shit. I thought he was Italian. What's going on?'

'No idea, and I still don't think we're talking about your Albanian gang infiltrating Cornwall. But I don't like coincidences. That's three bodies we've found now on Peneglos land that have some connection with Albania.'

Thoughts whirled around Jago's mind, but he was unable to catch hold of any of them. He'd heard enough weird, wonderful and crazy cases in court to know that coincidences did happen, but more often than not there was a connection and when investigated properly, it revealed something. He decided to keep his thoughts to himself. 'Any news on Dylan?'

A heavy sigh came down the line. 'He's a wily fox. He'll literally go to ground. Even though I'm not convinced he's responsible for any of these murders, my boss will soon be putting the pressure on me for a result. There's more to Dylan Bonnar than meets the eye, I swear it. I just can't find anything. If Olivia does hear from him, let me know, please.'

Jago glanced through the gap in the door to his room, where two of the most important women in his life were still talking, their heads close together.

'Okay.' Jago wasn't sure he would.

'Go easy on her, Jago. This has probably brought back a lot of stuff about last year's case. No surprise if she's feeling a bit sensitive about it all still.'

Jago's hackles rose. 'Thanks for the relationship advice, Ross, but stick to policing, eh?'

Trenow sighed. 'Just let me know if she hears anything from Dylan.'

---

Two pairs of eyes rested on Jago as he re-entered the room and closed the door behind him.

'Any news on Dylan?' There was no mistaking the concern in Olivia's voice.

'Afraid not. But they found another double-headed eagle tattoo.'

Maeve jumped on that bit of information. 'On Gabe Marotta?' She let out a low whistle. 'What's his connection with Albania?' Her gaze held his. 'There has to be one, James. We need to do a bit more digging in that direction.' She looked at her watch and tutted. 'Where's Monty when you need him?'

As if on cue, the door flew open and Monty, in best Harry Potter late-for-class fashion, burst into the room, laptop under one arm and a sheaf of papers under the other.

'I'm so sorry I'm late. I couldn't get my uncle off the phone.' His eyes took in Olivia and he blushed bright red. 'Sorry, I didn't realise you had company.'

Maeve tutted again. 'This is Olivia Wells, James's... partner.' As she chose the word, she sent a challenging glare in Jago's direction. 'Olivia, this is Monty Vaughan, my pupil and right-hand man of the moment.'

Monty stumbled over a chair in his eagerness to shake Olivia's hand, and blushed even more. 'Pleased to meet you.'

Jago watched the effect she was having on Monty and sympathised. She was everything the people the young man mixed with most days was not. Even today's outfit made her look like some angelic being in the midst of a sea of formal darkness. Jago didn't recognise the cream lace dress she was wearing, but it suited her exotic looks perfectly. Olivia was greeting Monty with a warm, friendly smile, and Jago knew he'd be eating out of her hand within minutes.

'It wasn't just a family catch-up with my uncle, Maeve. It's all relevant to the case, and very interesting,' Monty protested and sat down quickly on the other side of Olivia, starting to explain his delay, but Maeve silenced him with a look.

'Let's just go through things from the beginning, so we're all on the same page.' Maeve turned to Olivia. 'Monty's been running some basic checks on everyone who's involved at Peneglos Hall, present company excepted.' Maeve peered at her iPad through the lenses of tortoiseshell reading glasses perched on the end of her nose. 'Starting with Ruan Braithwaite and Lucinda Hayes, everything seems to check out with what James has already told us. It looks like they met while working at some sustainable luxury hotel in Mayfair, where one night's stay costs about the same as my eye-watering weekly nursery bill for two children.' She paused and scrolled through some more pages. 'Monty's confirmed that Gabriel Marotta also worked at the same establishment, as sous-chef in the kitchen. So that fits in with what we already know. And what it says on the Hall's website.'

'I think we should look some more into Marotta's background,' Jago suggested.

Monty made a note, and then looked up. 'Okay. But for now, according to his LinkedIn profile, he did his training at various hotels in Basilicata in southern Italy where he grew up. His last position was as commis chef in a Michelin starred restaurant in a city called Matera, so he was more than qualified to get a job as sous-chef at the hotel in Mayfair.'

Jago grunted, not impressed. 'I still think he was hiding something.'

'I think we've all gathered you're not his biggest fan, James,' Maeve commented mildly. 'I also think we should concentrate on the people who are still alive, don't you? Last time I looked, dead people don't commit crimes.'

Jago felt Olivia's eyes on him, but refused to meet her gaze. 'Okay, we'll come back to him.' He wasn't letting it go altogether. 'What did you find out about Dylan Bonnar?'

Monty's face brightened. 'His internet search brought up

much the same information as Ruan's. Same sort of jobs and work experience. All in the hotel industry. Like a mirror image of Ruan's on the hotel website. Which is weird.'

Jago's eyes swivelled to where Olivia was sitting, gazing out of the window at the gardens behind him. Her face gave nothing away but he could imagine the wheels turning inside her head. Whatever she was thinking, she was keeping it to herself.

'Did you know Dylan had been involved in the hotel industry?' he asked, more sharply than he intended. 'He certainly doesn't strike me as the type who enjoys dealing with people, which I would have thought comes pretty high up the list of skills you need in that business.'

'No.' Olivia finally met his eyes. 'I had no idea. He never talks about the past.'

'Anyway,' Monty butted in, his excitement growing, 'I thought it was all a bit odd so I went back further, found his school and university records and put together a complete timeline of his life. Until a few years ago that is, when he seemed to go off the radar.'

Jago's eyes didn't leave Olivia's face, which wasn't doing a very good job of hiding her feelings anymore.

'Before anyone says anything else, let me finish. The best is yet to come.' Monty was in full flow. 'I decided to do the same for Ruan. And that's where it gets interesting.' He paused for effect and Jago caught a glimpse of the successful barrister Monty could become.

'When you do a bit of deeper digging, Ruan did go to university in London at the same time as Dylan, but he went to the School of Oriental and African Studies in Bloomsbury and studied for a BA in Languages and Cultures, specialising in Middle Eastern languages.'

Jago frowned. He tried to imagine the fun-loving,

flamboyant Ruan Braithwaite he knew studying heavy-going Middle Eastern languages and failed. It was one hell of a swerve to go from that into the hotel industry. Judging by Olivia's face, she was having similar thoughts.

Maeve was more impatient. 'Get to the point, Monty, please.'

Monty looked wounded, but wasn't about to defy his pupil supervisor. 'Okay. A year after graduating, Ruan applied for army officer training at Sandhurst, passed the commissioning course with flying colours and joined the Intelligence Corps.' He paused again. 'And that's when it gets even more interesting.'

Jago and Maeve exchanged glances this time. 'Please, Monty.'

'Well, as he's obviously a retired army officer, I tried to find his military records, but I immediately hit a brick wall. It's all classified information.'

'What does that mean?' Maeve's tone was sharp.

'It means he was no ordinary soldier.' Monty's gaze swept them all, his eyes shining. 'But I have an uncle, the one I mentioned earlier, who works for the MOD, and as I've always been his favourite nephew he was happy to help me.'

'Jesus, Monty!' Maeve's voice rose an octave, her Irish accent stronger. 'I don't like the sound of this—'

'Just tell us the highlights,' Jago butted in. There was no way he was going to stop this now.

'He did five years in the Intelligence Corps and then passed selection to Special Forces.'

Jago felt his pulse quicken. 'SAS, SBS?'

'No.' Monty grinned. 'SRR.'

'What's that?' Olivia spoke up.

'The Special Reconnaissance Regiment. It's a relatively recently formed Special Forces Unit of the British Army and…' Monty read from his laptop screen. '…their main role is to support the SAS and SBS in their special operations by providing close target reconnaissance, surveillance and "eyes-on" intelligence.' He looked up. 'My uncle says very little information about them is ever leaked into the public domain.'

'Not a fighting force then?' asked Jago.

'Definitely not, although they're trained with the other Special Forces in some skills like close-quarters combat and advanced driving. But their role is to identify human targets through surveillance and infiltration so they can be attacked and eliminated by other Special Forces units. So, they plant bugging devices, hidden cameras and use covert methods of entering buildings and cars, and electronic surveillance gear for eavesdropping, etc.' Monty scanned his screen. 'Oh yes, and because of the nature of most of their work in the last decade with the War on Terror and so on, it is believed that many of the operatives are fluent in Middle Eastern languages. And they work closely with MI5, MI6 and other foreign intelligence organisations too.'

Silence fell on the room as everyone digested that latest bit of information.

'Let's recap a little.' Maeve was obviously struggling to cope with Monty's discoveries. 'You're telling us that Ruan Braithwaite, proprietor of Peneglos Hall, was in the UK's Special Forces. I wouldn't have thought the hotel business was the usual onward career path for someone like that.'

'No. He has the most amazing, unblemished military record. You name it, he's been there, according to my uncle, even places I doubt you've ever heard of. There's probably more information that you need top-level security clearance to find. Do you want me to ask my uncle to try?'

'No thanks' Jago said quickly, his mind still reeling. 'We get the picture. And we don't want to get your uncle into trouble.'

He turned to Maeve whose stunned expression was slowly turning to one of admiration.

'Jesus, James. We've unleashed a monster...'

'Thank you.' Monty grinned. 'Well, to finish up on Ruan, he finally retired from the army two years ago at the rank of Major, after twenty years' service.'

Another silence fell, and then Olivia spoke up. 'Do his military records contain any photographs of him?'

Monty cleared his throat. 'I have a copy of his official military ID photo. It may be from a few years ago and not the best quality but—'

'I'm not going to ask you how you got hold of that, Monty,' Maeve interrupted, her tone resigned. 'But this is the end of it. For now, anyway. I hate to think how many laws you've broken today and I don't want you to get the taste of the other side of the fence and decide you find it more exciting.'

'My uncle said not to worry about it, he's very good at covering his tracks.'

Jago sighed. He was way out of his comfort zone now. 'Show us then, Monty... we might as well be hanged for a sheep and all that.'

The four of them gathered around Monty and his laptop. Jago caught a waft of Olivia's familiar perfume and suddenly wondered what the hell they were all getting themselves into. But there was no going back now.

'Here he is,' Monty announced as he zoomed in on the grainy photo so they could all see it.

Jago took in the younger, slightly broader, smoother-faced man in full military uniform that looked pretty much like the Ruan Braithwaite he'd met on a few occasions.

'Is that him?' Maeve demanded. 'Get up the other photos we have of him, so we can compare.'

Monty did so and he, Maeve and Jago compared the photos one by one.

'Well, I've never met the guy,' commented Maeve, 'and I agree the military photo is a bit grainy, but they look the same to me. What do you think, James, you've met him?'

Jago sat back. 'I reckon it's the same person. Olivia? You know him best.'

Olivia pulled the laptop closer to her, having scrabbled in her bag for her reading glasses. She went very quiet.

'Do you agree, Olivia?' Maeve asked. 'Is that Ruan Braithwaite?'

'No.' Olivia's voice was so quiet they all had to lean in to hear her. 'I don't think it is.'

# 23

'Look at his nose, his ears, even his mouth. They're all different.' Olivia stabbed at the features of the two men, the images now side by side on Monty's laptop screen, as her telltale hot pinpricks began marching up her spine, through her neck and into her scalp. Something wasn't right. She watched as looks were exchanged between Monty, Maeve and Jago. Three faces turned to her, two of them bearing the same expression of confusion and incredulity. Jago simply raised his eyebrow, obviously taking her words seriously and making her heart lighten.

'They look pretty similar to me.' Maeve peered more closely at the screen.

'Is pretty similar good enough?' Olivia demanded. 'I'm telling you, those images are not of the same person.' She sent a desperate glance in Jago's direction.

He took one more look at the image and then leant back in his chair, the picture of calm.

'I think we should listen to Olivia. She's good with faces. Trust me.' Jago's expression became more intense. 'Show them your journal, Olivia, then they'll understand your attention to detail.'

It was the first time Jago had addressed her directly since they'd all started talking and Olivia looked at him. He knew she didn't like showing people her drawings, mainly because they usually revealed her thoughts about the people she was committing to paper as well as their faces. She'd stopped doing it after the murders in Penbartha, but had recently started again and was quite pleased with a drawing she'd done of Ruan and Lucinda during one planning meeting. Perhaps she could just show them that one, to prove her point.

Olivia pulled it out of her bag, opened it to the relevant page and put the journal on the desk.

'So, look at his nose. It's a totally different shape from the one in the photograph. It's wider, shorter, there's no bump on the bridge and the nostrils are wider.' Olivia pointed to the features on each picture. 'And look at his mouth. It's not as wide as on the military photograph, the lips are not as full and his chin is more pointed.'

'Wow, that's incredible, Olivia!' Monty was impressed with her observation skills.

'I drew this in a mind-numbingly boring planning meeting that I was just sitting in on to give my business partner moral support. It was the only way I could stop myself from falling asleep. Hence the detail.' She turned to Jago and Maeve. 'Do you see what I mean about his features?'

Maeve nodded. 'Now you've pointed it out in such detail yes, I do. The only explanation I can come up with off the top of my head is cosmetic surgery and I take it we're all happy to rule that out?'

Jago grimaced. 'I think that's extremely unlikely. Don't you, Olivia?'

She nodded. 'Yes. Those photos of who we think of as

Ruan from his London hotel days a few years ago show his features are the same as now. He hasn't had the time to undergo extensive cosmetic surgery. And I don't think he's the type.' Olivia pulled her journal back towards her, unwilling to share it any longer.

Maeve tapped her pen against her teeth, lost in thought. 'So do we all accept that Ruan Braithwaite in the military photograph is the real one?'

'I really don't think the military would go back and doctor ID photographs. Especially ones that aren't supposed to be in the public domain.' Jago shot a look at Monty, who reddened.

'Right,' said Maeve. 'So, we've got two mysteries here now. The murders that have taken place on Peneglos Hall land and the fact that the man we know as the proprietor, Ruan Braithwaite, doesn't appear to be the real Ruan Braithwaite. Are we all agreed?' There was a general murmur of consent, so she continued. 'Do we believe the two are connected? Or are they separate issues?'

Olivia's stomach churned. 'Are you saying that the man we know as Ruan might be behind the murders?'

'Well, he's obviously masquerading as someone he's not,' Maeve replied calmly. 'Whether he's a murderer is another question. I think we should concentrate on where the real Ruan is to begin with.'

'And we still don't know what's happened to Dy—' Olivia stopped mid-sentence, her brain racing as a sudden bolt of recognition hit her. She opened her journal, flipping through page after page of drawings, mind maps and lists until she found what she was looking for. She pushed the open journal back into the middle of the desk and pointed at the page, her heart hammering in her chest.

It was a pencil drawing of Dylan Bonnar, sitting cross-legged on the floor of his potting shed, oiling one of the estate's vintage wooden-handled forks. Olivia had captured the sun and the shadows of his sharply angled, bearded face and wild hair; his face a picture of sheer concentration.

'Who the hell is that? He looks like the wild man of Borneo!' Maeve exclaimed.

'It's Dylan. Dylan Bonnar.'

'Bloody hell! I wouldn't want to meet him on a dark night,' Maeve remarked, a little testily. 'But can we just concentrate on one missing person at a time?'

'No!' Olivia protested, suddenly annoyed. 'Look at the face: the bump on his nose, the lips, the cheekbones. I thought it was Dylan Bonnar, but it's not! It's Ruan Braithwaite. Look!'

The three barristers loomed over the drawing, comparing it to the military photograph. Jago was the first to concede that Olivia had a point. 'The hair and the beard cover up a lot of his face, but I agree the nose and the cheekbones are the same.'

Maeve was not so easily convinced.

'Let me try something.' Monty pulled his laptop to him, tapped a few keys, sucked his teeth and tapped a few more. Then he pushed his laptop back to the middle of the desk. 'There!'

They all leaned in again to see a series of photographs on the screen.

'Explain please, Monty.' Maeve still sounded annoyed.

'I've run some reverse imaging on the photos we think are of Ruan Braithwaite and then input this drawing. They don't come up as a match.'

'Is that a foolproof testing method?' Maeve's tone was beginning to grate a little on Olivia's nerves.

'I'm not sure it would stand up in court,' Monty admitted. 'But it's an indication and I can do some more digging,'

'The beard and the hair are an ideal disguise,' Jago

admitted. 'You don't really see past them when you meet him and he never hangs around for long enough to get to know him. I reckon Olivia's right. And it would tally with something Trenow said about not being able to find out anything about him.'

Olivia ignored Maeve's hiss of despair. 'I know I'm right and it makes sense of so much. He didn't like talking about himself at all and I can see why now.'

'Okay, okay.' Maeve sighed. 'Let's just accept that for some reason Ruan and Dylan have swapped identities, although it's a bloody weird thing to do in my opinion. But if they have, they have. Any idea when they started this?'

Olivia felt Maeve's green eyes pin her to the spot, and she immediately pulled back her shoulders and tilted her chin.

'I reckon it was before the old man – Charles Braithwaite – died. He would have had to be in on it to make it work. That's when Dylan, as I know him, came to live at the Hall and Ruan started work in London, after being abroad. That's what I was told anyway, I've only got to know him over the last few months. I always dealt with Ruan over the actual work to the Hall.'

'Do you reckon anyone else knows? Who's he close to? Any of the staff? What about the sous-chef he deals with in the kitchen?'

'Lexie Crawford checks out completely.' Monty referred to his notes. 'There's nothing to suggest she had any connection whatsoever to anyone at Peneglos Hall before she replied to an advert earlier this year for the position as sous-chef. She was working up in the Highlands of Scotland and only arrived in Cornwall six weeks ago, having been interviewed by the current Ruan.'

'Lexie's the only full-time member of staff so far, apart from Gabe.' Olivia winced and quickly told them about her being Gabe's supposed alibi. 'Dylan looked out for her, in a brotherly kind of way.'

Maeve sniffed. 'And what about Lucinda? Are she and Ruan in a relationship? Or are they business partners? Would he have told her about this identity swap?'

The questions came quick and fast and Olivia suddenly knew what it felt like to be cross-examined in court. Rather than appealing for Jago to object on her behalf, she stood her ground.

'I don't think Lucinda knows. She's too invested in the hotel. And totally committed to it,' Olivia replied, striving for a neutral tone. 'Would she be, if she didn't think Ruan was the real heir? It's a pretty big secret to expect anyone else to keep, isn't it? Surely the fewer people who know, the less chance there is of it getting out?'

'Don't they say that a secret's worth depends on the people from whom it must be kept?' Jago intervened mildly. 'Ruan and Dylan may have got to the point that they believe it themselves. I agree it would be interesting to know why they decided to swap identities, but if it was done openly and fairly and without any intention to commit fraud or cause harm, then I don't see they've committed any offence. Do you, Maeve?'

'It's still a bloody weird thing to do,' Maeve muttered. 'But I agree it's distracting us from the real issue here.'

'Do you think the real Ruan may have been acting undercover in an unofficial capacity to find out what's going on down there?' Monty suggested.

'Unlikely. Their decision to swap identities must predate all the stuff that's going on now,' Jago commented.

Olivia pushed back her chair from the desk and stood up to stretch her knotted muscles. She'd spent far too long confined inside and she wasn't used to it.

Maeve stood too, her smile trying to show there were no hard feelings. Just frustration. 'I think we need to take a break, stretch our legs, that sort of thing. I have a phone call to make and then I'll sort out tea and coffee. See you back here in twenty?'

---

Olivia found an empty bench under the shade of a tree and sat down heavily, trying to slow her thoughts down. After about five minutes a shadow fell across her and a familiar deep voice interrupted her peace. Her heart quickened. *Pull yourself together, Wells.*

'May I join you?'

She scooted up the bench silently.

'Don't let Maeve get under your skin. It's just her way.'

Olivia nodded, acutely aware that this was the closest she'd been to Jago in a while and yet here they were, acting like polite strangers.

'Can we talk later?' Jago's voice sounded uncertain. 'I think I owe you an explanation.'

'Yes, you do. That's one of the reasons I'm here.' She stared straight ahead.

'Not just for my top-rate investigation skills?'

She could tell he was trying to lighten the mood but she still didn't look at him. 'I'm really pissed off with you, Jago.'

'I know you are,' he said easily. 'And I don't blame you. But I would like the opportunity to explain. Then you can be properly pissed off with me, knowing all the facts.'

Olivia watched a bee buzz into the centre of a clump of pink roses in the border in front of them, and felt an overwhelming sense of tiredness and longing to be back in Penbartha.

'I'm tired. And I want to go home.'

'So do I.' The emotion in those three words made Olivia turn to him. He managed a small smile. 'Let's try and get to the bottom of this with the help of some of London's finest legal minds and then we'll go. Okay?' He held his hand out to her as if to shake it, but she let her hand rest in his for a few seconds.

'Okay.'

———

'Right, now we're all refreshed let's get back to the point in question and leave the business of the interchangeable identities of Ruan and Dylan to one side for a moment. All agreed?' Maeve suggested as they gathered back around Jago's desk.

'Good idea. I think we need to not lose sight of the fact that three victims, all with some sort of link to Albania have been found dead on Peneglos land.' Jago's solemn tone matched his expression. 'We have reason to believe that the first, Agnes Toska, may have been in Cornwall in some kind of unofficial protection set-up. Her parents, who still live in Albania, have confirmed her identity and that she came to the UK, apparently willingly, four months ago. The second is an unknown male with a double-headed eagle, the national symbol of Albania, tattooed on his left deltoid. And the third, Gabe Marotta, was found fatally stabbed, with a similar tattoo in the same place. And the weapon used was then conveniently placed in Dylan Bonnar's dwelling place and Bonnar himself has disappeared.'

'And now we know Dylan's real identity we can be pretty sure that he wouldn't be so stupid to leave a murder weapon in his hut and he's been set-up,' Olivia added.

'Well, I don't think the police are going to have much luck

finding him with his background,' Monty commented. 'He's been trained to sleep rough, live off the land and leave no trace of his presence, not to mention all his experience of surveillance. He'll be able to look after himself.'

A vision of Dylan's utilitarian hut flashed through Olivia's mind and she brightened. 'And it also means that the person who's set Dylan up will also have trouble tracking him down. Which is good news.'

'Before we get to that, we still need to work out how and why two of these three victims got to Peneglos Hall and what or who is the link between them,' Jago pointed out.

'Well, I guess the attraction for them was the same as for every other economic migrant wanting to come to the UK,' Maeve offered. 'More opportunities, higher wages, better standard of living, shall I go on?'

'We get the picture.' Jago sighed. 'Are we assuming they're here out of choice rather than fear? That they've come willingly, if illegally? The Fal Staff women didn't say they knew for a fact that Agnes had been forced here, did they?'

'I don't think they ask too many questions. I think they just got the impression she was trying to get away from someone,' Olivia confirmed.

'Okay. So assuming they're here willingly, how in God's name did they end up in Cornwall?' asked Maeve. 'Were they after the scenery, the weather or what?'

'Or is it because the usual Dover to Calais crossing is practically impossible to do now without being stopped by Border Force and detained, before being sent back to Albania under the new communique, so they're having to find new routes?' Monty suggested.

'I think you're clutching at straws a bit there, Monty-boy.' Maeve laughed. 'This could easily turn into *Eighty Days Around the World* if we're not careful. I think we need to refocus.

Whatever the reason they ended up in Cornwall, let's just accept they did and work from there. We're losing sight of the fact that we're looking into three murders. And we need to establish a motive, at the very least.' She turned her gaze to Olivia. 'Are you okay? You've gone a bit of a funny colour.'

Olivia nodded quickly. 'I'm fine, thanks. I had a sudden thought, but it's gone. And I agree we need to concentrate on the fact that whoever killed Gabe may be trying to find Dylan to do the same to him.'

'What makes you so sure of that?' Jago spoke up.

'Dylan had a real thing about Gabe. Didn't like him at all.'

Maeve's ears pricked up. 'Any reasons?'

'Apart from using Lexie as a false alibi? Dylan played his cards very close to his chest, and we know why now. He just said he had a feeling Gabe was up to no good. He kept finding him down by the cove, and when Dylan asked him why he liked swimming there he said it was because it reminded him of Italy. He was always asking about weather patterns and tides and the best conditions to swim.'

'Sounds fair enough. Cornish tides can be a real pain.'

Olivia looked at Jago in despair, suddenly overwhelmed with a sense of fatigue and helplessness. Her brain was jammed up with too many thoughts and her body was full of aches. She needed to rest and be alone with her thoughts.

'Actually, Maeve's right, I don't feel very well. Do you mind if I go back to your flat, Jago, and have a lie-down?'

Her ploy worked. Jago was at her side in an instant. It was rare for Olivia to plead illness and his face was full of concern. 'Of course not.' He turned to the others. 'Do you mind if we carry on with this another time?'

Maeve looked at her watch. 'Not at all. With a bit of luck, I'll make it out to Barnes for school pick-up and score some brownie points with Joey. Hope you feel better soon, Olivia.'

Only Monty looked disappointed. 'I'll do some more digging, James, if that's okay with you?'

'Fine. Just promise me you won't go infiltrating any more top-secret government files. We don't want you ruining a glittering legal career before it's even started.'

# 24

A door opening woke Olivia from a deep sleep in an unfamiliar but cool and shady room. She reared up from the bed in a panic, and then sank back down onto the pillows as Jago placed a tray with two mugs of tea and a plate of biscuits on the bed. *Of course, I'm in London. In Jago's guest room.*

'You've had two hours, so I thought I'd better wake you so you can sleep tonight.' He sat down on the edge of the bed and took his mug off the tray. 'How are you feeling now?'

Olivia sat up, stretched and winced. She ached all over. 'A bit better, thanks.' Her voice was husky. The result of being strangled by Martin. Whenever she was overtired, her vocal cords and throat betrayed her.

Jago's face tightened. 'You've been overdoing it.'

She lay back down again and gave him a look. 'There's been a lot going on.'

'We need to talk, Olivia. Please.'

'What about?'

'Us.'

She sat up again. 'Is that more important than trying to

find Dylan and getting to the bottom of what's going on at the Hall?'

'To me it is. Right now. And before you say anything, I'm pretty confident that Dylan will be able to look after himself for a few days.' He handed her a mug.

'That was a bit of a surprise, wasn't it?' She sipped at her tea, her mind wandering. 'But it makes sense of a lot of things.'

'Olivia, you're doing it again. Can we just put that aside for a moment, please?'

She looked at him properly then. His face, usually so difficult to read, was all tight with angular lines, but his eyes betrayed his emotions for once. Stress, tiredness, confusion, but mostly regret. Olivia's breath caught in her throat and she knew what she had to do. This was one of the reasons she'd come to London. To sort their relationship out.

She handed Jago her mug and got off the bed. 'Right, let's talk. We both have things that need to be said. But not in here.' She felt him following her silently into the sitting room where she sat down on one sofa and waved him to the other. She needed to keep him at arm's length for this.

He cleared his throat. 'I need to apologise.'

'Yes, you do, but first I need you to explain why you took off from Penbartha like a scalded cat. Leaving me behind with just a pathetic, measly note, wondering what the hell was going on and if I was even going to see you again!'

Jago avoided her eyes. 'I'm sorry. I didn't think it through.'

'No, you didn't. And that's not how relationships work in my book. I can't live my life not knowing if you're going to take off whenever it suits you, without any explanation.'

'It wasn't like that.'

'So, what was it like?'

And he told her. All about the Bregu case and how it had unsettled him, about the waitress's reaction to him at the party, Gabe's theory that she'd recognised him, his fear that Bregu was tracking him, and his decision to leave Penbartha in order to protect Olivia and keep her safe. By the time he'd finished speaking, his voice was wavering and he sounded nothing like the Jago she knew.

Olivia sat and stared at him, his words whirling round and round her mind until they eventually settled in the crack that had been in her heart since he left Penbartha. It was the cement she needed to see this through.

'I'm not a mind reader. I need you to tell me the things that really matter to you. I knew there was something wrong, something worrying you, but you wouldn't talk to me about it, no matter how often I asked. It felt like you didn't trust me.'

He bowed his head. 'I'm sorry. I didn't think it through. I was obsessed with keeping you safe and I thought the less you knew about it the better. I didn't want Bregu to realise how important you were to me and I thought that putting distance between us would put him off the scent.'

'I don't think you should have made that decision by yourself. If we're a partnership we need to do it together. Or else not bother.' She felt the tears burn at the back of her eyes and wiped them away angrily.

Jago was next to her in an instant, catching hold of her hands and turning her head to face him. 'Don't say that. Please. I realise now how stupid I was. But Bregu really got inside my head. I promise it won't happen again.' His blue eyes stared into her face, beseeching her to believe him, and Maeve's words about him floated into her mind.

'One of the reasons I came to London was because there's a big part of me that feels what we've got is far too special to throw away. I've shared everything with you. My hopes, my dreams, my bed, for God's sake! But I'm no longer sure you trust me. And you need to, Jago. Not shut me out. No secrets.

They're my non-negotiables.' She held his gaze and he nodded slowly, and her eyes moved to his mouth, where a tiny quiver of his lips betrayed his usual inscrutability. And she knew he understood.

'It's not a question of trust. I just don't always want to live through everything I've heard in court by talking about it. And I certainly don't want to pollute your mind with some of the things I've seen and heard. When I'm in Penbartha I just want to forget about it.'

'That's fine.' She managed a smile. 'Look, I knew what you did for a living before we got together. Okay, life might have been a lot easier if you really had been just a railway geek with a penchant for steam trains.'

'I'm an enthusiast, not a geek!' he protested.

She smiled again. 'Whatever. I just need to say this, Jago. I'm not blind to your work. I'm actually very proud of you. And I'm not too weak and fragile to be able to share some of it. If something is bothering you, I want you to talk about it rather than bottle it all up and behave like some macho man who can carry the weight of the world on his shoulders all by himself.' She took a breath. 'Because you can't. I know you too well now. And when you deny there's something wrong, I start doubting myself, and doubting whether I really know you at all. If we really are a partnership, let's act like one.'

There, she'd said it. The words and thoughts that had gone round her mind on a loop since she'd read his note. And here he was, sitting next to her, those blue eyes staring into hers. After a while, she wasn't sure whether it was her eyes or his that filled with tears. Everything went blurry and the next thing she knew he had pulled her into his arms and was kissing her wet cheeks.

'I'm so sorry. I just wanted to keep you safe,' he kept repeating.

She pulled away gently so she could look at him properly. 'I can look after myself, remember.' She told him about nearly taking Dylan out in the gardens of Tresillian. 'And now we know he's trained to kill with his bare hands, yet I still managed to hold my own.'

The lop-sided smile she loved so much flashed across his face and they both started to laugh, happy to release some of the tension they'd been holding in for so long. Jago sobered first, his face suddenly serious. 'Look, I know I've not said it before, but I really do—'

The bell pealed and Jago sighed impatiently. 'That had better not be bloody Penny from across the way. I swear she smells your shampoo and...' He heaved himself off the settee and went out into the hall.

He reappeared almost immediately with Monty in his wake.

'You won't believe what I've found out now.'

# 25

Jago had finished giving his order to the waiter and took a deep swig from his bottle of beer. 'That was a bit of a turn up for the books, wasn't it?'

Olivia was captivated by the bright Mexican folk art that adorned the walls of the most shaded restaurant they knew in Covent Garden. They could actually have been in Mexico, Olivia decided, with the low wooden ceilings and walls, dark tables and brightly coloured chairs, and the variety of languages and accents all around them. She helped herself to a nacho.

'There seems to be a never-ending supply of secrets and lies at Peneglos Hall.' Olivia zoned back into Jago's observation. 'Do you reckon anybody is actually who they claim to be?'

'Only Lexie as far as I can make out,' Jago replied, stuffing several nachos into his mouth at once.

'Dylan always reckoned there some complicated dynamic going on between Ruan, Lucinda and Gabe but he couldn't work out what it was.'

'In what way?'

'Ruan told him he didn't like the influence Gabe seemed to have over Lucinda sometimes. Apparently, he'd deliberately do the opposite of whatever Ruan suggested.'

'But Ruan, or whoever we thought Ruan was, is the owner. Surely what he says goes?'

'Lucinda seemed to think having Gabe as head chef was their key to getting the Michelin Green Star and putting the Hall on the UK sustainability map. So she was desperate to keep him happy. And Ruan always maintained that although he had more hotel experience than Lucinda, she had a better long-term vision for the Hall.'

'And did that cause friction between Ruan and Dylan?'

'Yes, it got to the point where they tried not to talk about Lucinda, which I didn't really understand at the time. I just thought Dylan was being a bit overprotective of his best friend. And perhaps a bit jealous that she'd come between them.' Olivia drank from her beer bottle. 'Now, in light of what we know, it makes more sense.'

'He didn't trust Gabe though, did he?' Jago caught hold of Olivia's hand across the table. 'I have to ask you something, but I don't want you to take it the wrong way.'

Olivia stiffened. 'Go on.'

'How can you be so absolutely sure that Dylan isn't at all involved in whatever's going on? It wouldn't be the first time that a murderer has tried to help out in an investigation, would it?'

Heat flooded her face and her hands automatically reached for her throat. 'I remember Martin Lambert very well, thank you. And I'm not going to make that mistake again,' she snapped and tried to pull her hand away, but he held it firmly.

'What is it that makes you so certain?' Jago asked gently.

Olivia hesitated. It was something she'd thought long and

hard about and still wasn't completely sure of the answer. Their meals arrived, giving her more time to formulate her response. She tucked into her chimichanga and murmured appreciatively.

'I've always been drawn to him, I guess.' She saw Jago's face tighten and she hurried to explain. 'Not in a sexual way. Not at all. He reminds me a lot of Mollie when he talks about plants and herbs and the old ways of doing things, so I enjoy spending time with him. Do you understand?'

Jago had taken another mouthful of food and nodded. Olivia knew he understood the way she felt about her godmother and how much she missed her. But there was more to it than that.

'I was intrigued about the way he lived, although he never explained it. Now I understand why he kept it all to himself, and it makes much more sense. He probably saw some pretty awful things during his time in the army and living the way he does gave him the opportunity to drop out of mainstream society, while still being connected to it through Ruan and the Hall.'

Jago looked at her, one eyebrow raised, and she knew she had to tell him. She took a deep breath. 'And he reminds me of my brother.' She shrugged. 'I can't explain why. It's twenty-five years since Aidan died and I don't remember that much about him really. But he was kind and funny and teased me in a way that only brothers do. And Dylan's like that. He's a lot like Aidan would be if he was still alive.' She remembered their conversation about just that and shared it with Jago.

He studied her face carefully, his eyes full of concern. 'You don't think it was finding Agnes's body that brought all that back?'

'No, I don't.' She met his gaze firmly. 'We already had some kind of connection. I know I've got Rocky and he's my oldest friend, but he never knows what to say when I'm upset or confused. He just hands me a grubby hanky, pats me on the back and runs a mile.'

Jago laughed at the expression on her face. 'God knows how he copes with Kitten and all her dramas.'

'He'll get there because he loves her.' Olivia was confident of that. 'Dylan just always knew exactly what to say to comfort me; what questions to ask to help me sort things out in my mind. Lexie said the same. I thought they might be an item at one stage but Dylan said she wasn't his type. Too high maintenance, apparently.'

Jago smiled and Olivia, sitting opposite him with her chin resting on her hand, realised it was a long time since she'd seen him smile properly.

'I'm really sorry I wasn't there for you.' His blue eyes held hers. 'It won't happen again.'

Her heart quickened. 'And you're okay with what I've just told you about Dylan?'

Jago thought for a moment. 'I think I can bring myself to feel grateful that he was there when I was being a total idiot,' he said slowly. 'So now all we have to do is find him so I can thank him in person.'

'Do you reckon he's okay?' Olivia couldn't keep the worry out of her voice.

'I have more confidence in Dylan being able to look after himself, with his Special Forces training, than anyone else I know,' Jago declared. 'And if I know anything, he'll be keeping a very close eye on everything that's going on at Peneglos.' He caught hold of her hand again. 'Do you have any way of getting in touch with him?'

She shook her head. 'He doesn't have a mobile, so I had to go looking for him if I wanted to speak to him.'

'And what if he wanted to get hold of you?'

'He'd borrow Lexie's mobile. Or Cassie's. Or just turn up and lie in wait for me at Tresillian.'

'Not helpful. But understandable.' Jago turned his attention back to his unfinished plate of food and Olivia did the same, suddenly feeling much lighter now she had shared her worries.

She waited until the table was cleared and the waiter had served them with coffee.

'So, what do we now?'

'We need to work out the connection between the murder victims and Peneglos Hall. What are the odds that one person from Albania and two who appear to have fairly strong links to the country would be found dead in the same garden within a relatively short space of time, unless they have a killer or something else in common?'

'Dylan reckoned Gabe murdered Agnes because it was him she recognised rather than you, but he seized on your reaction to her dropping the tray to deflect interest away from him. And the fact it wound you up just added to the thrill.'

Jago glowered into his coffee.

'And he was very suspicious of the fact that he was always hanging around in different parts of the garden, meeting various people, some who had no right to be there.'

'Who was he meeting?'

'Fairly often it was Lucinda but we assumed that was about menus and such like. They both liked the sun and were happy to have their meetings outside. He always said it reminded him of Italy.' Olivia paused. 'On one occasion, he told me he heard Gabe talking to someone on the phone. And he said he was pretty sure they weren't speaking Italian. That made him really suspicious.' The memory of them stalking Gabe and another man popped into her mind. And she reddened, hoping Jago wouldn't notice. But his eagle eyes didn't miss a thing and without even being asked, Olivia came clean. Being truthful worked both ways.

'So, what did this other guy look like?' Jago didn't comment on her actions, but his expression said it all.

'I didn't get as good a look at him as Dylan did. He had the binoculars. He wasn't as tall as Gabe, but broader and stockier. Dark, short hair, neat beard. He was wearing a tee shirt and jeans—'

'Tattoos?'

'Yes. On both arms. But I was too far away to see clearly.'

'And where were they in the garden?'

'In the woodland, at the bottom, before you go down to the cove—' Olivia stopped suddenly, trying to grasp the thought that was floating round the back of her mind, but couldn't.

When she looked up at Jago, he was watching her closely. 'What are you thinking?'

'I'm trying to work out what the connection is with the gardens. Why doesn't he meet these people away from the Hall, where there's less chance of being seen?'

'It's the summer, and we're in the middle of a heatwave. The gardens at Peneglos are huge from what I remember. It seems obvious, to me anyway, to meet there, and relatively easy to avoid any people. They were probably completely oblivious of Dylan, if he's as silent as you say.'

'You're right,' Olivia admitted. 'And he was a bit obsessed with all the stories of Ruan's ocean-faring ancestors who basically made most of their money from free trading.'

'Hmm.' Jago went quiet. 'Wasn't that just smuggling loads of treasures from wherever the packet ships travelled to?'

'Exactly.' The notion that had been niggling at her suddenly ricocheted to the front of her brain. 'That's it!' She turned to Jago, her entire body prickling in anticipation. 'I've just thought of something. It might be crazy…'

'What?' Jago sat upright.

'It's not the garden Gabe was interested in, it's the cove! What if he decided to use it for the same reasons? Perhaps he was smuggling goods into the cove?'

Jago went very still. 'What about the people who died?'

'Perhaps they were in on it too, and got greedy or threatened to spill the beans. If we're talking about a lot of money that would certainly give Gabe the motive to want them out of the way.'

Jago was quiet as he digested Olivia's theory. She sat on the edge of her seat, shredding her paper napkin.

'What treasures do you reckon they were smuggling?'

'Drugs? Wouldn't that be the obvious thing? Isn't it the most valuable commodity on the black market?'

Jago's knuckles went white round his coffee cup. 'Not anymore.'

Olivia stared, her heart thumping. 'What then?'

'People.'

---

Jago snapped back into barrister mode, called for the bill and paid quickly before ushering Olivia out of the door and into the humid London night.

She struggled to keep up with his long, determined strides and had to pull at his arm.

'Slow down, Jago, please! There's nothing we can do right now is there?'

He slowed his pace and took hold of her hand, tucking it into the crook of his arm. 'No, you're probably right. And we might be completely wrong.'

Olivia wasn't convinced. 'You don't believe that, do you?'

'No. Smuggling people has higher profits and lower risks

than smuggling drugs. It looks like Gabe found an ideal way to get around all the new legislation that's making it harder for Albanians to get across the Channel, by diverting to Cornwall and avoiding the Border Force patrols altogether. He must have been charging a fortune for that!'

'Do you reckon they were following the routes the packet ships used all those years ago and avoiding France altogether?'

Jago stopped in his tracks. 'I think you're right! If they can get the poor sods who are so desperate to leave Albania overland across the Balkans to the north-east of Spain, they can easily get to Falmouth by boat.'

'It would have to be done by some sort of motorised boat, as it's a twenty-four-hour crossing. To Santander anyway, probably longer to Corunna.' Olivia spoke with feeling, recalling unwanted memories of sea-sickness-filled journeys as a young child.

'Really? Well, I'm sure you can always pay some dodgy fisherman to do it and conveniently turn off their marine vessel tracking information at the essential moments.'

'And you reckon there would be a market for that in Albania?'

'A massive market. Gabe must have thought all his Christmases had come at once.' It sounded like he was grinding his teeth. 'Bastard!'

A couple walking past shot Olivia an alarmed look as they overheard Jago's outburst and looked at her questioningly. She smiled at them and pulled Jago by the arm. 'Let's get home, Jago, we're causing a scene.'

---

Once back at his apartment, Jago paced up and down.

'Something's not adding up, but as soon as we've joined all the dots I'm sure it'll make sense.

'Do you think it will have stopped, now Gabe's dead?'

Jago stopped pacing. 'Unlikely. Gabe probably stepped on some more important smuggler's toes and has been removed so they can move in and take over.'

'Dylan always said that Gabe was obsessed with high tides. That must have been when they brought them in.'

'When's the next high tide?' Jago's eyes pierced into hers and she fumbled with her mobile to get to the Tide Times app. She felt sick.

'Day after tomorrow.'

'Right. That gives us time.' Jago pulled his own mobile out of his pocket.

'Are you calling Trenow?' Olivia crossed her fingers.

'Too bloody right I am.'

# 26

Cassie gazed out across the creek from her balcony, trying to draw her usual energy and comfort from its constant movement, but the unease fluttering in her chest made it impossible to relax. As soon as Gabe's body had been found, almost the entire gardens at Peneglos Hall were cordoned off by the police. She and the volunteers had been told not to return until further notice so they could preserve the crime scene. This had given Cassie unwanted time to think. And for once, rather than thinking about other people, she had turned her thoughts inwards.

Cassie recognised she was the sort of person who liked to live on the edge of other people's lives and hated being the centre of attention. She'd enjoyed living her life vicariously through Kitten and Olivia since she'd been in Penbartha. Her girls, as she thought of them, seemed happy and settled. Cassie may have had a recent wobble about Jago's strange behaviour after the party, and she certainly wasn't impressed with the way he had taken off to London without any explanation, but she was full of admiration for Olivia going after him to sort everything out.

Was that something that she would ever do, Cassie wondered? She certainly hadn't in the past and now, sometimes, when Kitten was with Rocky and Olivia was with Jago, she felt like a third wheel. For the first time in years, she was beginning to think it might be good to be part of a couple and have someone to share her life with. Was she too old and set in her ways to change?

Cassie sighed as she faced facts. In all honesty, she was more likely to take up sleuthing than get involved with another man. And talking of sleuthing, she'd been turning lots of things that Dylan had said over in her mind. Why was she doing that? Was she just trying to take her mind off things, or was she trying to help him? Or, was she just trying to prove that there was more to Cassie Polmere than met the eye?

Mylor put his shaggy head on her bare knee, and nuzzled her hand, giving it a warm, wet lick with his gentle tongue. Poor boy, she thought, stroking his head gently. He was like her; only ever truly happy when all his favourite humans were together. Zennor, lying out in the sun, opened one eye and seeing that her brother was getting a fuss when she wasn't, leapt nimbly onto Cassie's lap and pushed her little nose under her free hand. Cassie's heart squeezed with the love she felt for them – the last living link she had to George and Mollie who had rescued her when she most needed it and given her a wonderful new start in life.

'Come on then, you two. We can either stay here and feel sorry for ourselves, or we can go for a walk. What do you reckon?'

The two dogs went crazy at the magic word, jumping up, whining and running around in excited circles, their tails wagging furiously. Cassie laughed as she walked into the house to fetch their leads. She was just picking them off the hook in the hall when both dogs stood still for a moment, heads cocked, eyes staring at the door. A split second later they set up a volley of barking, announcing a visitor. Cassie sighed.

'Sorry, is this a bad time?' She could just about hear Sam O'Driscoll's cheery tone above the noise and she shushed them quickly.

'A bit. I was just about to take the dogs out for a walk.'

Sam looked up and Cassie followed the direction of his gaze to a perfectly blue, cloudless sky. 'Isn't it a bit hot?'

Cassie stiffened. 'I'm going along the lane to the walkway and then down to the Waiting Rooms. It's all in the shade, so I don't think I'll be committing any dog cruelty offences, sergeant.'

O'Driscoll's face folded into an embarrassed expression. 'I wasn't suggesting that you were. God, I've done it again.' He rubbed the back of his neck. 'I'm so sorry. I'm always saying the wrong thing to you, aren't I?' He stood on the step, and looked at her, his mouth turned down, and under the thick expressive eyebrows, his hazel eyes were full of embarrassment. He was wearing a navy polo shirt, stone-coloured cargo shorts and trainers and she could see instantly that he hadn't let any of his boxer's muscles turn to fat, and then was cross with herself for noticing.

'Is this a business call?' She raised an eyebrow and opened the door wider to let him in.

'A rare day off. The boss has gone to meet the super and was good enough to spare me from the inevitable bollocking for not catching the killer yet,' he said, submitting himself to Mylor's thorough sniffing.

Half of Cassie wanted Sam to freeze and back away, but he

just bent down and patted the dog until he rolled over for a tummy rub.

'I wasn't sure you'd be a dog person,' Cassie admitted.

'Me? I love them.' Mylor sighed in delight and flopped down on Sam's feet. 'And what about you, pretty girl?'

This was the real test, Cassie thought. Mylor loved everybody, unless they were upsetting his favourite humans. Zennor was much more circumspect. A little like her really, Cassie decided, watching the dog with a smile. She approached Sam warily, much like she approached anything new, her little nose quivering with suspicion. Sam simply stood with his hands down by his sides, Mylor still sitting on one foot with his tail thumping against the floor. Zennor sniffed each bare leg carefully and circled Sam twice. Only then did she sit down and solemnly offer a dainty white paw to him. Cassie was astonished. Zennor didn't usually like men, with the exception of Jago, Rocky and Dylan. She had definitely not liked Martin Lambert. *Perhaps I should be more dog.*

Sam threw her a questioning look.

'You can pick her up if you like,' Cassie told him. 'Just be careful with her back.'

He bent down and murmuring gently to her, slipped his right hand underneath Zennor's chest and then, as he lifted her up, used his other hand to tuck her rump into his body. He was rewarded with a dainty lick on his nose from the little dog, who then gave his face and neck a thorough sniffing, before sighing contentedly, snuggling in and closing her eyes.

There was something about a man who looked like he'd be more at home in a boxing ring or with a Rottweiler on the end of a rope, holding a little white dog with comfort and ease. Part of the ice that had been packed round Cassie's heart for over twenty-five years started to melt and she had to swallow hard.

'Well, are we walking, or what?' Mylor erupted into another round of excited barking and even Zennor decided she'd had enough fuss and wanted to go out. Cassie handed Sam a lead. 'Coming with us?'

Sam looked taken aback by the friendly invitation. 'Only if I'm not intruding?'

'I think the dogs would be put out if you didn't.' Cassie headed down the steps. 'Especially as you seem to have passed their sniff test.'

———

They followed the grassy spine of the lane, now baked into a hard ridge by the sun, and walked along the south bank of the creek, keeping to the dappled shade of the ancient oak trees. They chatted about all sorts of inconsequential things as they walked and once again, Cassie found him surprisingly easy company and realised she was enjoying talking to someone who was distanced from the events that had clouded Penbartha over the last year. It made a nice change.

As they turned off the lane, they unclipped the dogs' leads and let them run ahead. Their conversation naturally followed suit.

'I had no idea you were so knowledgeable about dogs,' said Cassie.

'I grew up with them. We always had at least two and my mam and dad treated us all the same. Their parenting philosophy basically revolved around ignoring bad behaviour and rewarding the good.'

Cassie laughed. 'Sounds better than mine. It's a shame you

haven't got a dog of your own. But I suppose it wouldn't work with your shift patterns.'

'Well, we don't really do shifts in CID, just long, long days when we're on a case, so it still wouldn't be fair. I suppose we could have had one years ago, but my wife was allergic.'

Cassie's internal alarm system pinged. In the past, she would have immediately changed the subject, or run a mile. But not anymore. He'd mentioned his ex-wife before, and this time she wasn't going to let it bother her. She could do this. She took a deep breath, pushed her sunglasses up her nose and tried to speak in a normal voice.

'I'd forgotten you'd mentioned you're divorced. How long?'

Sam stopped walking. 'I'm not divorced…'

Cassie speeded up before he got to the end of his sentence, her heart suddenly in her mouth.

'It's not like that, let me finish… please, Cassie.' He caught hold of her arm and spun her round.

She pulled away instinctively, but stood in front of him, her mind totally blank. 'You don't need to finish. Or explain. We're just going for walk.' Her voice was unnaturally high, but Sam didn't seem to notice.

'I'd like to explain. My wife died four years ago. We'd been married for six.' He spoke calmly, but Cassie could see a flash of sadness cross his face.

'I'm so sorry.' She reached out and touched his arm. 'Let's carry on. We go left here, inland onto the old railway line.'

He nodded and they were soon in the cool of the huge trees and bushes that lined the network of trails so popular with walkers, cyclists and runners. Sam eventually broke the silence. 'Sorry to tell you like that. But I wanted you to know.'

Cassie just nodded.

'Ovarian cancer. There were no signs. Until it was too late and it had spread.'

'What was her name?'

Sam stopped and stared at her. 'Most people don't ask me that. They don't see her as a person. They want the gory details of the cancer. Cecilia.' His voice broke as he said her name and he tried to cover it with a cough.

'That's a lovely name. Unusual.' Cassie started walking again, hoping the distraction would help him and then added, unnecessarily, 'She's the patron saint of music, isn't she?'

'She is, yes. And thank you. We met while I was still in the army, but when we got married, I decided to join the Met. She was a real city girl and loved London. The army life wouldn't have suited her.'

'How did you meet?' Cassie had the feeling Sam wanted to talk about Cecilia.

He smiled at the memory. 'At an army charity rugby match. I was captain of the winning team. Two of her brothers were playing for the opposition and we were all in the scrum together.' He chuckled. 'You get to know someone pretty quickly that way.'

Cassie laughed. *Ah, he was a rugby player, not a boxer. So that explains the bashed-in face and the muscled body.*

'Do you still play?'

'Not since Cecilia died. I'm too old and battered now. Although I like keeping in shape and I've found a great gym in Truro. In fact, I'm pretty sure I've seen Olivia there, at some of the advanced martial arts classes they run. I think she's a blue belt. Way above me.'

Cassie found herself telling him the tale about Olivia breaking her attacker's arm on this very walkway, as well as Mylor's heroic role in sinking his teeth into the man's upper thigh, leaving him with easily identifiable injuries.

'What a hero!' Sam laughed easily and bent down to pat the

shaggy dog, whose tail was wagging proudly at the mention of his name.

'They make quite a pair,' Cassie agreed. 'Now, the Waiting Rooms are just around the next bend. Fancy a coffee or cold drink?'

'Great idea. And I've been wanting to visit here ever since the boss told me about the cakes. Isn't this where your daughter works?'

'Yes, she's the manager.' Cassie could hear the pride in her voice and smiled. She'd never thought Kitten would settle down to a regular job. In the past she'd always been eager to drop whatever she was doing and rush off to join a march against sewage, plastic, second homes or any other cause she aligned herself with. Now, everyone agreed she was doing a great job at the Waiting Rooms, keeping it fresh and buzzing, while still promoting her causes, but in much more low-key, more inclusive and, quite frankly, more successful ways.

As they rounded the bend, the Waiting Rooms came into view and Sam let out a low whistle. Cassie hadn't stopped to admire it for a long time, but now she saw the beautiful granite building through Sam's eyes.

It sat raised above the walkway on the original platform and blended beautifully into its wooded backdrop. The main building was low, with four arched windows either side of its central double doors and a decorative cream wooden awning stretched the length of the station roof and overhung the platform, giving much-needed shade to today's customers.

Sam let out a low whistle. 'It's what I've come to expect from Olivia and Rocky. They are so talented.' He stood back and let Cassie lead the way up the slope onto the busy platform. 'After you.'

'We'll go inside. It's cooler and quieter.' She saw his expression as the dogs ran to her heels. 'They're welcome.'

Almost every table was full of walkers, tourists and locals enjoying refreshments, and Cassie, spotting a family leaving, hurried over to the sofas under an open window in the far corner while Sam went to queue for their drinks, hoping they would both avoid the eagle gaze of her daughter.

Within seconds Kitten appeared beside her. 'Hey, Mum! Fancy seeing you here.'

Cassie followed Kitten's gaze over to the queue where Sam was chatting good-naturedly to the man in front of him. 'And Sam too! I thought you weren't keen?'

'We're just walking the dogs, Kitten. Nothing more.' She narrowed her eyes. 'Although, as I recall, you were the one who suggested I talked to him about the case to see if I could get any information out of him for Olivia.'

'Is that what you're doing? Really? That doesn't sound like you.'

Cassie smiled.

'Well don't go upsetting him, Mum.' Kitten laughed, unperturbed. 'He looks like he's got a good right hook.'

'He's a rugby player, actually. Not a boxer.'

'Really?' Kitten's eyes went back to the queue. 'Well, whatever he is, have you seen the way he's looking at you?'

Cassie glared. 'More importantly though Kitten, have you seen me looking back at him in any particular way? No! We're just having a walk together. That's all.'

Sam arrived back at the table with a full tray and Kitten turned her thousand-watt smile on the unsuspecting policeman.

'Cappuccino for you, Cass.' He placed it on the low table. 'And puppuccinos, whatever they are, for our four-legged friends. I've been assured they'll be very welcome.'

Mother and daughter took the small paper cups filled with

whipped cream and held them while the dogs devoured them with gusto.

'Good choice, Sam. You've made a friend for life.' Kitten winked at her mum and sashayed her way back to the counter.

———

An hour later, they continued down the walkway past all the other station buildings, with a running commentary provided by Cassie.

'I was right when I said you'd make an excellent guide.' Sam was still laughing at one of her tales. 'Only, now I don't think you should just stick to gardens.' He rubbed the back of his neck. 'Look, Cass, I was wondering if you'd like to go for a drink at the village pub sometime? Or further afield if you'd prefer?' He coughed. 'As long as you don't think it's bad timing or a terrible idea or anything?'

'It's not a terrible idea.' Cassie gulped and then pulled herself together. *What's wrong with two adults wanting to get to know each other?* There was no pressure for it to become anything more, and it probably wouldn't, but it was nice to feel wanted again. She felt a bit of a glow and decided the time had come to seize the moment.

'Yes, let's and before we do, you can update me on any major developments in the case, if Inspector Trenow has been hauled in to explain himself.'

Sam brightened and then sighed. 'We seem to be taking one step forward and two steps back when it comes to trying to locate Gabe's next of kin.'

'That's a shame.'

'It turns out that his real surname wasn't even Marotta, it was Murati, which puts quite a different spin on things.'

'Oh?'

'It seems that his family moved to Italy when Gabe was about ten. He only changed his name to Marotta when he started working in the kitchens in southern Italy, so it took longer to track his family down.'

'Why did he change his name? They don't sound that different to me.'

Sam sighed. 'I really shouldn't be telling you this, Cass. But he's dead, so most data protection regulations don't apply anyway. Can I trust you to keep it to yourself?'

Cassie felt her heart starting to thump. 'Of course.'

'Gabe's family came from Albania.'

Her heart thumped more loudly. 'So that's three people linked to Albania who have met grisly ends in the gardens at Peneglos Hall and you have absolutely no idea what's going on?'

'No.' Sam sounded defeated. 'I don't want you to think I'm underestimating what you've got here and I agree Peneglos Hall is a fabulous setting, but it's not exactly prime Albanian mafia turf, is it?'

'I certainly hope not.'

'So, what has Peneglos Hall got to offer some random Albanians that they can't get anywhere else. Any idea, Cass? Because I'm damned sure I haven't.'

A lightbulb went off in Cassie's head, with what felt like a blinding flash. 'I think I might have, actually.'

Sam's head snapped round to look at her. 'Care to share?'

Her mind was whirring. 'Not yet. I need to talk to Olivia and Jago first.'

A small smile crumpled his teddy bear face. 'You do know that withholding information from the police is an offence?'

She couldn't help but smile back. 'So, arrest me, sergeant.'

# 27

Three nights later Olivia and Cassie were sitting anxiously in the orangery at Tresillian, the lights flickering in the latest storm that was battering the house and creek. They'd given up the pretence of distracting themselves by watching television, as the noise of the rain hitting the windows and the trees thrashing outside made it practically impossible to hear anything else. And so they sat in silence, each clutching a dog for comfort and Steren between their feet, sending anxious glances to each other, not sure what they were hoping for.

It had taken the combined forces of Olivia, Jago and Cassie to persuade Trenow, O'Driscoll and their superiors that the cove at Peneglos Hall was being used for smuggling, either of drugs or people or both, and that because of the tides, the next drop of goods was imminent. Border Force, HMRC and the police had finally been given the green light to conduct a hastily arranged operation to monitor the cove. Everyone was sworn to absolute secrecy.

Nothing had happened for the last two nights, apart from a lot of people getting extremely wet and cross at being out in the stormy weather, on what was beginning to look like a fool's errand. Tonight was the last night all the different agencies were prepared to attend. Feelings were running high.

A huge gust of wind hit the orangery with such force that all the windows rattled, and Olivia and Cassie jumped, each thinking of the men and women who were waiting down in the cove. From beneath a cushion beside Olivia, her mobile rang and she snatched it up.

'Olivia! You need to come now. Dylan's hurt and he needs you!'

'Lucinda? Is that you? I can't really hear you.' Olivia jumped to her feet, phone to one ear, her finger jammed in the other, and ran to the part of the house with the best reception.

'Please, Olivia, come now.' Lucinda's voice rose. 'I'm scared and Dylan really needs you!'

'Okay, okay, stay calm.' Olivia tried to placate an increasingly distraught Lucinda, while her own heart was racing at the thought of Dylan being hurt. 'Have you called an ambulance?'

'Of course I have! But they're overwhelmed and don't know how long they'll be.'

Olivia mimed calling 999 to Cassie, who did as she was asked and then held her own mobile out helplessly as it failed to connect.

'Where's Ruan?'

'I don't know! He went out before the storm started and I can't get hold of him.'

'Where are you?' Olivia rushed to the boot room and started pulling on her waterproof with one hand. 'At the Hall?'

'No! At his hut. Olivia, you really need to…' Lucinda's voice tailed off in a wail and the line was cut.

'What was that all about?' Cassie clutched Olivia's arm as she reappeared in the hall, her eyes wide with panic.

'Dylan's turned up at his hut, hurt.' Olivia grabbed her car keys from the hall table and then hunted for the torch that usually lived there. 'I'm going to help.'

'I'm coming too.' Cassie grabbed her own coat.

'No!' Olivia shouted. 'Sorry, Cass, but no. You need to keep calling 999 and get help for Dylan. You stand more chance of that from here. And then see if you can contact Sam.'

'But he's down at the cove with the rest of the operation. They'll be busy. And the reception's lousy there.'

'Busy doing nothing if the last few nights are anything to go by. They'll be really pissed off and more worried about their budgets than anything else. And now this storm's in full swing, they'll reckon the boat won't risk the crossing.' Olivia wrestled with the back door. 'See if you can get hold of Jago too. He's probably not as far down the gardens as the rest of them.'

'But what can you do to help?'

Olivia stopped in her tracks. 'I have no idea, but if Dylan and Lucinda need me, I'm going. Just keep trying for an ambulance!'

It was lashing down as Olivia drove along empty country lanes to Peneglos Hall. She abandoned her car by the stables, grabbed her torch and ran roughly in the direction she remembered, gusts of wind soaking her with salty rain. Eventually her eyes fastened on a distant smudge of light she hoped was coming from his hut and she stumbled towards it with relief.

Lucinda was standing outside, completely drenched and hopping from foot to foot, her own torch guiding the way.

'Thank God you're here!' she cried as Olivia got closer. 'Please hurry.' She stood back to let Olivia into the hut first and hurried in behind her, pulling the door closed.

The hut was empty. No sign of Dylan.

Olivia spun round, her mouth open. The look on Lucinda's face as she turned the lock on the door made her breath catch in her throat.

'What the hell's going on, Lucinda? Where's Dylan?'

'I was rather hoping you could tell me that.' Lucinda was leaning with her back against the kitchen counter.

'How would I know?'

'I thought you were the famous sleuth around here, not that you seem to have got very far this time...' Lucinda stared, her face suddenly unfamiliar. The usual friendly mask slipped and Olivia was horrified by the venom displayed underneath.

'So I thought it was time we had a little chat and pooled our theories.'

'What theories?'

'Don't mess with me, Olivia. Ruan's convinced you're going to get to the bottom of what's been going on. I'm just interested in how far you've got and who else you've told.'

Olivia's heart began to bang against her ribcage. 'Is Ruan in on this?'

Lucinda's face twisted. 'Of course not. He's far too much of a goody two-shoes. Won't do anything without running it past Dylan for some reason. And now his friend has disappeared, Ruan's like a lost soul. Although, funnily enough, he's still not asking too many questions about where the extra money's coming from.'

Olivia felt the skin on the back of her neck prickle. 'What extra money?'

Lucinda laughed, but it didn't make its usual musical sound. 'Let's just say I've developed quite a lucrative side hustle since I've come to Peneglos Hall.'

A vision of Agnes's bloated face rushed into Olivia's mind and she swallowed hard. She needed to get out of here. And fast. Unfortunately, Lucinda was between her and the door. *Schoolgirl error.*

'And before you think about running away…' Lucinda shifted her position, so the large hunting knife in her right hand was clearly visible, its curved blade glinting in the artificial light. '…this might make you stay a while and listen to me for a change.'

Olivia eyed the knife, adrenaline coursing through her body. Then she eyed Lucinda. Could she get past her? Her mind weighed everything up quickly, the way she'd been taught in her classes. The first rule of self-defence was to run. But there was nowhere to run without getting close enough to Lucinda for her to use the knife. Better to let her talk first.

'Okay, I'm listening.'

Lucinda waved the knife towards the chairs furthest away from the door.

Olivia did as she was told, but remained standing. 'I know you're using the cove for smuggling. So, what's your side hustle? Drugs?'

She laughed unpleasantly. 'You've been watching too much TV, Olivia. Do you really expect me to spill my guts to you now?'

'Sorry. I thought that was what you wanted to do. Tell me how clever your side hustle is and how you've been smuggling whatever treasures you have into the cove at high tide. Am I right?'

'You don't know what you're talking about,' Lucinda scoffed. 'You might think you've got it all worked out, but you're way off beam.'

'Tell me then.'

'It started off as a philanthropic mission, actually.' Lucinda glared. 'Don't look at me like that. Gabe had a cousin in Albania who was pretty much imprisoned in his own home because of a blood feud. Do you know much about them?' When Olivia shook her head, she continued. 'It's an Albanian thing and they can last for years and years. Basically, if anyone kills another person, then a male member of the bereaved family is obliged to kill a male member of the murderer's family in order to salvage their honour.'

'Nice.' Olivia did not take her eyes off the knife.

'Yeah, well, it can go on for generations. Gabe's grandfather murdered someone, so Gabe's dad fled to Italy with his own family, leaving Gabe's uncle and cousin behind in hiding. His uncle recently died leaving his cousin Niko as the last man in the family. Niko was making Gabe feel bad about the whole thing, so he agreed to help and paid people smugglers to get Niko overland via the Balkans to Spain.'

'Why Spain and not Calais?' Olivia asked, although she thought she knew the answer.

Lucinda snorted. 'Everyone knows that the Calais crossings are too well manned to be successful these days. They just get picked up by Border Force and sent straight back to Albania.' A cunning look crossed her face. 'So I thought, if it was good enough for some dumb Cornishmen two hundred years ago to divert their routes away from France and sail direct from Corunna, it was good enough for us. Gabe found a Spanish fisherman who was happy enough to turn off his radar and get them to just off the cove, and Gabe went out to meet him in a borrowed boat.'

Olivia nodded. That all made perfect sense. 'So why did you do it again? Why not quit while you were ahead?'

'Niko wanted to pay Gabe back the money he'd spent on his overland crossing and the boat.' Her eyes gleamed. 'Do you know how much people are prepared to pay to get from

Corunna to a secret cove in the UK? Seven grand each, that's how much. And you can get at least twenty immigrants on a standard fishing boat, more if you cram them in.'

Olivia did the sums in her head. 'So he must have easily paid Gabe back in one trip?'

Lucinda smirked. 'Yes. And there was more than enough left over for the swimming pond. Which was an ideal way to clean up some slightly dodgy money. It's amazing how many workmen are prepared to accept cash.' The smirk turned into a glare. 'Present company excepted.'

Olivia ignored the jibe. 'And the swimming pond gave you the excuse not to restore the steps down to the cove?'

'Yes, and of course we had to make sure that Dylan and his bloody hut were out of the way. So I persuaded Ruan to get him this one and position it up here.' Her eyes swept it. 'He's done a surprisingly good job. Perhaps I could have used him to fit out our eco-pods after all.'

'Was the waitress who died one of the people you trafficked on that second trip?'

'We're not traffickers,' Lucinda snapped. 'We're smugglers. There's a moral difference, which I'd like you to remember. We're providing a service to people who are more than happy to pay for it.'

'So, was she?'

Lucinda shrugged. 'I don't know. And Gabe wasn't sure if she recognised him personally or just guessed he was Albanian. But it wasn't a risk we could take.' She narrowed her eyes. 'Don't look at me like that. If you hadn't gone nosing into our business, no-one would have ever found out who she was.'

'You begged me to help!'

'No, Ruan begged you to help,' she corrected. And I had no choice but to go along with it, to put you off the scent. I'm sure Olivia the super sleuth would have been very suspicious if I hadn't been as desperate for help as Ruan was.'

'So what about the second body? Was that from another trip?'

Lucinda shifted her position and the knife wavered. 'Yes. Niko said the guy panicked and jumped from the boat before it got into the cove. The waves took him away, so he probably just drowned.'

Olivia gasped. '"Probably just drowned"? He was a person, Lucinda. A desperate person. Didn't it occur to you that his body would be washed up in the cove?'

'Why would it?' Lucinda bristled. 'What do I know about Cornish tides? And Gabe was bloody useless. He should have found that body before Dylan did, but he could never get up early enough.'

Olivia's eyes never left the knife. 'Is that why you killed him?'

'Because he wouldn't get up in the morning? Give me some credit. No, Gabe was getting cold feet. He said we'd done enough and he wanted out.'

'Really? Even though you were providing such a valuable service to his fellow countrymen? Or was there more to it?'

A sly look crossed Lucinda's face. 'We may have diversified a bit…'

'What? Into trafficking?'

'Will you stop calling it that? We just upped our prices and then offered different payment terms.'

It was Olivia's turn to sneer. 'What? Like come and work for someone we know who runs cannabis farms or brothels upcountry, until you've paid off your debts? Although you probably never will because we're charging exorbitant rates of interest?'

'We charge the going rate.'

'What? The going rate among smugglers? Listen to yourself, Lucinda. What have you become? You had a successful job in the hotel industry, a great vision for the Hall and now you've turned into a people trafficker!'

A sudden clap of thunder rocked the hut and both women briefly lost their footing. As Olivia grabbed the back of a chair, Lucinda lunged forward with the knife, catching the left side of her face.

'Shit!' Olivia reared backwards, her hand automatically reaching for her cheek. Blood dripped through her fingers.

'See,' Lucinda jeered. 'I do know what I'm doing. I wasn't aiming for your carotid artery that time.' She moved forward, still waving the knife in front of her. 'I'll save that for next. Or your heart. I haven't decided yet. But I want you to listen to me first, for once. I've had enough of you judging me.'

'Do you blame me for judging you?' Olivia wiped more blood away, her eyes never moving from the knife. 'You've basically admitted to people trafficking and killing Gabe.'

'Gabe knew too much. He wasn't going to just walk away. He wanted to have his kitchen here and be the award-winning chef Gabe Marotta. Except he would have had a hold over Niko and me and I'm not going to be blackmailed for the rest of my life.'

Olivia thought fast. 'Why don't you just tell the police that Niko and Gabe were behind everything? That it was all their idea? And they forced you into helping?'

Lucinda's face went still. 'Why would I do that?'

'You'd get off with a lesser sentence. And you'd be doing the right thing.'

'"The right thing"!' Lucinda mimicked her. 'What do you know about that, Olivia? Have you ever had to choose between doing the right thing and doing the best thing for yourself?'

'Aren't they the same?'

'Of course not,' Lucinda spat at her. 'It's everyone for himself in this world.'

'Even Ruan?'

Lucinda's face hardened. 'Ruan's fun but weak. He's not strong enough to run the Hall by himself. He'd be nothing without me.'

Olivia watched her carefully. 'But if you get married, the Hall will be yours anyway.'

'We won't ever get married! Or if we do, it won't be for long.'

'What do you mean?'

Lucinda laughed. A high, but hollow sound. 'Because he's in love with Dylan for some unknown reason. He can't even admit it to himself, he's such a public-school boy.'

Something that had been buzzing around Olivia's mind for several days now finally clicked into place.

'Does Dylan feel the same way about him?'

'Who knows? And who cares? They're as repressed as each other.'

'But you didn't know when you first tracked Ruan down to that hotel in London?'

Shutters came down over Lucinda's face. 'I don't know what you're talking about.'

'Yes, you do. You found out who Ruan was and got yourself and Gabe jobs at the hotel he was working at.'

'So what? I found him online, checked him out. Saw where his family home was and thought why can't I have a bit of that myself? I made myself indispensable to him and his plans for this place and the rest is history. That's not a crime, is it?'

'Not as such. But I know the real reason you tracked him down in the first place.'

'You know nothing.' Lucinda yawned. 'Look, I'm getting bored. I need to finish up here.'

'So, what's your plan? Come on, Lucinda, you might as well tell me now.'

She yawned again. 'No.'

'Even if I tell you that I know Ruan's actually your brother and you were both adopted as babies, but Ruan got the better end of the deal?'

Lucinda snapped to attention and moved closer to Olivia, pointing the knife directly at her chest. 'How do you know that? Who told you? No-one else knows. Not even Ruan.'

Olivia silently thanked Monty and his questionable research skills. 'I have my sources. What are you going to do?'

Lucinda waved the knife. 'Well, I suppose I might as well tell you now. As a reward for all the hard work you've obviously been doing.' Her face contorted with anger. 'There'll be so much evidence against Dylan that he won't see the light of day for years, especially when they find your body here too. And then, I have two options. One,' she held up a finger, 'either Ruan and I will get married and he'll probably have an accident on our honeymoon, so I get to claim the Hall that way. Or two, if he won't play ball, and we don't get married because he's really not into me, he'll have an accident and I can reveal I'm his next of kin and claim the Hall anyway.' Her face hardened and she smirked at Olivia. 'See, I've got all eventualities covered.'

Olivia wiped more blood away from her face. 'That won't work. Either way.'

'Why not?'

Olivia's eyes fixed on the hunting knife, waiting for the right moment. She chose her words carefully. 'Ruan isn't your brother. He and Dylan swapped identities years ago.'

Lucinda's mouth dropped open and she swayed. Olivia

shifted her position, whipped both arms in front of her and struck her palms either side of Lucinda's wrist simultaneously, as she'd practised so many times in her classes. The knife flew into the air and Lucinda fell backwards, smacking her head on the wood burner. In that split second, Olivia knew she had to run rather than look for the knife. She scrabbled with the lock, one eye on Lucinda's inert body, and with a final wrench pulled open the door and fell into a pair of sturdy arms.

'Okay, everyone, stand down. We'll take it from here.'

## 28

**Three weeks later**

'Are you sure it's okay for us to dress this casually?' Sam asked for the tenth time, looking down uncertainly at his clothes.

Cassie laughed at the expression on his face. This was the first time she'd seen him show his nerves, other than the night of their first date at a pub in Falmouth, two weeks earlier.

'Dylan made it very clear that everyone was to wear their most comfortable things – preferably shorts. They want to make sure this gathering is as different from the last party as possible. I think it's very brave of him and Ruan to go ahead with their plans for the Hall and the least we can do is support them.'

Sam scratched the back of his head. 'I get that, I'm just not used to socialising with members of the public I've met through work. It all feels a bit weird.'

'But they're not just any old members of the public, are they? They're my friends, and people you're going to see a whole lot more of if you're planning on sticking around.' Her words almost caught in her throat, and Sam kissed her gently.

'I most certainly am sticking around.' He held her at arm's length. 'My official transfer came through yesterday. So you're stuck with me now.' He laughed at the look on Cassie's face. 'I think that's why I might be feeling nervous. I want to make a good impression on everyone.'

She was puzzled. 'But you already know most of them.'

'Yes, but that's as DS O'Driscoll. This is different. We're going public with our relationship for the first time and I want them to...' He petered off.

Cassie's skin tingled all over. 'Want them to what?'

Sam turned to her, his face pink. 'I want them to think I'm worthy of you. To know that I want to make you happy.'

'Oh, Sam!' She threw her arms round his neck, breathing in his now familiar, but still delicious cologne. 'They know that already. Everyone says how happy I look. Even if they don't know the reason why yet.'

'And you're absolutely sure Kitten's okay with it?'

She kissed him firmly on the mouth. 'Positive.' Kitten, Olivia and Dylan were the only three people Cassie had confided in so far. They'd all been delighted and Cassie couldn't believe how happy she was. 'We're going to have a lovely time and I'm going to be so proud to have you by my side.'

---

Jago took the dogs across the gardens and down to the creek while he waited for Olivia to get ready for the gathering of friends at Peneglos Hall. Like Sam, he was feeling nervous. Although it was early evening, the sun was still strong and he gave thanks for being able to wear shorts and a cotton shirt rather than the formal dinner suit that had been stipulated last time. He still couldn't fully get his head around everything that had happened that fateful night at the Hall and wasn't sure he ever would.

He felt vindicated that their theory was right about the new smuggling route from Corunna to Falmouth and the cove being used as the drop-off point. The police, Border Force and other agencies involved had been getting antsy after three nights waiting in stormy weather and making their doubts increasingly obvious. Jago was becoming seriously concerned they were about to call the whole operation off when a fishing boat overloaded with thirty desperate migrants had eventually dropped anchor at the cove. Dozens of uniformed men and women had sprung into action, boarded the boat and swiftly arrested everyone. The man Jago now knew to be Niko Murati had initially claimed he was also a victim of trafficking, but it wasn't long before the truth came out. He was now in custody, awaiting trial.

What Jago hadn't been prepared for, however, was Olivia's involvement in the night's action. He'd come up from the cove to find her dripping in blood and fighting to get away from the paramedics trying to persuade her into an ambulance, and Lucinda in handcuffs, being forced into the back of a car by two police officers.

*Would Olivia ever stick to a plan we've agreed upfront?* Probably not, he decided with a wry smile. That's what made her who she was. At least she hadn't been too badly injured this time. The cut on her face was long but surprisingly shallow and had been treated on the scene with Steri-Strips. Three weeks on, the wound had healed well and was already fading. Olivia seemed to be back to her old self: busy and happy and her eyes were sparkling again. She'd even decided to take a month off work while they sorted things out. Jago knew he still had some serious thinking to do on that front.

Lucinda had obviously listened to Olivia's advice and tried to accuse Gabe and his cousin of being behind the whole venture while she was just another of their victims. Unfortunately for her, Dylan had installed some of his specialist listening equipment in his hut, and there was a crystal-clear recording of the whole incident. Dylan and Ruan had been cleared of any wrongdoing in swapping identities, but there was still some way to go to sort everything out. Jago sighed. *Why do people make life so complicated?*

And life was complicated, Jago decided. There was a part of him still dealing with the fact he was once again emotionally involved in an investigation where he knew the victims and witnesses personally. It was a far cry from his life at the Bar, where he'd always been able to approach his cases with logic and emotional detachment. Until the Bregu case. And although he was confident that Bregu had nothing to do with the people smuggling being carried out at Peneglos Hall, the awfulness of the coincidence would worry him for a long time.

The three dogs suddenly stood still, heads cocked, and then took off up the garden. Seconds later, Olivia appeared and Jago's knees went weak. She looked beautiful in denim shorts that had butterflies and birds embroidered over them and a white vest. Her dark curls were caught up in a messy bun, a few tendrils carefully covering the faint scar on her left cheek. Her usual obsidian pendant and a pair of dangly earrings completed her outfit – ideal for the grounded, sassy and utterly gorgeous woman she was.

'Are you ready to go?' she asked with a wide smile. 'We're going with Cassie and Sam, and Dylan made me promise we wouldn't be late. He's got a little surprise for us, apparently.'

Jago's heart sank. 'I think I've had enough surprises in the last few weeks to last a lifetime.'

Olivia laughed, one of her deep infectious laughs that always made him feel warm inside. 'Who was it that said life is all about experiencing the joys and delights of the unexpected?'

'No idea.' He rested his arm along her shoulders as they stood watching the sunlight dancing across the creek. 'But they've obviously never met you.'

Apart from the twinkling fairy lights threaded through the pergolas on the terraces and the warm evening, Peneglos Hall could have been a completely different place from the last gathering, Olivia thought as the four friends automatically walked to the back of the house. And she meant everything. About twenty people, nearly all of whom she recognised, were sitting in relaxed groups on the terraces, chatting away happily, renewing old acquaintances and making new ones. Low classical music played from a speaker just inside the doors, and a simple table stood under one pergola bearing buckets full of beer and wine and some tasty-looking snacks.

Two figures wandered across to greet them and Olivia did a double take. 'Dylan, is that really you?' She looked from face to face. More similar now they were both unshaven, but still different in so many ways.

There was a lot of squealing, shrieking and hugging. Dylan eventually extricated himself from Cassie's grip and stood back, smiling shyly at Olivia. The overgrown beard had gone, revealing sharp cheekbones and a firm jaw, marred only by a thin scar running all the way down the right side of his face, and his hair was short and neatly trimmed. For the first time since she'd known him, he wasn't dressed in earth-coloured, scruffy clothes, but looked good in combat shorts and a slim-fitting white tee shirt, which hugged his torso and showed off his muscles. The transformation was amazing.

Olivia felt tears prick her eyes. He looked just how she imagined Aidan would at his age. Dylan caught hold of her and hugged her close. 'It's not that bad a surprise, is it, Olli-o? And at least we have matching scars now.'

She knew he understood and was grateful for his attempt to make her laugh. She hugged him back fiercely. 'We do. I'm just so used to you looking like someone who's been chained to a dungeon wall for ten years that I'm struggling to take it all in.'

'Cheeky!' He stood back and turned to his friend. 'Ruan knew it was all there underneath.'

Olivia intercepted the look that passed between them and her pulse quickened. 'Have you sorted things out?'

'We're getting there. We realise we've both been in denial about our feelings for each other for years. I suppose I should have realised how Ruan really felt when he agreed to go along with our identity swap. That was a massive thing to do.'

Ruan stepped forward and stood close to Dylan. 'And we realise we owe you all an explanation for that, but tonight we'll just give you the basics. Dylan, as you now know, was in the Special Forces and unsurprisingly saw, heard and experienced some pretty awful things during his years spent overseas.'

'What Ruan is trying to say is that I was a mess when I finally left the SRR. I had PTSD, among other things, and had to go into intensive rehabilitation. When that was finished, I still wasn't able to function in the real world and I came here to Uncle Charles. Ruan came down to see me as often as he could, full of tales of hotel life and this wonderful new sustainable place he was working at. He and Uncle Charles came up with the idea of turning the Hall into a hotel in order to save it from complete ruin, but there was no way I was ready, either mentally or physically to take that on.' Dylan shuddered, and Ruan took over.

'Charles suggested we swapped identities, in order to save a lot of complications. We took legal advice, anonymously, to make sure we weren't breaking the law. And so that's what we did. I wasn't being quite as altruistic as Dylan makes out. It was my opportunity to run my own hotel, the way I wanted to. And help my best friend out as well.'

'Someone's going to ask you where Lucinda and Gabe came into all this,' Jago spoke up. 'So it might as well be me.'

Ruan reddened. 'That was entirely my fault. And I'll regret it until the day I die. We were all working at the same hotel, just by chance, or so I thought. Gabe was an excellent chef and very keen on getting his Michelin Green Star. Lucinda was brilliant at her job and I just thought the three of us would make a dream team here.' His voice suddenly wavered. 'I honestly had no idea about their plan. I was stupid and naïve.'

'No, you weren't. How on earth were you to know what they were up to?' Dylan slipped his arm through Ruan's and turned to the others. 'There was never any personal relationship between Lucinda and Ruan, apart from in her head. She persuaded Ruan it would make everything at the Hall more conventional and acceptable if people believed they were a couple. So Ruan went along with it, in public.'

'It was just easier,' Ruan said quietly. 'There was so much going on with the building work and getting everything ready, I kept putting off thinking about it. I'm so sorry.'

Olivia's heart went out to both of them. 'I think that's enough for now. We can continue this some other time if we have to. I just want to know that you're happy together and are going to sort everything out between you.' She caught Jago's eye and he winked.

'Is that Maeve and Joey over on the terrace?' he enquired.

'Yes.' Dylan seized on the subject change. 'It's been really good for us to meet Maeve and Joey and talk things through with them. They're making the most of being child-free for a few days and are going to stay on with us.'

'That's a great idea.' Jago clapped Dylan on the back and turned to Cassie and Sam. 'C'mon, you two, let me introduce you all.' They wandered off with Ruan, tactfully leaving Olivia and Dylan behind.

'Monty's here too,' Dylan told her and laughed at her expression. 'Yeah, we've already agreed that we won't discuss his unorthodox research methods, but I have suggested his talents may be wasted at the Bar…'

'Don't say that in front of Maeve,' Olivia hissed. 'She'll be furious with you!'

'Only joking.' He nudged her repeatedly until she laughed.

'Oh, Dylan.' She checked herself. 'Or should I be calling you Ruan now? It's going to take some time to get used to all of this.'

'Of course it is.' He smiled, and once again Olivia marvelled at how much younger and happier he looked. 'Ruan and I are happy for people to call us whatever they like, within reason of course.' A shadow crossed his face. 'It's not your fault we've misled you.' He coughed. 'I wasn't well enough at the time to realise why he was doing it for me.'

'But you do now?' Olivia felt a rush of affection for both men.

Dylan nodded.

'And you're happy?'

He nodded again, tears filling his eyes. 'It's just awful that it's taken three deaths to make us see what's been staring us in the face for the past twenty-five years.'

Olivia looked at him. 'Yes, it is. But that was all beyond your control. Or Ruan's.' She hugged him close. 'Let's just enjoy tonight, eh?'

He brightened. 'I'm so pleased we invited Mina and Esmé and their husbands. We've already decided to sign the estate cottages up to Frank Hughes's holiday lettings company, and we can support Esmé's girls more proactively that way. We just need to sign the paperwork on Monday.'

Olivia beamed and then winced. 'Does that mean Kitten's met Esmé?'

'Oh yes. Firm friends already.' Dylan looked sideways at Olivia. 'At least it should take Kitten's mind off her mother's love life for a while.'

Olivia brightened. 'Don't they make a lovely couple? Sam is absolutely besotted with her and I've never seen Cass look so happy.'

He grinned. 'She deserves it. And I think they'll be good for each other.' He held out the crook of his arm for Olivia to slip her hand through and they walked up the garden. 'And Lexie's totally on board with taking over in the kitchen, so that just leaves you, Olli-o. Have you sorted things out with the big man yet?'

'He's a man of few words, Dylan. Let's not rush things.' A sudden flash of white caught her eye. 'Is that my gorgeous godson on the terrace with Willow and Mina?' And she was off, leaving a laughing and bemused Dylan in her wake.

As the sun slowly lowered into the ocean and the sky turned into a fiery mass of oranges and reds, Willow and Frazer took baby Dougie home to bed and Kitten pleaded a headache, so left with Rocky. Olivia sat chatting with Maeve, Joey and Monty, pointing out the beautiful scents of the night stocks and phlox as they glimmered in the borders behind them, all refreshed by the dampening of dusk. It was an idyllic evening, thought Olivia, seeking out Jago's silver head and broad shoulders. He caught her eye and nodded, tilting his head across the lawn. She nodded back, made her excuses and slipped away.

Seconds later, she felt familiar arms slide around her waist and she leant backwards into his solid warmth.

'Hey,' he whispered into her ear. 'Enjoying yourself?'

'Mmm.' She turned in his arms, stood on her tiptoes, snaked her arms around his neck and kissed him. She leant back and waited for the lop-sided smile that crinkled into the corners of his eyes and made her insides quiver with anticipation. It did its usual trick. 'Are you?'

He untangled himself from her arms and stood, slightly apart from her.

A sudden chill swept through Olivia and she shivered. 'What's the matter?'

'I've been thinking.'

Her stomach clenched. 'What about?'

He looked at her, his own face a picture of uncertainty. 'Us.'

'What about us?'

He moved from foot to foot, obviously deeply uncomfortable. 'When we were in London, you were talking about us being a partnership.'

'Yes.' Olivia had no idea where this was going.

'I've been thinking that we might want to put our partnership on a more legal footing.' His blue eyes were earnest. 'I think it would help.'

She blinked. 'I'm sorry?'

'There are all sorts of legal benefits,' he began to explain. 'Inheritance rights, joint assets, pensions, all sorts of next of kin issues—'

'Stop right there!' Olivia's heart fell and her voice rose at the same time. 'What the bloody hell are you on about, Jago? Are you asking me if I want to draw up some kind of legal partnership agreement?'

'Not exactly.'

Olivia turned away. 'I'm getting cold and Ruan said he was lighting the fire pit. I don't want a ridiculous conversation about legal niceties just at the moment.'

'Neither do I.' The anguish in his voice stopped her and she turned back.

'What are you trying to say, Jago? For someone who's allegedly always so brilliant in court, you have your moments.'

'I'm trying to say that I think we should get married.'

'I'm sorry?' She stared at him; her mouth open. 'What? You and me?'

'Of course you and me. Who else would I want to marry?'

She looked at him closely. Fear, uncertainty and anguish were written all over Jago's handsome face and a strange sensation ran through her.

'That has to be the most unromantic marriage proposal in the history of mankind,' she told him crossly.

'I'm sorry. I didn't really have the chance to prepare what I was going to say.'

'Obviously.' She thought for a moment. 'Do you love me?'

'Of course I love you!' His eyes had never looked more serious.

'You've never said so. Not once.'

'I try to show it. In the everyday things I do, the way I am with you, how I treat you. Isn't that more important than words?' His eyes never left her face. 'You've never told me either, but I know you do.'

A fizzing feeling ran through her. He was right. 'Yeah, I reckon I do.' She moved closer and kissed him, feeling his mouth curve into a smile beneath hers.

'I don't want a big wedding,' she warned him.

He shuddered. 'Good God, no.'

'Or a white dress.'

'Me neither.' He kissed her.

'Or any fuss.'

'Absolutely not.' He kissed her.

'And I don't even want to tell anyone, until we've talked about it properly.'

'Me neither.' He kissed her again and she moulded herself into his body.

*Oh, to hell with it. This is the twenty-first century.*

'Jago?'

'Yes.' He didn't seem to want to stop kissing her.

'Will you marry me?'

She felt the rumble of laughter travel through his body. 'I thought you'd never ask.'

---

In the back seat of the taxi, on their way home with Cassie and Sam, Olivia recognised the dark eyes twinkling at her in the rear-view mirror.

'Hiya, Olivia. It is you, isn't it? I wasn't sure without all those tassels and beads and things.'

'It is, yes. How are you doing, Jack? Did your daughter get anywhere with a job at Peneglos Hall?'

He beamed. 'She did, thanks. And she's proper happy about it. Starts next week.'

'I'm so glad.'

'So am I.' He winked at her. 'And how about you, love? You certainly look happier than you did the last time you were in my cab...'

Olivia felt Jago's fingers curl around hers and squeeze tightly.

'...in fact, you almost look like a different person.'

She exchanged a smile with Jago and then grinned in the mirror at Jack.

'Thanks. I am.'

## ALSO BY JANE MCPARKES

**<u>Olivia Wells Mysteries</u>**

A Deadly Inheritance

# ACKNOWLEDGEMENTS

Thank you so much for reading *Deadly Treasures*. I hope you enjoyed it.

While my concern for the environment is very real, *Deadly Treasures* is meant to be an uplifting, escapist read, making the most of the freedom that the cosy mystery genre allows. Climate solutions are in action throughout the story, but are mainly incidental to the main plot, whose purpose is to entertain and inspire readers. If you take on board any of the sustainability ideas and tips that are included in the story, I will be thrilled! If you want to let me know, please do.

If you enjoyed reading *Deadly Treasures*, please tell your friends and family about it, or give it a mention on social media. Or please leave a quick review on Amazon or Goodreads (or both). Before I became an author, I wasn't aware of how important recommendations and reviews are, but believe me, they really are.

While writing *A Deadly Inheritance*, the first book in the Olivia Wells Mysteries series, felt like a very solitary experience, writing *Deadly Treasures* has been the complete opposite and I've been overwhelmed by the contrast at times. Being published gave me the confidence to dip my literary toe into all sorts of writing groups and associations where I've always been met with kindness, help and support, and I have learned so much. There really are too many people to mention by name – but thank you all!

I owe particular thanks to my lovely, patient editor, Abbie

Rutherford, whose kind words and encouragement meant that I thoroughly enjoyed the editing process, and for helping to make this book the best it can be before it goes out into the world. To Lorna Hinde whose proofreading and support has made the whole process even more painless. And to Ken Dawson for bringing my vague ideas for the cover to life. I really feel part of a proper team now.

I must also thank my non-writing friends for always cheering me on and understanding when I haven't been as present as I usually am. It's nothing personal, promise!

And of course, to all my readers. I have been delighted by how many of you enjoyed *A Deadly Inheritance* and have invested in the characters' lives and storylines. Your appreciation confirmed my belief that Olivia and friends deserved a series. There's much more to come, so please do stay around and enjoy the journey with me.

To my immediate and extended McParkes clan. Thanks for all your love, support, encouragement and help. I couldn't have done any of this without you, but I would have finished much sooner if you hadn't kept interrupting me.

Finally, to Margot and Geoffrey, who have watched me write every single word of this book, listened to all my worries and woes and never once doubted me. Every writer should have dogs as writing buddies.

# ABOUT THE AUTHOR

Jane McParkes is the author of the Olivia Wells Mysteries, a cosy crime series with an eco-twist which combines Jane's love of Cornwall and her interest in the environment, sustainability and creativity.

The first book in the series, *A Deadly Inheritance*, was a finalist in the international Wishing Shelf Book Awards.

To keep up to date with all Jane's news, special offers, promotions and books, please join her newsletter here. Or, for photos of Cornwall, her dogs and behind the scenes glimpses of Jane's writing life, she's on Twitter, Instagram and Substack all @JaneMcParkes.

Lastly, if you have enjoyed *Deadly Treasures*, please leave a review on Amazon, or post something nice on social media. It really does make all the difference!

Printed in Great Britain
by Amazon